For two gay men in the Deep South, fighting for love and family can lead to one beautiful, sexy, and unexpected knock out . . .

In college, an "are you sure you're gay?" experiment with his (female) best friend left Sterling Harper married with a baby on the way. Eleven years later, his life is flipped upside-down—his wife has died, his "little boy" is transitioning to her new life as a girl, Alexa, and his embittered in-laws have proven too transphobic to babysit for the summer like they'd planned. They're fighting for custody of Alexa, though, so Sterling can't afford to give them more ammunition. If only there were a nice, conservative, trans-preteen-friendly nanny available on short notice . . .

Jericho Johnston doesn't do "conservative," but Alexa takes to him immediately. He's got a teaching job lined up for the fall, a killer smile, and loads of charisma . . . but he is not going back in the proverbial closet. It doesn't take long for the two men to go from comrades-in-arms against their rarified community to two men in love. This kicks off the looming custody battle with Sterling's bigoted in-laws, though, and the idea of two gay men raising a trans daughter isn't going over well with anyone. Now, with so much to lose, Sterling and Jericho must fight harder than ever—for themselves, for Alexa, and for their future.

Books by Wendy Qualls

The Heart of the South
Worth Waiting For
Worth Searching For
Worth Fighting For

Published by Kensington Publishing Corporation

Worth Fighting For

The Heart of the South

Wendy Qualls

LYRICAL PRESS
Kensington Publishing Corp.
www.kensingtonbooks.com

Lyrical Press books are published by
Kensington Publishing Corp. 119 West 40th Street New York, NY 10018

First Electronic Edition: August 2018
eISBN-13: 978-1-5161-0188-7
eISBN-10: 1-5161-0188-X

First Print Edition: August 2018
ISBN-13: 978-1-5161-0189-4
ISBN-10: 1-5161-0189-8

Printed in the United States of America

For Bea

Chapter 1

"Dad! You came! I knew you would." Alexa came barreling through her grandparents' foyer and practically tackled Sterling with a tight hug. She was in jeans and an oversized white polo shirt, which wasn't what she'd been wearing when he dropped her off at school that morning. "Please, please can we go home?" she asked, muffled against his chest. "Grandma Butler is mad because I won't let her cut my hair, but she keeps yelling at me and I don't *want* a boy cut, I want to let it get longer—"

"Hey." Sterling drew back and got a good look at Alexa's hair. She'd been growing it out for months, trying to get it long enough to pull back into some semblance of a feminine style, but now there was a conspicuous chunk missing from the left side. Even Sterling, who'd kept the same basic haircut since he was twelve and couldn't tell a fashionable style from bedhead, could tell it wasn't fixable.

Vivian Butler, Sterling's mother-in-law, came around the corner from the living room while Sterling was examining the damage. She flashed him a blatantly fake smile and hurried over to offer a side-armed hug. "Sterling! Oscar didn't tell us you'd be home early."

"My name isn't Oscar," Alexa growled through clenched teeth, "and I called him to come pick me up. Dad, can we leave now?"

"You need to go grab your backpack," Sterling said. "And I want to talk to your grandma for a minute first, okay? You can go out and wait in the car if you want to—the door's unlocked."

Alexa nodded and went to the kitchen to retrieve her things. Sterling took Vivian's arm and drew her aside, out of the hall, so they were out of Alexa's way when she headed outside.

"You're not doing that boy any favors by encouraging him, you know," Vivian said in a low voice. "I can't believe you let him go to school wearing pink this morning! I had to pull out one of Lawrence's old shirts for him to wear instead."

Sterling closed his eyes and counted to ten. They'd gone round and round and *round* on this, but his in-laws still refused to call Alexa by her new name or to use feminine pronouns. "Alexa is welcome to wear whatever color she likes," he said for what was probably the hundredth time. "And if you keep calling her by her deadname, I swear I'm going to keep her home this summer and you won't get to see her unsupervised ever again."

Vivian crossed her arms and glared at him. "Dana would have been ashamed of you both. Oscar was a perfectly healthy little boy before—"

"Before my wife died. Thank you so much for bringing that back up," Sterling snapped. "You don't think I miss her the same as you do? Or Alexa does? It still doesn't give you the right make those decisions on behalf of my daughter."

"If you refuse to parent *our grandson*—"

Goddammit. "Know what? I can't do this anymore." Sterling was seriously resisting the urge to hit his mother-in-law; heaven only knew how long he could keep his hands to himself. Not that he'd *actually* hit her, but it would be so satisfying…

"It's embarrassing!" Vivian exclaimed. "What am I supposed to say when my friends at Bible study ask how Oscar is doing? It's bad enough you never take him to church anymore. I can't tell them my grandson is being dressed up like a girl and is demanding everyone call him 'Alexa'!" Her tone softened a bit. "I know Dana loved you very much," she added. "And I know you worked hard at making her happy, regardless of… circumstances. But can you honestly tell me you think Dana would have approved of this? You know as well as I do she would have been mortified to have everyone gossiping about Oscar behind your backs. Lawrence and I are just trying to help him get back to the real world and stop all this sexual confusion nonsense. He's *ten*. Nowhere near old enough to be thinking about sex yet."

That argument was frustratingly familiar too. Sterling took a deep breath, formulating a reply—and then decided it wasn't worth the effort. She wouldn't understand. She hadn't understood Alexa in forever and hadn't understood Dana and Sterling's relationship for a lot longer than that. Vivian and Lawrence's refusal to honor Alexa's social transition was clearly hurting Alexa more than Sterling had realized, and his in-laws were both being more stubborn about it than even the worst-case scenario he'd envisioned when Alexa first came out as female. It always boiled down to them insisting her transition was a phase, or some red flag for sexual deviance, or a cry for help because Sterling's parenting skills were somehow inadequate. They refused to see the perfectly healthy girl finally getting to express herself the way she wanted. Her gender had nothing to do with wanting sex.

There was a zero percent chance his late wife's parents would bother to learn the difference between the two, or even care about getting it wrong.

"Goodbye," Sterling said, in lieu of something much ruder. Many somethings, if he let himself give her the tongue-lashing she deserved. He left Vivian standing there in her living room and took a tiny bit of satisfaction in letting the screen door slam on his way out of the house.

Alexa was already buckled into her seat in the back when he got to the car. She'd shed her grandfather's oversized shirt and was back in the pink butterfly-print tank top she'd been wearing that morning. "Thanks for coming, Dad," she said softly. "Grandpa keeps telling me I'm being disobedient, but I'm *not.* Now that I'm finally…but they keep telling me I'm wrong."

"I know. And I'm really, truly sorry for not putting a stop to this earlier. I didn't realize they were still doing this to you when I'm not there." It was one more failure he could tally up, courtesy of being a single dad. God only knew how they'd have handled Alexa's transition if Dana were still alive, but she wasn't and he'd had to come to terms with that ages ago. "I kept hoping they'd eventually come around," he added, "but your grandparents are…" *Big damn narcissists? Self-absorbed jackasses?* "…slow to change."

Alexa grimaced. "Did you see what she did to my hair?" She turned her head to the right, and Sterling tried not to react too badly. He'd only gotten a quick glance at it inside, before his mother-in-law distracted them, but now in the passive afternoon light he could identify the damage more clearly—a big hunk was missing over her left ear. Everywhere else was still a gender-ambiguous length, but that one spot looked ridiculous. She'd been trying for *months* to grow her hair longer to look more feminine, but Dana's parents were more concerned about what people would think of their "grandson" than about what Alexa wanted. *Goddammit.*

"Grandma Butler did that?"

"Yeah." Alexa's shoulders slumped. "She made an appointment to take me to the barber today. To get a boy style. I flat-out told her no, so she got the scissors from the kitchen and chopped off a big hunk of my hair out so I'd have to go." She fingered the ragged cut. "I can't leave it like this," she whispered in the direction of her lap, "but now it's gone and I can't grow it back."

"You'll have longer hair eventually, but I promise you don't have to leave it uneven in the meantime." Sterling started the engine and backed out of his in-laws' driveway. He headed east, toward downtown instead of home. "I'm sure we can find a stylist who doesn't require an appointment—let's see what they can do."

"You think it's fixable?"

Sterling locked eyes with Alexa in the mirror and willed her to believe the sense of calm competence he was trying to project. He didn't have the first clue how to fix the whole mess, but at the very least he could get Alexa a nice, shorter-but-still-feminine haircut. "It is," he declared firmly. "And I'll see what I can do about your grandparents."

Chapter 2

Jericho got to the little coffee shop about ten minutes early. Other than when he signed up with TeachUniversal three years earlier, he hadn't had an interview in…well, ever, really. He'd only had the one job at Uncle René and Tante Brielle's summer camp, and even though he'd stuck with it for several years running, there'd never actually been a formal interview. The whole offer had been more like "Your mom said you're good with kids! Want to come to Florida for the summer and entertain them? We'll pay you!" The application process for TeachUniversal had been more in-depth, but still culminated in something less like a job interview and more like a personality test. Apparently there were a lot of people who wanted to work with special needs children in exotic locales whose enthusiasm didn't correspond with the right ability or temperament.

On the subject of temperament, though…*coffee*. Coffee would be heavenly. It was almost eight a.m.—presumably prime time for pre-work caffeination—and the shop had a busy drive-through but only three other customers inside. That was good, both because there was no line and because the dining area was seriously tiny. Any more people and he'd be having his interview two feet away from a random stranger. Jericho covertly scanned the room while pretending to look at the menu. The spot near the front window would be the best place to sit for a one-on-one, but it was already occupied by a clean-cut white dude in a suit. Blondish-brown hair, square-rimmed glasses, kind of a hot lawyer look. The guy wore it well, but his knee was bouncing madly under the table. He looked almost as jittery as Jericho felt. Maybe the table near—

"Good morning," the suited man said, standing and approaching him. "Your name isn't Jericho Johnston, is it? I'm supposed to meet him here at eight and you're the only one I've seen come through who fit my friend's description."

Oh, he's got a nice voice too. Jericho plastered a confident smile on his face and offered a handshake. "You must be Doctor Harper."

The man nodded and smiled back. "Call me Sterling, please. Being on a last-name basis all summer would get to be a bit much, don't you think?"

Starting off on a first-name basis felt equally weird, but Sterling couldn't have been *that* much older than Jericho was. Four or five years, maybe. If this hadn't essentially been a job interview, the informality of the whole first-name thing would have felt like an opening for some subtle flirtation. As it was, though, Jericho was more than willing to keep his trap shut for the next two and a half months if it meant having somewhere to live and hopefully some money left over at the end.

"What did Irene tell you, then?" he asked his potential employer. "Tall, bald, and cheerful?" There was a good chance "really dark" was part of her list too, but since Jericho was six foot three—which tended to be his second most noticeable feature, after his skin tone—it was possible she'd stuck with "tall."

"Something like that," Sterling hedged. *So yes.* "It let me pick you out of this total lack of crowd, at any rate. You want to…?" He gestured back toward the table.

"Okay if I grab myself a coffee?"

Sterling waved him toward the counter. "Oh, sorry, of course. Take your time. The caramel mocha's amazing."

Jericho wasn't in a mood to make more decisions than absolutely necessary, so he got himself the caramel mocha like Sterling suggested. The second barista had his coffee ready to go almost before he was done paying. There was something weird about knowing that Sterling probably had eyes on him the whole time, waiting and assessing, but Jericho reminded himself that appearances and confidence were merely one more part of the interview process.

Nothing to stress about. You've got this. He had good credentials and could pass a background check with flying colors. Paul and Brandon, the friends he was staying with while job hunting, had finally taken pity on him after his third wardrobe change of the morning and essentially pushed him out the door with a pat on the shoulder and a sincere "Good luck!" In short, Jericho knew he was a damn good find for a summer nanny, and this interview was a chance for him to show that to Sterling. If it didn't work, no biggie—he'd find something else. Another year at Camp Ladybug would be interesting too, wouldn't it? Almost like going back in time to his high school and college summers. That would be fun.

Maybe if he told himself that enough times, he'd start to believe it.

"Sorry," Sterling said when Jericho got back to the table. "I tend to run early more often than late, but I didn't mean to accost you before you got your breakfast. Don't let me rush you."

"It's fine. I run early too, usually." He would have gotten actual food and ordered something a little less sweet to drink, in other circumstances, but the caramel mocha wasn't terrible and Jericho was too hyped up to eat more anyway. "Pleasure to meet you."

"Thanks. Good. We've got the nice-to-meet-yous and beverage-acquisition part out of the way." Now that introductions were over, Sterling seemed to be relaxing some. Jericho decided to take that as a good sign. "Long story short," Sterling explained, "my daughter is ten years old and her last day of school is this coming Friday. It's just me and her, and I can't always predict when I'm going to have to stay late at the office—I'm a dentist and my partner has dropped back to part-time, so I end up taking over most of the trickier issues. Seems like nowadays I'm there late more often than not. Alexa's old enough not to burn the house down, but I'm not comfortable leaving her alone every day for the next two and a half months."

"Of course." He wanted Jericho to start work in less than a week? "Is there a reason you're not interviewing candidates further in advance, if you don't mind me asking?"

"The original plan was for her to stay with my in-laws while I'm at work, but some changes have come up unexpectedly. I assume Irene told you a bit about what I'm looking for?"

She had, but not much. This referral had totally been a chance connection. Jericho's college roommate, Chris, had dated a girl named Irene off and on for ages. Ultimately the two had split but remained friends. Chris became part of Jericho's core social group in Atlanta; Irene got promoted to office manager at the little health clinic she'd been the receptionist for in downtown Atlanta and then more or less dropped out of their lives. Facebook said she'd ended up in a posh little town a bit south of the Florida-Georgia line, at what turned out to be Sterling Harper's office. Her job tip came completely out of the blue after almost three years of no contact—she'd thought of Jericho when she learned that this single dad, a rich dentist, was looking for a live-in sitter ASAP. It was a convoluted connection, but the timing couldn't have been better. "Only the very basics," Jericho admitted. "No details other than your daughter's age and that you need someone for the duration of the summer."

Sterling pinched his lips and nodded. "That's…well. The first thing I should mention is that Alexa is on the spectrum. She doesn't always make the most logical decisions, so you may end up spending half the summer reminding her not to take stupid risks in the name of curiosity. She also gets fixated on the strangest things and wants to talk about the same topics over and over again. It's not always blatant—she's mainstreamed in school and everything—but it throws adults off sometimes. You've got experience working with kids who have Asperger's, don't you?"

Extensively. "It's generally all called Autism Spectrum Disorder now, but yes," Jericho assured him. "My degree is in teaching special education, but I've spent the last three years in Haiti working at a school for children who have a variety of special needs. ASD was one of them."

Sterling nodded. "You mentioned that on your resume. There's another thing, though. It's very recent—Alexa is only starting her public transition now—but Irene may not have called attention to it. I only told everyone at the office a few weeks ago, and they all seem determined to tiptoe around the topic."

She hadn't mentioned anything else, Jericho was sure, but he'd have given even odds she either didn't want to prejudice him or guessed he wouldn't care. "Your daughter is transgender?"

"Will that be a problem?"

Jericho shook his head. Saying "some of my best friends are trans women" would make him sound like a jackass, but there was no question he'd be better-equipped than most to deal with questions an LGBT kid might ask. Age-appropriate answers, even. It wouldn't surprise him if Irene *had* intentionally passed on the job tip without mentioning that Sterling's daughter was transgender—it would be just like her to recommend him specifically without saying why. "I haven't worked with any trans kids that young," he confessed, "but her gender identity won't make a difference to me. If that's what you're asking. The summer camp I worked at all through college was initially designed for youth with a wide variety of disabilities, but really it was for anyone who needed a one-on-one experience. Some of the teens I worked with were nonbinary or transgender and came to Camp Ladybug because they didn't feel comfortable going to other, gender-segregated summer programs."

Sterling's eyed widened enough to show Jericho had surprised him. "Damn, I hadn't even thought about that issue for as she gets older," he admitted. "Right now it feels like we're still struggling with one step at a time. You may hear me slip up and call her Oscar occasionally—I'm trying to work on that."

"The fact that you *are* trying is a huge deal to her, I'm sure."

"I hope so."

"I'll never have known her as Oscar," Jericho added, "so that might make it easier for you. I'm guessing you don't talk to each other in the third person much. Practice will help."

"True." Sterling let out a long breath and flashed Jericho a much more honest smile than they'd exchanged at the beginning. "Figured I should get that out of the way first, just in case. I did read your resume—sounds like Camp Ladybug was a good fit for you, wasn't it? Five summers there, bachelor's in education from Georgia State with a focus in early childhood development and special education, and three years in Haiti with TeachUniversal? Did you have a classroom there?"

Christ, did he have Jericho's resume memorized? Jericho wasn't sure whether that was a good sign or just intimidating. "Not exactly," he said, "but I did interact a lot with the kids." He'd only been back in the States for a few weeks and he already missed them like crazy. "TeachUniversal is a nonprofit that sends teachers with special needs training to underprivileged parts of the world, mostly in countries where there's no mandated education system and no schools in place capable of handling neurodiverse kids. I was initially only going to be there for a year, helping train the other teachers who would then run this new school, but I ended up staying two more years working for the director as a program manager. It was amazing and exhausting. When I get my own class here in the States—somewhere—it'll probably feel luxurious even if I end up in the poorest inner-city school ever and have next to no budget. We got good at making do."

"That's your plan for fall, then?"

"If all goes well, then yes. Although obviously it's not entirely up to me." Haiti had been amazing—stunning beauty and incredible poverty juxtaposed together. Jericho was more than ready to come back to the US after three years there, though. The kids were great, but the complete and total ban on homosexuality was stifling. It got claustrophobic in that closet, fast. "I've got an offer to substitute teach up in Brunswick starting this fall," he added. "It's about an hour north of here, I think? I'll be at an elementary school, where the regular special needs teacher is going to be out on maternity leave for a while—possibly most of the year, since rumor has it pegged as a high-risk pregnancy. My certification is in Georgia and my ties are to Atlanta, so I'll probably end up closer to that part of the state eventually, but Brunswick is still a reasonable drive from my aunt and uncle's summer camp, and it would be nice to have family within visiting distance. I have no other obligations until the middle of August, though, so you can see why this opportunity is such a good fit for me."

"You'll be a good fit for Alexa too, I suspect," Sterling declared. "I'm not saying yes yet, because I'm still looking at other options, but what do you expect in terms of salary? And time off, and benefits? I'd like to get an idea of what you're willing to do before we finalize anything."

It wasn't a "yes please, let me hire you," but it felt very, very close. Jericho had to bite his cheek to keep from grinning. *Perfect summer job, here I come.*

* * * *

Alexa really did look cute in a pixie cut, Sterling decided. The stylist at the swanky boutique salon downtown had suggested the cut, feminine but short, and showed her how to mousse and gel it into a few different variations. If they didn't leave for school within the next fifteen minutes Alexa was going to be late, though, and neither of them had eaten yet. How was it possible for a shorter style to take his daughter *more* time in front of the mirror? She'd been picky about her hair for ages, well before the word "transitioning" ever came into their vocabulary, but now that Alexa was "out" she'd started obsessing about her looks to an insane degree. *And she's only ten. Christ.*

"You look great," Sterling called through the partially opened bathroom door. In the visible sliver of the mirror, he could see Alexa adding one last touch of gel to her pixie spikes before she nodded proudly at her reflection and came out into the hallway.

"You always say that," she grumbled, but she gave him a little hug as she went past. Still barefoot, Sterling noticed. "If you'd let me wear makeup—"

"Not a chance in hell. Not until you're sixteen."

"—then I wouldn't have to work so hard on my hair. What?"

Sterling cleared his throat and looked pointedly down at her bare feet. "If I go downstairs to finish making your lunch, will you get yourself the rest of the way ready in time?"

Alexa launched into her "I'm not a little kid" speech again, so Sterling left her to it. She was turning eleven in January—he still wasn't crazy about the idea of her getting into makeup yet, but maybe she'd like to get her ears pierced. Earrings would show well until she grew her hair out longer, and she'd probably have a blast deciding what her style was. *Christ, my kid has a "style."* It wasn't all that different than her usual clothing preferences were back when she was going by Oscar, truth be told, but Sterling had let her spend as much as she wanted buying new clothes online when she first started talking seriously about transitioning. Suddenly a large part of her wardrobe became pink, purple, and rainbows.

The phone rang—of course—right as Sterling had four eggs frying in the pan and two frozen waffles finishing up in the toaster. He picked it up and immediately put it on speaker.

"Hey, Little Buddy," his mother chirped. She was the only one who ever called him that, had since he was little, but he'd never actually gotten around to telling her how much the nickname bothered him. Over the years it became less annoying and felt more like an inside joke. Having your only child living nine hours away would be tough on anyone, and his mom deserved some happiness in her life. Sterling could deal with a childish nickname.

"Getting Alexa out the door in a few," he answered, "but hey to you too. When did you become such an early riser?"

"Helen decided we'd get more early foot traffic if we opened at eight instead of nine. She put me on the morning shift."

When Sterling was a kid, his mother had worked two jobs. She cashiered at a little tourist trap store during the day, walked him home from school, made them both dinner, then got up at two a.m. to clean corporate offices until it was time to wake him up again. She'd hated the cleaning job for as long as he could remember her having it. He did eventually convince her to cut back to only the store, and part-time at that, but she was still stubborn about being self-reliant. Even though her son was now a dentist, making actual money, and she didn't need to be.

"You know you don't have to work there, Mom. I've offered—"

"Helen needs me," she chided gently. This was well-worn territory. "If she can keep working at her age, so can I. It's not so bad. Anyway, I was calling to congratulate Alexa on starting summer break. Is she up yet?"

"You're a bit early, Nana," Alexa declared in the general direction of the phone as she swept into the kitchen. "Break starts Friday afternoon for me."

"Well, happy advance congratulations. Are you looking forward to it? You'll be spending the summer with your other grandparents while your dad's at work, right?"

Alexa looked up at him, her eyes wide, and Sterling abruptly realized he hadn't told her about his whole hiring-a-nanny plan yet. There'd been no point in getting her hopes up if there weren't any candidates who were a good fit on such short notice. If it came down to it, he'd cancel all his patients so he could stay home with her and do all the things a good father should have been doing with his kid instead of working so much. There'd only been a handful of applications for the last-minute position, anyway, and only the one interview. Jericho Johnston. Whom Sterling had purposely left dangling, despite how the guy was obviously an amazing find, in case he had second thoughts.

Second thoughts wouldn't help Alexa, though. Neither would shipping her off to a summer camp, or waiting the month it would take to have a home help service send out someone formally vetted and qualified to babysit. Jericho was more than qualified. Plus, charismatic and attractive and friendly. Also, the fried eggs were on the verge of being overcooked.

"We've had a change of plans," Sterling said casually. "Lawrence and Vivian are starting to slow down some, even though they don't like to admit it. They're not at a good place right now to take on a ten-year-old girl for a whole two and a half months, so I found a nanny who will be coming to stay with us." *I'll need to tell Jericho he's hired.*

Alexa ran across the kitchen—still barefoot, Sterling noticed belatedly—and clung to him in a silent hug. Sterling hugged her back and bent down to press a kiss to her spiky, gel-flavored hair. Just as well he'd already turned off the burner and dished out two eggs apiece onto the two waiting plates; he'd definitely be burning them now.

"That sounds like a fun summer," Sterling's mother declared. "Alexa, have you met her yet? Is she nice?"

"It's a 'him,' Mom. And no, she hasn't, but I'm hoping he can be here Friday evening so he has a chance to settle in before I'm back at work on Monday and he and Alexa start their hanging out time."

Alexa wrinkled her nose at him. "Kids don't 'hang out' anymore, Dad. It's called chilling."

"I thought that was a euphemism for…never mind."

"What's 'euphemism' mean?"

Sterling gave her a poke, which quickly turned into a tickle. She squealed and twisted away right as the toaster oven dinged. Sterling glanced over at the clock on the oven, saw the time, and barely contained his comment to something kid-appropriate.

"Sorry, Mom, we really do have to go. And if you're supposed to be at the shop at eight, you probably need to get moving too. Don't worry—even though this was a last-minute decision, we've got it all under control."

"You always do, Little Buddy." He could hear the smile in her voice as she said it. God, he and Alexa needed to get back down to the Keys and visit her sometime soon. "A live-in nanny, though? A man? That'll be an adjustment for both of you."

She didn't ask whether Jericho was "cute," which was a relief. Or whether he was gay. Sterling kind of suspected he was, based entirely on first impressions, but it wasn't going to make a difference because no matter who Sterling was attracted to, his little social circle would *definitely* have issues if Sterling suddenly started dating a man. Nobody could replace Dana, thankyouverymuch, and Alexa didn't need a substitute mother. A sputtered denial wouldn't convince anyone, in any case.

Alexa waited to ask her questions until they'd said their goodbyes, eaten their hasty breakfast, she'd *finally* found her shoes, and they were in the car. Then Sterling was a captive audience. There was more time to talk later, but obviously Alexa wasn't willing to let this turn of events go.

"Did you really hire me a babysitter? You know I'm ten, right?"

"He's not really a babysitter, and believe me, I'm *definitely* aware that you're ten. Going on eighteen. I'm not going to make you spend your summer with Grandma and Grandpa Butler, though. Especially now."

"They're going to hate you for implying they're old."

"I know." Sterling and Alexa shared a grin in the rearview mirror. "Let's hope you get Nana's genes for not going gray until you're fifty."

She was silent for a minute. Then, in a small voice… "Is the nanny going to call me Oscar like Grandma and Grandpa do?"

Christ. Sterling would have been perfectly happy to cut his in-laws out of his life entirely. Would have already, if it didn't feel like he'd be cutting out Dana's memory as well. "He won't," Sterling promised her. "I told him about your transition, so he wouldn't be surprised, and it turns out he actually worked a while at a summer camp with some trans kids. Well, teenagers. And he's going to live in the guest bedroom at our house, so you and I will both get to know him as well as he gets to know us. I really hope you like him—I think I already do."

"That's good." She slumped back in her seat. "That you like him, I mean. You almost never like annoying people. When do I get to meet him?"

"Hopefully Friday evening, like I told your nana. We can invite him over for dinner."

"Okay. You'll pick me up after school today, though?"

"Of course, Pup. I'll always be there for you." He'd already called into the office and asked the receptionist to reschedule all his patients past three p.m. for the rest of the week. There would be some grumbling, but Sterling purposely kept a few empty slots in his otherwise busy schedule for occasions like this and Alexa came first. She had to. "The way I see it," he added, "we've got the next few afternoons to ourselves. We're going to spend some of that getting the guest bedroom ready, but there will be time for fun stuff too."

The rest of the drive was taken up by a rousing sing-along of Bon Jovi.

Chapter 3

Jericho got to Sterling's house a bit before the agreed-upon four o'clock on Friday afternoon. His new employer was plenty well-off; that would have been apparent from the neighborhood even if the guy hadn't been offering six hundred bucks a week plus free room and board for a live-in babysitter. Unlike either the ugly brick apartments where Jericho had lived when he was a student or Paul and Brandon's cute white-picket-fence ranch he'd been crashing at for the last week and a half, this house was an impressive multistory affair with a landscaped yard, a balcony over the front porch, and what looked like a two-and-a-half-car garage. Jericho had barely rung the bell before the door was opened by a girl with short, spiky hair, a sparkly shirt that would do Lady Gaga proud, and an intense look in her eyes as she bluntly examined him up and down.

"Hi," she declared. Apparently he passed inspection, then. "I'm Alexa. My dad's in the kitchen right now because today was my last day of school and he took the whole afternoon off and we made cookies but he accidentally set the timer for eighty-eight minutes instead of eight minutes on the last batch so now the kitchen smells like smoke and he wanted to air it out before you got here. You're ten minutes early."

"Is that too much? I can wait out here until I'm regular old 'on time,' I suppose."

Alexa shrugged, then ducked back inside a moment. "Dad!" she yelled. "He's here! Can I sit outside with him until you're done in there?" Jericho couldn't hear his new employer's reply, but Alexa left the door open a crack and stepped out on the porch. Barefoot. She was wearing sparkly purple toenail polish to match her sparkly shirt, Jericho noticed. There was a wooden swing hanging from one side of the roof overhang, so Jericho claimed one end and indicated for Alexa to take the other.

Lord, she was going to be interesting to spend a summer with. The delightful "sharing every thought that comes into her head with no filter whatsoever" thing was a common quirk of ASD, and one Jericho had never minded in previous kids he'd worked with. Alexa talked at twice the speed she needed to, was outgoing enough to answer the door even when her father was in another part of the house, and was now sizing Jericho up with a little cock of her head. Other than her bluntness, though, her body language was friendly and perfectly polite. That was encouraging.

"What do you want to talk about?" she asked. "When you meet someone new, you're supposed to talk and get to know each other. Dad told you that everyone used to think I was a boy, right? That weirds some people out."

"He did, and I'm not weirded out," Jericho assured her. "In fact, it will probably be easier for me to not misgender you because I didn't know you when you were presenting as male. I'm sure everyone else is trying their best."

She wrinkled her nose at him. "Not Grandma and Grandpa Butler. They still call me Oscar."

Jericho made a mental note to ask Sterling about that later. It sounded like there might be a story he was missing. "That's got to be frustrating," he said. "Even if they get it wrong, though, you're still you. I have an idea—want to take turns getting to know each other? I'll tell you something about me and then you tell me something about yourself?"

Alexa pulled her feet in toward herself so she could rest her chin on her knee, but she made a vague sound of agreement. "Okay, but I'll start. Does 'nanny' mean you're going to be my babysitter?"

That was a good one to get out of the way right at the beginning, Jericho supposed. Truth be told, he didn't know *what* Sterling wanted to call him—"nanny" sounded a bit Mary-Poppins-ish, but "domestic help" or "live-in childcare" didn't really fit either. "I'd like to be your friend," he answered honestly. "A friend who can drive, and cook, and knows first aid just in case, and who helps make sure both of us survive the summer without maiming ourselves or destroying the house. Sometimes I'll be a *bit* like a babysitter, sometimes I'll have to tell you no we can't do something, but I promise I'll always give you an explanation afterward if you ask. You're old enough I don't have to treat you like a little kid as long as you don't act like one. Sound like a good compromise?"

"Yeah, I guess so." She shrugged, chin still on her knee. "What should I call you? Mr. Jericho? Mr. Johnston?"

Jericho smiled. "Mr. Jericho or Mr. J, if you want. 'Mr. Johnston' would feel like I'm your teacher at school, and I bet you're ready for a break from that. My turn now." He mentally flipped through several general questions, finally settling on "What was your favorite subject this year?"

"Science," she answered immediately. "And math too. They're kind of tied together. Dad says there's a lot of math in science."

"That's definitely true." Math had never been Jericho's favorite subject, but they could probably come up with some kid-friendly science experiments to do if Alexa wanted to. Even nature walks might be fun on the rare occasions Florida stopped being so ridiculously hot and humid. The city of Willow Heights was only half an hour from Camp Ladybug, which was conveniently the one area in the entire world Jericho felt confident he could identify 90 percent of the flora and fauna he and Alexa would be likely to encounter. He'd certainly done enough wilderness hikes with campers to pick some things up here and there. "So…you like rocks? Weather? Flowers? Catching lizards?"

She giggled. "Yeah, all those I guess. Mostly animals, though. I'm gonna go to college and maybe be a dentist like Dad is, but what I *really* want to be is a dental zoologist. That's a person who takes care of animals' teeth instead of having to look in people's mouths all the time. I'll work in a zoo because I'd get to see all kinds of interesting animals and teeth. Now me: how old are you?"

Abrupt and blunt change of subject, in that way ten-year-olds excelled at. "Twenty-five," Jericho said. "I'll turn twenty-six next month. My next question is, why a dental zoologist, specifically? I've never heard of that before, but it sounds interesting."

Alexa's entire face lit up. "That's because it is! Animals get different tooth problems than humans do, you know. The two biggest reasons people lose teeth are dental decay and gum disease, and animals don't get either of those. Tooth decay happens because the plaque on your teeth sometimes gets acidic bacteria in it, which end up eating away the tooth and causing cavities. And the most common kinds of gum disease are caused by the toxic waste products of the microorganisms in the plaque—it's like germ poop." She wrinkled her nose. Fair bet that dental zoology was one of the strange topic fixations Sterling had warned him about. "The chemicals irritate your gums and make them get sick," Alexa continued in what seemed like one long breath, "but wild animals don't eat processed sugar and carbohydrates the same way we do so they don't get plaque. Even when they do, bacteria on their teeth don't develop the same way ours do unless they're a pet and eat a lot of people food. I've already done a lot of research on my own—Dad says he'll take me to San Diego to see the zoo there someday. It's the biggest in the world." She bit her lip. "So my next question is, ummm…what's your favorite color, I guess?"

That was easy. "Royal purple." Coincidentally the same color as Alexa's toenails. "And since that was such an easy answer, I'll tell you my favorite food too: it's chocolate. Chocolate milk, specifically. Which I'm sure is bad for my teeth."

"Don't remind Dad about that, or we'll never be allowed to have any. I like it too."

"Good We might end up keeping some around the house for special treats, then." Assuming Sterling didn't mind—food was another thing Jericho would need to ask about. He was accumulating a dauntingly long mental list. "My next question is a bit more personal, but something I really should ask: is there anyone you're not 'out' to yet? Anyone I should be careful not to use your name or any pronouns when we're around them? Sometimes manipulating the conversation like that is hard to do, so I want to be prepared."

Alexa thought a moment, then shook her head. "Not everyone knows yet, but I don't want to pretend anymore. Dad and I talked about it a lot since Christmas. That's when I really started to think about transitioning for real. Not—not surgery or anything, but I…"

"I get it. Transitioning socially is a big enough step all on its own."

"Yeah." She flashed him a tiny smile. "I don't know if he believed me at first, but last month I finally picked my new name and Dad has been trying really hard to remember to not call me Oscar. That's a boy's name, and I'm not a boy." Her curled-up position caused her skinny jeans to ride up, drawing attention to the tiny purple flowers embroidered on the hem. They matched the tiny white flowers on her toenails. "We decided… this was my last week of school, and then it will be a whole two and a half months before I see my friends again. This week was the first time I wore girly clothes, instead of plain jeans and t-shirts, and today I told everyone my new name. Dad said it would probably help if they had the whole summer to get used to it."

"Yeah? How'd it go?"

"Fine."

That was an awfully quick answer. Jericho arched an eyebrow at her. "Really?"

"…No." She hugged her knees tighter to herself. "But don't tell Dad, okay? He's gonna have to come into the school office and do some kind of paperwork to change my name in the teachers' computers, and I don't want him mad at anyone. He keeps saying he's proud of how I'm being so brave and strong, but sometimes it's really hard. And kind of scary."

"It's okay not to feel strong all the time." God, how well Jericho knew that struggle. "I'm not going to promise you I'll keep secrets from your dad if he asks me directly or if I think he really needs to know something, but I'm not going to go blabbing about any private stuff you tell me either. Friends, okay?"

Alexa hauled in a deep breath, then nodded. "Friends."

"Wanna see if your dad has conquered the cookies yet?"

She perked up at that. "I can see if we have Hershey's syrup in the fridge—then we could make chocolate milk too."

"That sounds wonderful."

* * * *

Sterling was almost finished airing out the kitchen when Jericho knocked on the door. Alexa answered before he could get to it, though, and she and Jericho seemed to be perfectly content to chat outside for a bit. The reprieve meant Sterling was able to transfer the burnt cookies to the trash and scrub the charred crumbs from the baking sheet before they came inside. The lasagna was done, sitting on the warming shelf over the range, but the chocolate chip cookie smell was supposed to be a homey touch. So much for that.

When Alexa and Jericho did come in, several minutes later, Alexa was already talking a mile a minute and giving an abbreviated, nonlinear house tour. Jericho flashed a smile and a silent nod of greeting to Sterling before returning his attention to her.

"—because my room is upstairs, and Dad's study is next to me but really it's more like storage for some of Mom's things we haven't dealt with yet. This is the living room, there's the TV, and Dad's bedroom is the door over there. There's a really big closet and a bath that's like a hot tub, but if you want to use it Dad says you have to wipe it out afterward or else it gets gross and he gets mad. Hey, Dad—Mr. J is really nice. We sat on the porch swing until he was on time instead of early, and he and I have the same favorite color. So this is the kitchen—"

"I think he figured that out," Sterling interrupted, raising a significant eyebrow. Alexa took the hint and stopped rambling.

Jericho smiled at her, though, which kept her from reacting too dramatically to the mild chastisement. "You have a beautiful home," he declared. "The whole neighborhood is gorgeous, actually."

Alexa wrinkled her nose. "The neighbors next door are grumpy old snobs, but some of the other people on our street aren't terrible. I wish there were more kids."

There were several children within a few blocks of their house, Sterling realized, but none of them spent much time playing outside. Including Alexa. Maybe having an adult with her one-on-one for the summer—someone *other* than her transphobic grandparents—would help give some social interaction she'd be lacking otherwise. Sterling tried not to notice how a long-dormant part of his libido greatly approved of Jericho living with them for the next few months. Not that anything could happen between them, of course, but it wouldn't hurt to have eye candy like that around…

"I'd tell you not to say unkind things behind someone's back," Sterling said, jerking his train of thought back to a more acceptable track, "but in this case I'd agree with you. Luckily our grumpy snowbird neighbors are already in New Jersey and probably won't be back until October. Alexa, would you please help set the table? Maybe show Mr. Johnston where everything is in all the cupboards so he can start learning his way around?"

She did it without complaining, which was a relief, although she narrated her every thought the entire time. Sterling set himself to portioning out the lasagna. Jericho managed to wedge in a few answers in between Alexa's questions as she went, sounding genuinely interested, but he sidled closer to Sterling at the same time.

"I told her she was welcome to call me either Mr. Jericho or Mr. J," he said in a low enough voice for Alexa not to overhear while she prattled. "I assume that's all right? If you'd rather she call me by my last name, more formally—"

"It's fine," Sterling said quickly, trying to match Jericho's quiet tone. "Thanks for asking, though. I assume you don't have to leave right after dinner? You and I probably ought to hash out more details after Alexa's in bed, now that you've met her."

"Absolutely." Jericho nodded toward the plates. "Want me to help pour drinks, or…?"

"I've got it," Alexa chimed in as she breezed past them. "Dad, do you want water or orange juice? I found the Hershey's syrup, so Mr. J and I are both gonna have chocolate milk."

Sterling raised an eyebrow at that, but Jericho shrugged. "She's being a good hostess," he said. "I did happen to mention that chocolate milk is my favorite food. Well, favorite drink."

There wasn't really any way to argue with that. Alexa voluntarily helping in any sort of useful way was a novelty already. "Water for me," Sterling replied. "And—oh, I guess I'll have a glass of chocolate milk too. A *small* one."

It felt decidedly odd to have three people at the dinner table again. It didn't occur to Sterling to pause and say grace until after the moment had already passed; luckily Jericho didn't seem to expect it and Alexa didn't comment. That brief nod to religion was one of the many things he and Alexa had slacked off about in the two years since Dana's death. Alexa did remember her table manners, though, which was encouraging. He'd half worried that the etiquette part of her education had atrophied too.

"Tell me more about what you like to do, Alexa," Jericho prompted. "Anything you're looking forward to having time for this summer?"

She paused and gave it some thought. "Watching TV," she finally said. "Playing videogames. Drawing. Staying up later, doing…*stuff.* Things that aren't like school." She took another bite. "Oh, and shopping. If that's okay? I do have some new clothes already—Dad let me buy them online—but picking out t-shirts on Amazon isn't the same as getting to try things on. I really want a sundress." She beamed up at Sterling with a cherubic smile. "I've always thought they look really comfortable."

"Oh dear," Jericho murmured, a smile in his voice even though he managed to keep his expression serious. "Is *that* what this summer's going to be like? Well, I'm not an expert clothes-shopper, but I have friends who are and I'm a quick learner. I'm sure we can come up with something."

"Something reasonable," Sterling interjected. "Appropriate for a ten-year-old. We can talk more about it later."

"Sure thing." Jericho nodded decisively. "Different question, then: any foods y'all particularly do or don't like? I mean, I'd be perfectly happy eating this lasagna for dinner every night, but you might like a bit more variety."

They hadn't discussed him taking over the role of cook, but they probably should have. Maybe Jericho thought playing chef was an obvious part of his duties as not-exactly-nanny. Sterling cleared his throat. "Yes, well… don't be too wowed. It was frozen and came in a box."

"Dad *can* do real food," Alexa chimed in, "but most of the time he doesn't. We eat a lot of fish sticks and takeout."

When she put it that way, Sterling sounded like a terrible father. Even if the accusation had more truth to it than he wanted to admit. "I thought you liked fish sticks."

"I do! But we eat them a lot."

"Do you cook for yourself then?" Jericho asked her. Totally taking the "my dad is a crap cook" thing in stride, apparently. There was no judgment in his tone either, no underlying hint of "I can't believe your father can't even provide healthy food for you." Which was…surprisingly reassuring. Sterling hadn't realized how much he'd been stressing about Jericho approving of him as a parent until the half-expected criticism didn't come. And hey, if Jericho was volunteering to cook sometimes, he'd take it.

Alexa nodded vigorously. "I can do hot dogs, mac and cheese, and stuff that goes in the microwave as long as it has directions on the package. Mom always said"—she glanced over at Sterling—"that as long as I had the four food groups and my dinner wasn't too dessert-y, it would all balance out eventually."

"Your mom is…not living with you anymore?"

Jericho was clearly trying to feel around the edges of what was okay to ask about, but he needn't have worried. "My wife passed away almost two years ago," Sterling explained. "It was very sudden at the time, but Alexa and I muddled through it the best we could. We make a good team, don't we, Pup?"

She slid out of her chair to come give him a tight hug. Jericho pointedly averted his gaze, giving them their moment. "We do," she whispered quietly against Sterling's temple as she clung to his neck. "I still miss her sometimes, though."

"God, me too." More than he'd ever thought possible. Their marriage had never been a grand love affair, but Dana was a funny, genuine person and it had hurt like hell to lose her. Sterling cleared his throat and gently shooed Alexa back to her seat. "So," he declared. "If everyone's done with their lasagna, we do happen to have a batch of cookies which survived the Great Fire. Alexa, would you like to be the hostess?"

The cookies didn't taste even a little burnt, which was a huge relief. Not that Sterling *had* to impress Jericho—especially not with his cooking, since Alexa had been painfully honest about his lack of aptitude in that area—but those cookies were made from scratch and therefore at least one thing for the evening had gone according to how he'd planned it. Jericho complimented him on the taste. Then complimented Alexa on the proper ratio of chocolate to milk when she got everyone a refill, which made her preen. *Yeah, they'll get along like a house on fire.*

Soon enough they all had empty glasses and nothing but cookie crumbs and tomato sauce smears on their plates. Sterling peeked at his phone: nine o'clock. Usually Alexa's bedtime, at least during the week. No doubt the three of them would have to work out something different for the summer. Still, though… "Alexa, Mr. Jericho and I are going to be talking business for a while. Go brush your teeth and you can read for twenty minutes before lights-out, okay?"

Her facial expression made it clear it was *not*, in fact, okay with her. "Why can't I stay up and talk with you?"

"Because it's going to be boring details about who cooks and how often, and transportation, and when Mr. Jericho wants his vacation days, and when lights-out will be between now until August. Pouting now is only going to make me assume you need an earlier bedtime."

She rolled her eyes. "It's not like I have school tomorrow," she argued. "And I want to stay up and hear what you two are talking about. It's my summer, after all. Mr. J wouldn't be here at all if it weren't to play with me!"

God, she really took after Dana at times like this—petulant and stubborn, but in the most adorable manner possible. Maybe like a teenage Dana must have been, all attitude and frustration and undirected rebellion. There was no *way* Dana hadn't pulled that exact same eye roll on her parents, once upon a time. The familiarity didn't make it any less annoying, though.

"I might have something important to say," Alexa pressed. "I'm not a little kid—"

"We all know you're not," Jericho cut in gently. "But your dad is going to be my boss now and I'll be his employee, so we have to talk business things. Some of them will be private. Some of them will be boring. And you are tired; I can tell." He raised an eyebrow at her, somehow managing to look stern and congenial at the same time. "Tell you what—how about you and I clear the table and help your dad put the leftover lasagna away, then you can show me where my room is going to be and what the rest of the house looks like. You can be thinking of more things you want to know about me while you're getting your pajamas on and brushing your teeth and we can play another few rounds of our question game before you go to sleep. Deal?"

She held eye contact for a few moments, then nodded sharply. "Deal."

Sterling had to blink a few times to make sure he'd just seen what he thought he had. *Well, damn.* Jericho talked Alexa into voluntarily helping clean up? If the man's child-wrangling expertise hadn't already been impressive before, Sterling was definitely impressed now. Alexa was usually easygoing—in a ten-year-old kind of way, and in an extremely liberal use of the concept—but she rarely went along with anything that smacked of "chores" without at least a token grumble. Here she was, though, bussing plates without a fuss. God, was Jericho some kind of sexier, trans-friendly Mary Poppins? Sterling silently put the leftovers in the fridge and hung back to listen as Alexa gave Jericho the rest of the tour.

"This way." She waved for him to follow her the short distance past the dining nook and down the back hallway, all trace of her earlier petulance gone. "This used to be the guest bedroom, but we don't have anyone except Nana come to visit anymore—that's Grandma Harper. She's my dad's mom. She lives all by herself down in the Keys, but she's always really busy so she usually can't come up here and we have to go down there to visit her instead. That's your bed. Your closet is over there but it's kinda little. It was full of Christmas decorations but Dad and I moved those to the garage for you yesterday. I was helpful!" She squared her shoulders, pride evident in both her voice and her posture. "You have Mom's old dresser in here too, so you have more space to put your stuff. It still smells a little bit like her perfume if you put your face right in the top drawer, but not as much as it did when I first spilled a bottle in there when I was little so I'm okay with you using it. You have a bathroom in there"—she pointed toward the en suite—"but it's sorta small. I wanted to move the guest bed into Dad's study upstairs so you'd be next door to me, but Dad said I'm ten going on eighteen and I hog the bathroom too much so even though this one's not very big, you'd probably want to have it to yourself."

"Astute of him," Jericho replied gravely. "And you never know. Maybe I hog the bathroom too and we'd always be fighting over it. That'd be awkward, wouldn't it?"

Alexa made a face. "You couldn't," she countered. "You don't have any hair and you don't wear makeup. Dad won't let me wear it yet either, not until I'm sixteen. It's totally not fair—Mom would have let me." She sighed. "But okay, in the hallway back here is the door to the garage and past that is the washer and dryer." She waved toward the mud room. It was clean and sparkling and not at all muddy, for once, because Sterling and Alexa had spent the better part of the last two evenings trying to get this end of the house in order. Her help may have been more symbolic than helpful, but clearly she took pride in playing hostess and Lord knew Sterling wasn't going to discourage her. "Dad said we each have to do our own laundry because you're not here to clean up after us," Alexa continued. "I can't reach all the way down inside the washer, though, so I might still need a *bit* of help."

Jericho nodded, but he shot Sterling a subtly surprised look. Apparently laundry was one more thing they'd forgotten to discuss in their back-and-forth emails. Sterling wasn't sure he could handle learning whether Jericho preferred boxers or briefs, though—it was going to be hard enough to keep himself from looking and probably drooling if and when he ever saw Jericho without a shirt. The man was tall, thin, and moved with an easygoing grace Sterling couldn't help but appreciate. In an entirely professional, employer-employee way, of course.

"I'm sure we can work it all out," Jericho assured Alexa. "May I see the upstairs? I bet you've got your room all decorated exactly like you want it."

Alexa huffed. "There's still a lot of 'Oscar' stuff and it's all boy colors, but I'm working on decorating it better. It's up here."

Sterling trailed after them as they all mounted the stairs. The smaller second floor had only Alexa's room, Sterling's study, a small bathroom, and a walk-in storage closet, but the central landing opened up into a cozy reading nook and had double doors leading to a balcony overhanging the front porch. The space currently glowed orange from the sunset sky radiating through the glass doors. Dana had always loved the play of light across the little nook—it had been her favorite place to set up her easel and paint. One of the first things Sterling had done after she was gone was to go through the canvasses she'd deemed "not good enough" and pull out several to hang up throughout the house.

Jericho oohed and aahed appropriately as Alexa chattered at him about the various treasures in her room. Dana had never wanted to let Oscar decorate in a "girly" way—despite occasional pleas to the contrary, which probably should have given them a hint years ago—but the result of their constant tug-of-war over it was a color scheme which definitely veered more toward blues and grays than pink and lace. Pink and purple and sparkles and rainbows were 100 percent what Alexa was going to want, surely. Maybe Jericho would help her decide on something new and tasteful. Sterling truly hadn't had the time to help Alexa actually repaint and redecorate since her transition, but they were going to have to do something one of these days. A weekend project, perhaps. *Lord knows I don't spend enough time with her as it is.*

"You go ahead and get yourself ready for bed," Jericho directed, jolting Sterling back to the moment, "but your dad and I will both come back up here to say goodnight, okay? You can ask me…hmmm. Let's say two questions."

Alexa crossed her arms and stuck out her chin. "Four."

"Three."

"Deal. We'll be back in a bit." Jericho turned, hiding his triumphant expression from Alexa.

"I'm impressed," Sterling admitted once they were out of Alexa's earshot. "Irene said you were good with kids, but…well, I guess it's only fair warning to say she's usually not that compliant. You're exactly what Alexa needs, I think." Exactly what Sterling needed too, even if he'd only be silently imagining the possibilities from afar.

"Oh, I hope so. She's a sweet girl." Jericho chuckled. "She reminds me a lot of my sister Tamara—observant, blunt, and interested in *everything*. It's exhausting even imagining what living like that every day is like."

Neither Irene nor Jericho's resume had mentioned anything about his home life. "Older sister or younger?"

"Oh, younger," Jericho answered immediately. "I'm number four of eight."

"Seriously?" Sterling couldn't hide his surprise, which probably wasn't very polite of him. Still, though…eight kids ought to be a handful for any parent, even to someone who shared genes with Jericho. "Did a lot of babysitting, I'm guessing?"

Jericho nodded toward the living room. "Let's sit down and I'll tell you about it."

Chapter 4

Talking about siblings was a nice, safe suggestion, Jericho decided. It was a good way to ease into all the other stuff. They'd already hashed out some of the details via email over the last few days, which was good, but there were definitely some things he still needed to ask about. Not that there was a chance of him turning Sterling's job offer down. Hell, he'd probably hang out with Alexa all summer just for the free room and board, which would still be a heckuva lot better than Atlanta-level rent. Timing-wise, this was the perfect summer job.

The "how to be a live-in nanny" advice sites all emphasized the importance of negotiations and getting everything down on paper, though. Then before Jericho drove down for the interview, Brandon lectured him about the legal things he needed to worry about. It was a long list. Also a huge departure from the carefree, easygoing friend Jericho remembered from before going to Haiti. Brandon and his boyfriend Paul were only three years older than Jericho, but now they were settled with their own house and expecting a baby via Paul's twin sister acting as surrogate. It sometimes felt like they were from a completely different generation. Crashing with them meant getting advice on adulting whether Jericho wanted it or not.

"Want a drink?" Sterling asked, veering toward the kitchen. "Coke, apple juice, or beer?"

"Whatever you're having would be fine." Jericho leaned up against the counter and watched as Sterling pulled out two Cokes, then they shifted over to the armchairs near the enormous flat-screen TV. Sterling sank down with a sigh, closed his eyes, and appeared to be savoring his Coke like it was a fine whiskey. The silence was oddly comfortable.

"So the fourth kid out of eight," he finally ventured. "What's that like?"

"Hectic," Jericho answered without having to think about it. That probably wasn't a surprise. "I've got five sisters and two brothers, ranging from my sister Naomi who's seven years older than I am all the way down to Malachi who's a senior in high school this year. And before you ask, it wasn't a religious thing—my parents just love kids. Dad runs a consulting firm and Mom edits for some of the major textbook companies now that most of us are out of the house. Naomi was still in high school when Malachi was born, though, so they had eight kids all under the same roof at the same time. Everything got a little crazy. My father's sister lived with us for several years and helped tame the pandemonium a bit, but…yeah. You said you're an only child, right?"

Sterling nodded. "Guessing my childhood was a bit different."

"Oh, I'm not complaining." There were times he missed the controlled chaos, actually. "I wouldn't say I ever formally 'babysat' my younger siblings, but we were all expected to help out when my parents or my aunt needed it. Some of my cousins live in the New Orleans area too, so whenever we had family get-togethers, the older kids got to keep an eye on the younger ones. That was one drawback to going to Georgia State—I'm certified to teach in Georgia, not Louisiana. I mean, it's not *that* hard to transfer my qualifications, but I went and put down roots away from most of the rest of the family."

"That's tough." Sterling shook his head. "For me, it was always just me and my mother. A two-person family. I have vague memories of grandparents when I was still pretty young, but Mom was an only child and my biological father was never in the picture. Mom dated occasionally, but never anyone who stuck around. The idea of such a huge, busy family is totally beyond my ability to compute."

"And now you and Alexa are your own two-person family?"

"Yep."

There was a world of sadness in that single-word response. Sterling looked exhausted. Like a man who was overworked, overstressed, and never got the chance to simply sit down and watch Netflix or play a few rounds of whatever videogame was the most popular that month. There was an old Nintendo Wii under the TV, but if Jericho had to guess, he'd say it was probably Alexa's. Sterling probably was more the curl-up-and-read kind, Jericho decided.

He got the impression that Sterling could have really used a vacation a while ago but was too afraid to let his guard down. For Alexa's sake, presumably. God, the man looked like he needed a good cry, a good hug, a good fuck, or some combination of the three. And dammit, sex wasn't a particularly professional thing to be thinking about. *Focus.* He cleared his throat. "There's probably a bunch of important employer-employee things you wanted to discuss," he said, "but if you don't mind… Would you be willing to tell me a bit more about your late wife? In regards to her relationship with Alexa, at least?"

"God, you're not easing into this, are you?" Sterling hid his expression behind his raised glass. "I guess it's a natural first question."

Crap. Way to go, me. Excellent social skills. Jericho shook his head. "Really sorry, I should have—"

"No, it's fine. Nothing you could ask me I haven't been asked already, and by people with far less tact." Sterling frowned into his Coke for a minute. "Dana was…well. Calling her 'the life of the party' makes it sound like partying was all she cared about, but she was always so *alive*. She and Oscar—sorry, Alexa, told you I still screw that up sometimes when I'm talking about her before her transition—they were always trying to come up with ways to make me laugh. They had about as healthy a parent-child relationship as anyone could ask for. I was home a lot less, first for dental school and then once I started working, but Dana didn't mind being a stay-at-home mom. She really did love it, as far as I could tell."

Jericho could absolutely imagine Sterling with a bubbly, laughing woman on his arm. It was easy to see how they'd complement each other. "She passed away before Alexa transitioned?"

"That answer's a bit more complicated." Sterling sighed. "Dana had a cerebral aneurysm on June 24, 2016. It was a Friday. We'd only moved here to Willow Heights two years earlier, when I joined my partner's practice. It was so sudden—I was at work, Alexa was at school, and Dana was out shopping with her mother. By the time I got the call, she was already gone."

"I'm sorry for your loss." The platitude felt like a totally inadequate response, but it was heartfelt. To have to experience that, and with a kid… *Damn.* "You don't have to go into detail," Jericho said, choosing his words carefully, "but I assume that's something Alexa's still working through? In some form or another? I'm not a psychologist, obviously, but I want to be prepared to give whatever support you think she's likely to need."

"I think we've both gotten most of our initial grieving out of the way by now," Sterling said softly. "Not a day goes by that I don't miss her, but it's not…it's not sharp anymore, I suppose. And back to your original question—Oscar had never really been into stereotypically 'boy' things like dinosaurs or sports or toy guns. That bothered Dana a lot more than it bothered me. I don't want to say she'd have objected to Osc—sorry, *Alexa*—being trans, but I don't think she'd have had a particularly easy time getting used to it either. Alexa didn't really put a term to her dysphoria until well after Dana was gone." He grimaced. "It's been a tough process."

I'll bet. "I've got a few friends who are in the process of transitioning," Jericho said. "For some of them it has to be one part of their life at a time, and it's taken ages. It's not an easy thing to do." Hell, one of his closest buddies from college was still on the fence about publicly transitioning, almost three years after she first told him she was nonbinary. At the moment she had a complex set of rules for which pronouns were to be used where and at what time, who she was out to and whether they thought she was a cisgender gay man or knew she was a bisexual trans femme, the whole shebang. It was hard to even imagine having to keep life that segmented. Then again, Jericho's entire extended family had accepted him without question—and without surprise—when he came out, which was far from a universal experience, so…

"We're learning that." Sterling's tone suggested "not an easy thing to do" was a massive understatement. He eyed Jericho critically for a moment, assessing something, then nodded sharply. "I'll tell you the whole story, but it's with the understanding that you won't let Alexa find out. Okay? She doesn't need to know all the details, at least not yet."

Jericho took a gulp of his Coke. Whatever "the whole story" was, it sounded like he'd be needing the fortification. Caffeine, if not alcohol. "I promise."

"Good. So." Sterling copied the gesture, emptying his own glass before setting it back down onto the end table beside him and slumping a bit in his chair. "Damn, you're literally the first person I've ever admitted this to out loud. It leads into why I was looking for someone to watch Alexa at the last minute this summer, though." Sterling's gaze was fixed on the wall somewhere over Jericho's left shoulder. Thinking, or avoiding eye contact? The silence stretched long enough to become awkward.

Maybe this whole mess could wait for another time. When they knew each other better, perhaps. "I really didn't mean to be nosy—"

"So the thing is," Sterling said, talking right over Jericho's awkward apology, "Dana's family has always been extremely class-conscious. Her parents are—to be blunt—really freaking rich. I mean, I've been doing okay since finishing dental school and actually being in practice, but Dana was…well, she was a product of her upbringing."

That sounded an awful lot like code for "spoiled." Or, at the very least, "incredibly privileged." If Sterling's giant house and posh neighborhood were merely him doing "okay"… "Not an upbringing you shared, I take it?" Jericho prompted.

Sterling let out a startled laugh. "Oh, Lord no. It was all my mom could do to keep the two of us afloat and to put a roof over our heads. I was homeschooled from sixth grade on, but she did that on top of her regular two and a half jobs. The only reason I got out of the Keys at all is because the University of Florida offered me a full ride plus a stipend for room and board—and even then, it was a work-study program. Marrying Dana was a huge adjustment."

Damn. "I can imagine."

"My mother and I were never particularly church-going people," Sterling continued, "but Lawrence and Vivian—Dana's parents—have always put a lot of stock in their church. Which reminds me, by the way, I'd be happy to put you in touch with someone here if you want to find a congregation. Don't feel like you have to abstain on our account."

Oh, bless the Bible belt and the near-obligatory offer to help newcomers find a church family. "Thanks," Jericho demurred, "but that's not necessary. I'm only here for the summer anyway." Three years of mandatory six-days-a-week chapel with TeachUniversal was plenty. Christianity was fine, in a general way, but he'd never been quite as gung-ho for Jesus as everyone else he worked with in Haiti was. *Surely God will forgive me taking a bit of a break after that.*

Sterling gave a little "whatever" shrug. "No problem. I mean, it's fine either way. I've always… I shouldn't make assumptions about anyone's private beliefs, but I've always had the impression that Dana's parents' church relationships were more about community and appearances and keeping up with the Joneses than they were about God. Hell. I'm a terrible person for saying that about my own in-laws, aren't I?"

"Candid, maybe, but not terrible," Jericho countered. "I guarantee you they're not the only ones who do that. In fact, I'd guess 'the Joneses' they feel they're competing with are probably there, at least in part, for the same reason."

Sterling laughed again, a quieter huff than before. "Probably," he conceded. "In any case, Dana was always more of a free spirit. I think that was why she was willing to hang around with me when we first met. I was totally different from her high school friends, and she had a pretty sheltered life before college. I'm not one to talk—I was an awkward scrawny know-it-all who didn't exactly get out much either—but *anyway.* Dana was more open-minded than her parents about a lot of things, but she never did lose that 'what do people see when they look at me?' awareness. She tried hard not to show it, but she still noticed. And of course, her parents were forever taking her to task over anything she did that they disagreed with."

Of course. Jericho knew the type, had seen a few when they dropped off their teens at Camp Ladybug. Every time, he'd said a silent prayer of thanks that his own parents weren't like that. "They live nearby?"

"About a mile from here. One of those huge houses bordering the prestigious members-only golf course."

"Ah." Jericho vaguely remembered reading something about Willow Heights and golf, some top ten list of famous places to play. Dana's parents living in that neighborhood lent credence to the "grew up really stupidly rich" thing.

"You can imagine what their friends are like," Sterling continued. "So. As I said, Dana was a lot more easygoing than her parents are, but sometimes she didn't even realize her prejudices until someone called her out on them. We got married less than a year after we first met, because she found out she was pregnant." He grimaced. "I know it's a cliché, but that's how it happened. We were both so young..."

Damn. Jericho made a vague sympathetic noise.

"She was a junior and I was a freshman," Sterling explained. "But since I went to college a year early, I had only just turned eighteen."

Wait, *eighteen*? Seriously? Jericho had been still trying to navigate Atlanta at that age—far from home, brand-new college, finally 100 percent out of the closet, and tentatively starting to build a social life with his crazy roommate's Georgia Tech friends from the Pride Alliance there. He hadn't known then that those friendships would be the ones that stuck with him, more so than with any of his classmates at Georgia State. Growing up so close to New Orleans didn't really do much to create a sheltered upbringing, but Jericho remembered vividly how being all alone in a new place had taken a long time to get used to. "Sorry," he said, realizing Sterling was waiting for some sort of reaction. "I'm trying to imagine myself in that situation at eighteen years old. There's no way I was ready to be a parent back then."

Sterling offered him a small smile. "We weren't, either, but at that point it was less about *if* and more about *when*. Dana only had one more year of school left, but she dropped out to take care of our son. Daughter. Her parents had a fit."

That wasn't hard to imagine, given what Sterling had already told him. "Couldn't you have put Alexa in daycare?"

"Probably. In theory. Dana and her parents certainly had the money. I honestly don't think Dana really wanted a college degree in the first place, though. She'd always dreamed of being a stay-at-home mom. I know a lot of college-age young women would choose not to have the kid, in that situation, but she wanted to keep the baby so badly…"

He didn't mention whether his own opinion factored into her decision. The subsequent marriage proposal kind of spoke for itself, though, didn't it?

"We were dead broke," Sterling added, "but I still had free tuition and board. We got married that summer so campus housing would put us into the family apartments they usually kept for international grad students who come here with spouses and kids. I switched to the University of Florida's accelerated dental track because that meant I could finish a year early. We moved here when Alexa was six, and I finally started to earn money instead of accumulating debt to my in-laws whenever we had an unexpected expense. Their financial help was always presented as a gift, not a formal loan, but you know how those things can go."

Jericho nodded. His own student loans weren't too bad, but that was because his parents and his oldest sister—who was now a lawyer—had paid off a big chunk of them as a graduation present. His TeachUniversal stipend had gone toward the remainder of the loans too, since he hadn't exactly been spending a lot of money while living in rural Haiti. His parents' and his sister's contribution had been a gift, a totally unexpected one, but plenty of his friends were stuck in that emotional-debt-to-family cycle. The situation really sucked, especially for those with less functional families.

"They pushed for us to move here, to Willow Heights, because they couldn't wait to see more of their grandson. I mean, of Alexa. Sorry."

Oh, Lord love the man for trying to get it right even when Alexa wasn't in the room. *That*, Jericho thought, was the key to Alexa surviving the whole coming out thing without too much emotional baggage. "You'll get used to it eventually," he reassured him. "I'm sure she understands."

Sterling flashed a wan smile. "Thanks. I think you're right about what you said at the coffee shop on Tuesday—you'll be good for her, not having known her when she was presenting as a boy. So *anyway*, the long story made shorter: Dana would have tried to get Alexa's pronouns right, but Lawrence and Vivian won't. Aren't. They refuse to accept Alexa's gender identity, her new name, any of it. I honestly don't think they object to the trans thing as a religious issue, it's more that other people might find out. The whole 'keeping up with the Joneses' thing again. They want a grandson to continue the family lineage, blah blah blah, and a trans granddaughter isn't good enough. Especially since Alexa is the only grandkid they're going to get."

Jericho felt an unexpected surge of protective instinct wash through him. Alexa deserved better. "They're that openly transphobic? Seriously?"

"Pretty much." Sterling's tone made it clear he'd argued his point with them and had been rejected. Probably multiple times. "We'd planned for Alexa to go to their house while I'm at work during summer break, but I don't want to put her through that. If they can't call her by her new name, they don't deserve to spend time with her."

"Agreed."

Sterling sighed. "Vivian and I argued about it last week," he said. "I said they weren't welcome here until they stopped misgendering my daughter, and I admit I vented about it later that afternoon to a few of the hygienists. The next day, our office manager—Irene—recommended you."

That, all by itself, was a miracle. "I didn't know she even still remembered me," Jericho admitted. "We're friends on Facebook, but we don't keep in touch. When I first got the call about this potential nanny thing from my friend Chris, he neglected to mention that the connection came courtesy of his ex. I didn't find that part out until right before our interview."

"Maybe she thought you were worth rekindling the connection for? Or that Chris was, I suppose?"

"Oh, I doubt it was for me." More like *not a chance in hell*—he and Irene were still barely more than acquaintances. "Chris and I were roommates back in college," he explained. "Irene and Chris dated on and off for ages, but she and I were never really friends. Most of what I remember about her is that she's frighteningly organized when she wants to be, and also that she and Chris were a terrible match for each other."

A hint of amusement appeared on Sterling's face. He looked younger when he was smiling. "Dr. McClellan and I tend to get left out of office gossip about ex-boyfriends and how men are terrible," he said. "I can verify that Irene is still frighteningly efficient, though."

"No, I guess she'd leave the ex-boyfriend part out." Jericho hoped, for Sterling's sake, that she'd done some growing up since she and Jericho last saw each other. "Irene knew that Chris is bi and I'm gay, but she totally refused to accept that we might share an apartment yet not be attracted to each other. Most of their fights were because she was jealous of anyone else getting his attention."

Jericho paused, giving Sterling a moment to let the "I'm gay" part sink in. It seemed to be a slow process—Sterling's face was frozen in a puzzled expression, but he didn't answer.

Crap. "Will that be a problem?" Jericho prompted. "My orientation?"

Sterling immediately shook his head. "That's…no, it's fine. I had—well, I'd wondered, after meeting you in person. I just wasn't expecting you to lay it out there like that. We're LGBT-friendly in this house, obviously."

It was exhausting, having to specifically "come out" to everyone in his life individually, but necessity meant Jericho had eventually gotten used to it. He'd have to do it again with his fellow teachers once he started his new job in the fall. "I mention it because it's not something I intend to hide any longer," he said. "Three years of playing straight in Haiti was enough for me. It doesn't impact how well I can care for your daughter, obviously, but if you're worried about 'what people will think'—"

"That's my in-laws' issue, not mine," Sterling declared firmly. He paused. "I'd prefer you not…bring anyone back here while Alexa's around…but I'd say that for female dates too. It's really—it's all fine." He looked like he wanted to say something else, but the silence between them stretched until it started to get awkward.

"Good. Okay." Jericho nodded, even though Sterling hadn't really asked a question. *Glad to get that part over with, though.* "On that note, shall we both go up and say goodnight to Alexa? I notice we didn't actually get to any of the employment contract stuff, but it's been a lot longer than the twenty minutes we told her after dinner."

It was a blatant change of subject, but Sterling seemed just as eager to grasp it as Jericho was. Jericho climbed the stairs slowly and hung back so Sterling could go into his daughter's room first.

"You reading something good, Pup?" he asked her softly.

Alexa *hmm*ed and handed him the book she'd been so engrossed in. "The pictures in that one aren't very detailed," she declared, "but it's got lots of good facts. Did you know turtle shells are actually made from their ribs and vertebrae fused together? Their shell is covered with keratin, the same thing fingernails and bird beaks are made of."

Jericho had to crane his neck to see around Sterling and read the book's title—he couldn't make out the smallish font, but it had a snake skeleton on the cover. The volume was impressively thick for a ten-year-old to be reading too. *Guess I'll have to brush up on my biology.* To keep up with a ten-year-old. *Yeesh.*

"I didn't," Sterling answered, "but I do now. Thank you. It's lights-out for tonight—"

"Wait!" Alexa sat up and looked right at Jericho, eyes wide. "We were going do three questions and I haven't even thought of mine yet!"

That sounded like a play for more time if there ever was one. Luckily, having four younger siblings meant Jericho knew all the tricks. He came around to sit at the foot of the bed so they could all see each other. "How about this," he suggested. "You tell me three true things about you and I'll tell you three true things about me. Would that work?"

"Dad has to do it too."

"Of course! It's only fair." *And I'm curious.*

Sterling shook his head, but he was smiling. "Okay, you two, bossing me around. Who's going first?"

Neither of them were chomping at the bit, so Jericho volunteered. "I've got seven brothers and sisters, I can speak French and two kinds of Creole, and I'm just over six feet three inches tall. Everyone always asks if I play basketball, but I'm terrible at it. You next."

Alexa thought seriously for a moment. "I have no brothers or sisters, I'm four feet six inches tall, and my birthday is on January first. That's also New Year's. And a fourth true thing—I hate when people lump my birthday and Christmas together into one party because it's not fair. I got my picture in the newspaper for being the first baby born that year, though."

"My sister Abby has a December birthday, and she would agree with you." Their family had finally instituted a *no Christmas decorations before the 15th* rule, so Abby could have an actual birthday party before red and green everything took over. "Dr. Harper, your turn."

Sterling gave him a funny look over his shoulder, but tough. Jericho wasn't gonna call the guy by his first name in front of the girl who called him "Dad."

"I went to middle school and part of high school at home with Nana, I once read the entire Lord of the Rings trilogy back-to-back all in one day, and I've got the *silliest daughter in the world*." He punctuated this with a few strategic tickles that left Alexa wriggling under the covers. "I'm also a grumpy old man and want to go to bed because someone wore me out this afternoon. Sleep well, Pup, all right?"

She curled back up on her side. "I'll try, Dad. Goodnight. And goodnight, Mr. J. I think you're nice."

"I think you're nice too," Jericho said. "And I think we're going to have a really good summer."

Chapter 5

Sunday morning, Alexa was totally unable to sit still. She bounced and chatted a mile a minute from the back seat while Sterling picked his way through over an hour of back roads. The drive should have been closer to half that, but apparently Jericho's aunt and uncle lived so far out in the boonies that even Siri couldn't figure out where the heck they were. Alexa was the first one to spot the "Camp Ladybug" signs with helpful arrows pointing them through the last few turns. The entrance to the actual camp had a red-and-turquoise arch over the gravel road, with large wooden ladybugs staked into the ground at random intervals alongside. Sterling took the first left past the arch, as Jericho had directed, and pulled up to a little off-white house framed by neatly landscaped flowerbeds. Jericho was already waiting for them on the front porch.

"You found it! Excellent." He opened Alexa's door for her and herded them both inside. "Tante Brielle made a fresh pitcher of mint lemonade, if you want some. She and Uncle René will be back in a bit—they went up to deal with something in one of the cabins, but Tante Brielle said it was probably a five-minute fix. They did want to say hi to you before we left, though. Mind if I go ahead and put my suitcase in your car?"

Sterling pointed his keychain remote toward the door and popped the trunk. Modern technology was really nice sometimes. "I flipped down one of the back seats, so hopefully there's room for everything. It may take a bit of Tetris depending on how much you have, sorry—my Crosstrek isn't really built for hauling. What can I help carry?"

"I got it." Jericho grabbed the handle of a smallish rolling suitcase. "I pack light. This and my laptop, and I'm all set."

"Seriously?" The suitcase was *maybe* enough to hold two weeks' worth of clothes. And yes, the guest room was already furnished, but Sterling had assumed Jericho would want to bring more than the absolute basics.

"Seriously." Jericho slung the laptop bag over his shoulder and hoisted up the suitcase to carry it down the stairs. The already-sticky morning air brought a bit of eye-catching shine to the lines of his bicep, and Sterling's brain went to static at the sight. Unexpected, and gorgeous. His mouth probably dropped open too, so it was just as well Jericho was headed out the door instead of in. The trunk opened and closed, then Jericho came back inside all smiles and friendly and oblivious to Sterling's helpless ogling and started pouring lemonade.

Uncle René and Tante Brielle did return a few minutes after Sterling and Alexa and Jericho had all sat down at the kitchen table. René Johnston was built like Jericho; the family resemblance was unmistakable. Both men were tall, slender, and moved with an odd sort of grace that belied their long limbs. Tante Brielle had slightly lighter skin, short curly hair, and her head only came midway up her husband's chest.

"We'll be sad not to have Jericho around here this summer," Tante Brielle said as she and her husband joined them at the table with their own glasses of lemonade. She looked petite and delicate, dwarfed between her husband and Jericho. "We're getting our first crop of campers this afternoon, and some of our repeat visitors have been asking when Mr. J was coming back. Jericho, when you end up with your own classroom somewhere up in Georgia, you're always welcome to come down for the season while you're not teaching. We'll find a place for you."

"Thanks," Jericho said, pulling the smaller woman in for a sideways hug. "I'll miss you too, but I get to spend this summer with my fun new friends. Speaking of which, I didn't do introductions. Uncle René, Tante Brielle, this is Sterling and Alexa Harper. Sterling and Alexa, this is my uncle René and my aunt Brielle."

"You called her 'Taunt,'" Alexa said, confusion on her face.

"'Tante' means 'aunt' in French," Jericho explained. "And 'tant' is aunt in Louisiana Creole, which is the other language most of the people in my family can speak. It's kind of like English and French smushed together. I can teach you some, if you want."

"How do I say 'hi my name is Alexa'?"

"*Je m'appelle* Alexa. *Mo pele* Alexa. *Mwen rele* Alexa." Jericho coached her through the phrases, one at a time. "There, now you can introduce yourself in France, Louisiana, and Haiti." He added something else, a long, fluid phrase that made his aunt snort into her lemonade, but he didn't offer a translation.

Alexa grinned and nodded, already done with the topic now that her question had been answered, but Sterling's thoughts were decidedly slower to move on. Prior to that moment he would have said Jericho had a nice enough voice. On the deeper side, with a tiny hint of an accent he hadn't been able to place, but normal enough to not particularly notice it as a defining feature. It suited him. Hearing that smooth voice take on an almost musical element speaking something other than English, though… Sterling had to take a long drink to keep himself from reacting too obviously. Maybe it would have been worth sticking with a foreign language in school after all.

They all made polite small talk for a few minutes—Sterling talking less than normal, not that anyone noticed—but then it was time to go. Jericho thanked his aunt and uncle for the hospitality and said his goodbyes, then he and Alexa and Sterling started the hopefully-not-quite-as-long drive back to Willow Heights.

"We have a surprise for you when we get home," Alexa announced from the back seat before they were even past the camp's entrance gate. "It's more Dad's surprise than mine, but I got to help pick it out."

Jericho raised an eyebrow at Sterling, a half smile on his face. "Something good, I hope?"

I hope so too. "Something you'll need," Sterling said. It was a nonanswer, but tough cookies. He and Alexa had spent two hours at the dealership, picking out something appropriately safe and reasonable for Jericho to drive over the summer. If Alexa wanted to surprise him and gauge his reaction, Sterling wasn't going to say no. "It's something I realized we mentioned in our initial emails and never really hashed out details for. I hope you don't mind Alexa and me taking the initiative."

Jericho playfully tried to badger an answer out of both Sterling and Alexa for the rest of the ride home. He didn't guess it until Sterling pulled into the driveway, alongside the silver Mazda already parked there, and tossed a set of keys into Jericho's lap.

"It's a car!" Alexa declared, as if he couldn't see it himself.

"It's not a stupidly expensive gift, don't worry," Sterling said, before Jericho's eyeballs *actually* popped out of his head. "You'll need something to drive this summer, though, so Alexa helped me pick out something we can lease for a few months. This one was reviewed well for tall drivers and had a good safety rating. We'll have to fill out a few last bits of paperwork tomorrow to make you the primary driver as far as insurance goes, but otherwise it's yours to use while you're here. Alexa crawled around all the back seats at the dealership to find one that met with her approval."

Jericho still hadn't stopped staring at the Mazda 3. "I've never… I mean, *wow.* You hinted that transportation would be 'covered,' but I assumed that meant borrowing an old beater or you lived near a convenient bus stop or something. This is…wow."

Truth be told, Sterling felt rather the same way. It really did look pretty, all sparkling and new in the morning sunlight. He'd never been much of a gearhead, but at the dealership the previous day he couldn't help but gravitate toward the nicer end of the lot. He and Dana had shared his cheaper—and much older—Ford Focus all through dental school. Dana nicknamed it "Margo." They'd traded Margo back and forth for six years, the whole time they were trying desperately to make married life work despite Sterling studying his ass off when not at school and Dana being at home with the baby. Eventually Dana's parents decided not to cut her off after all and money stopped being so tight, but they didn't get a second car until Sterling passed his boards and finally got to add "D.D.S." after his name. They sold Margo, Dana picked out a sedan big enough to transport her canvasses and art supplies in, and Sterling eventually let himself be talked into the little SUV he had now. *Probably drive it until it dies before buying a new one*. No point in dropping fifty grand on something that ultimately just gets you to the office and back. The Mazda was a bit of an indulgence, but Alexa had fallen in love with it and Sterling found himself really, really wanting to see Jericho's face when he got the keys. The experience didn't disappoint.

Alexa had absorbed more of the salesman's patter than he'd thought too. She demonstrated it now, chattering to Jericho about the parts she'd found interesting: the sound system, the infrared camera that helped with parallel parking and backing out of the driveway, the legroom.

"They put a paper on the window with lots of numbers," she explained to him. "And some of them are the same on all the cars but some are different. The salesman was mostly busy talking to Dad, so I got to go read a bunch of them and this one had a sticker saying it had the most legroom and headroom of all the cars in that part of the parking lot. I remembered that you were six feet three inches tall."

"You do have an excellent memory." Jericho looked from the car, to Sterling, and back again. His skin was too dark to tell for sure, but Sterling could have sworn there was a bit of a blush on those cheeks. "I want to bring in my suitcase and put my things away," Jericho said, "but then can we come back out? You two can show me what it looks like on the inside."

He'd packed so light there wasn't even anything for Sterling to offer to help carry. Instead, Sterling ended up trailing behind on the way into the house, trying not to let himself feel inappropriately giddy over having made Jericho smile like that.

* * * *

Jericho set his suitcase and laptop gently on the bed, far enough from the edge that Alexa's excited bouncing around wouldn't knock them off. He hadn't really thought about having "packed light" until Sterling mentioned it, but now that he noticed...*damn.* His whole life, the last three years of it anyway, fit in a mid-sized suitcase he could lift with one hand. There had been plenty of opportunities to stock back up on clothes, books, and other things once he was back in the States and crashing with Paul and Brandon, but he just...hadn't. The bedroom was three times the size of his room in Haiti, though, with a lot of dresser and closet space to fill. Maybe it was time?

"Alexa," Sterling said from the doorway, "I think Mr. Jericho needs some time alone to get settled. Why don't you come out here with me and we can write down as many useful tidbits for him as we can think of? That way he won't have to ask if he wants to know where something is."

Jericho caught Sterling's eye and nodded his thanks. Having Sterling and Alexa observe as he unpacked would have felt awkward—they didn't need to see his entire life on display one item at a time. Even though he was moving into their house and they'd probably see most of it eventually anyway. There were still some everyday things he needed to pick up, a new razor and soap and deodorant and other "personal" supplies, but... *Oh!* That meant he had an excuse to drive the new car.

"I can help," Alexa argued, not moving from her spot. "I wanna see what Mr. J has. Any good books? Did you bring toys? I know you probably don't have *little kid* toys in there, but sometimes Nana packs—"

"Alexa."

"Dad." She glared at him and copied his tone of voice perfectly, albeit with a hint of an eye roll at the end. "I *am* being useful. We can write things down after. And I can help later, because Mr. J and I are spending the whole summer together. That means I'll always be around and can tell him things or help with—"

"Out. Give him some space." Sterling lowered his chin in what Jericho recognized from his own childhood as the *don't you give me lip young man or you gonna regret it* look. Sterling wasn't as good at it as Jericho's mama had been. Then again, she and his dad had eight kids' worth of practice.

Despite Sterling's stern tone, Jericho could see Alexa digging her metaphorical heels in. She wanted to be "helpful"? Jericho didn't think he really had any not-safe-for-Alexa-to-see possessions—not counting his browser history, maybe—but still. *No.* Hell, Sterling had already told her to get out, so now her refusal was about more than respecting boundaries.

Jericho puttered around with sizing up the bathroom cupboards and the empty dresser drawers for a bit, mostly to get himself out of the way while Alexa and Sterling had their standoff. The two glared at each other, Sterling repeated himself, Alexa refused. They kept the cycle up for an uncomfortably long time. Alexa didn't budge from her claimed spot on Jericho's bed, but she did up her volume in a way that suggested her full-fledged meltdowns were probably an impressive affair. She'd settled into a pugnacious pose kneeling on the bed, chin high, and obviously not taking in a word of what Sterling was telling her. Sterling, on the other hand, was leaning on the doorway like he was already tired and regretted getting drawn into a battle of wills with his ten-year-old. Which he appeared to be losing, Jericho realized.

"Alexa." Speaking up was going to make things awkward—it wasn't really Jericho's place to interfere with the father-daughter power dynamic—but he was going to have to sort out the best discipline techniques for Alexa eventually. Might as well take it on while Sterling was around. "When your father tells you to do something, you do it first and argue second. Even if you're right and he's wrong. Even if it's hard. Even if you don't want to stop whatever you were doing before."

She twisted around to pout at him too. "I only wanted to help…"

"You wanted to disobey your dad." Jericho cocked an eyebrow and gave her an "I'm not taking that attitude" look. Another one to thank Mama for. It was something that transcended the language barrier, as he learned early on at TeachUniversal when he first got to Haiti and was faced with a random assortment of students and brand-new teachers. It worked on Alexa too, thank goodness—she blinked at him, but kept her mouth shut. The silence stretched.

Jericho was weighing up the pros and cons of delivering a lecture on listening versus potentially overstepping his employer's boundaries when Sterling finally pushed off the door frame and came closer. Alexa kneeling meant the two of them were closer in height. "Pup," he said softly, "you're listening well right now and I'm proud of you. I'm sure Mr. J is happy about how well you're managing your emotions, even though we told you no. What does Miss Susan always say?"

Alexa's shoulders sagged. "Think twice, talk once," she mumbled.

"And what was your think twice this time?"

She heaved out a long breath. "That Mr. J didn't say I can stay."

Sterling gathered her up into a hug. "Go on up to your desk, find some paper, and think of what useful things we can write down, okay? I'm going to talk to Mr. J for a minute and then I'll be right out with you. I'm sure he's got a few questions."

Alexa was strangely quiet after her little rebellion, but she flashed Jericho a tight smile and slipped past Sterling out of the room. Sterling hung back in the doorway until they could hear her flop onto the sofa in the living room before he met Jericho's eyes. His obligatory smile looked surprisingly similar to Alexa's.

"I can fill you in more about this later," he said softly, "but that right there was actually a pretty big deal. One of the ways Alexa's autism spectrum diagnosis manifests itself is in angry meltdowns when she doesn't get her way. Or more accurately, I guess, when she gets reprimanded for something. Even something little. She was having trouble coping after Dana died, so I found her a therapist."

"Someone named Miss Susan?" Jericho guessed.

Sterling nodded. "Oscar—Alexa—was never a *calm* child, but as far as I can tell we dealt with an average number of tantrums. After Dana was gone, though, every little thing turned into a massive fight. Miss Susan worked with Alexa on it. Quite a bit, actually. Her meltdowns aren't as frequent or as dramatic as they used to be, but she still has a really, really hard time calming herself back down. For future reference."

Autism manifested itself in so many forms and flavors it was impossible to catalogue them all, but temper issues weren't impossible to overcome. "Does she get violent when she's having a meltdown?" Jericho asked. "Sorry there's no way to put that more delicately."

Sterling shook his head. "Not like I'm sure you've experienced in the past, if you've dealt with other autistic kids. Not usually, anyway. Like I said, I don't mind telling you more specifics later, but just...be aware, okay?"

Recent gender transition, autism spectrum, and lost her mother. *Damn.* Jericho might have his hands full this summer, but there was no question Alexa was a kid who could benefit from an adult to talk to. Therapist or not, Jericho could at least do that much.

Chapter 6

Irene and Ellen were both already in the break room when Sterling finally got a few minutes to eat early the next week.

"Staying for lunch again, Doctor?" Ellen asked. She was halfway through a salad and a Diet Coke, which—extrapolating from past experience—was a big red-flag warning that she was about to start a new fad diet. Those inevitably led to her scrutinizing everyone's caloric intake for however long her enthusiasm lasted. The rest of the hygienists tolerated it with a bit of annoyance and a lot of patience, since Ellen epitomized the stereotype of "sweet Southern charm" and was by far the oldest woman in the office. She pre-dated Sterling's partner Dr. McClellan, even. Ellen saw it as her motherly duty to impart her wisdom upon the younger generation and nobody had the heart to tell her what the word "hangry" meant and why she really ought to self-examine a bit more. "Seems like we never saw you when you weren't with patients before," she added, "and I *know* you never brought leftovers for lunch."

"Probably because there never used to be any." Leftovers were one of the many lovely changes since Jericho moved in. Previously, Sterling's lunches had usually been hastily eaten sandwiches in the office he and Dr. McClellan shared while reviewing patient charts. Jericho's food deserved more attention than that, though. Today, lunch was the last few barbecue ribs—which were just as good cold as they'd been when Jericho pulled them out of the oven the night before—and the remainder of Alexa and Jericho's joint attempt at corn casserole from the night before that. Faced with the choice of packing leftovers, a sandwich, or trying to get carry-out from somewhere nearby and dashing back to the office, there was really no contest.

Irene's cheerful expression turned a *tiny* bit smug. She had leftovers for lunch too, he noticed. They didn't smell anywhere near as good. "New nanny's working out, then?" she asked.

"You found someone?" Ellen motioned with her fork in a "come on, spill the details" gesture. "Oh Lord, is Osc—your kid out of school already? I swear it was still March an hour ago."

Sterling forced a tight smile. She was trying, and it was important to recognize that as a positive step. A big one for somebody who grew up in Alabama in the '50s. She and the rest of the staff still weren't entirely sure what to think of Alexa's transition, though, despite Sterling making a point of telling everyone individually so they all had time to get used to the idea before it became office gossip. Most had reacted with blank looks. Irene, the office manager and—apparently—ex-girlfriend of Jericho's ex-roommate, was the only one to simply respond with "okay." Now, over a month later, she was still the only one who didn't default to "kid" whenever Alexa came up in conversation.

"Alexa finished last week," he answered her. "And yes, Jericho is turning out to be an excellent fit for her. I really do appreciate the recommendation. I can't imagine anyone else having clicked anywhere near as quickly. Alexa said she and Jericho are making you a surprise as a thank-you—they won't tell me what it is, though, so I'll be just as surprised as you are."

Irene wriggled her shoulders in a little chair dance. "I knew he'd be perfect. Oh, that's great. I haven't seen Jericho for a few years—did he tell you how we met?"

Ellen frowned, thinking. "Is he the guy you dated when you were back in Georgia?"

"His roommate. The one studying to be a special ed teacher."

"Oh! Tall Black guy with the amazing abs, right?"

"He mentioned it in passing," Sterling interjected, before they could start talking more about either Jericho's abs or Irene's varied and extensive dating history. Maybe it would be better to escape back to his desk as soon as the corn casserole was done reheating. Irene and the hygienists were all ridiculously invested in each other's lives, but Sterling was one of the owners of the practice and thus their boss. The women rarely included him or Dr. McClellan in office gossip and that was probably for the best. Still, though, this sounded like the best chance he was ever going to get to find out more about Jericho without actually having to ask outright. Asking Jericho directly would lead to him wondering why Sterling was so interested. "Didn't give any details, though," he added. Hopefully that came across as innocently matter-of-fact but with an implied "...so fill me in please." There wasn't really any way to be more subtle about it. "During the interview he mentioned having known you from college, but not much more than that."

Irene nodded. "He was in college; I was a receptionist at the student health clinic near campus. The Georgia Tech campus, I mean—Chris was at Georgia Tech, Jericho went to… I forget, was it Georgia State? They're practically right next to each other."

"That sounds right." He'd spent a ridiculous amount of time staring at Jericho's resume after that interview, trying to decide whether entrusting this stranger with Alexa was the best or the worst idea ever. *Also whether I'd spend the summer with a constant hard-on, guy like that under my roof.* The verdict was still out on that one.

"So—oh, I do remember." She put her fork down, the better to gesture with her hands as she told the story. "I guess we must have seen each other in passing a few times when Chris and I were first dating, but the one I really remember was on Halloween. Chris's apartment complex was sponsoring some sort of haunted house party for the neighborhood kids, because it's not like they could trick-or-treat in downtown Atlanta. Also because most of the people who lived there were students and I think they wanted an excuse to dress up in costumes and make idiots of themselves. They had the meeting room downstairs all decked out with fake spider webs and plastic skeletons, and Chris had volunteered me to help him with clean-up. He always did that kind of thing—good intentions, but he usually assumed everyone would want to do whatever charitable task he was signing up for. Anyway, he and I and some other girl were pulling decorations down and wrangling trash cans and Jericho was doing face-painting. He had a line all the way out the door, because he was *good*. Like, true actual artwork. It was amazing. The party was supposed to be over, but he kept going until he got through everyone. It took him probably an extra hour, the whole time we're cleaning up. And then he stands up and I see he's got this bright pink scribble all over his cheek and forehead, and he laughs and says one of the kids was scared so he let her draw a design on his face first. He and Chris and I hung out together after that, once in a while, but I'm never going to forget him with that toddler scrawl all over his face."

Sterling didn't find that mental picture hard to visualize. Not in the slightest. Jericho acted like a perfectly normal guy most of the time, from what Sterling had been able to observe in the last several days. When he and Alexa got to goofing around, though, Jericho had no sense of dignity whatsoever. Alexa *loved* it. Tuesday night the two of them had played a two-person game of charades while Sterling did dishes, making up the ideas as they went. It got more and more outrageous until Alexa laughed so hard at Jericho's rendition of "angry, charging bull accidentally falling in a lake" that she cracked her forehead on the corner of the coffee table. She had an impressive goose egg for quite a while afterward. Sterling came home the next night to find Jericho and Alexa had drawn a face and arms on the no-longer-painful bump and were in the middle of making paper-doll-style outfits Alexa could tape to her face. Sterling took a mental snapshot: Alexa laughing, Jericho looking slightly embarrassed but mostly pleased with himself. Sterling hadn't realized until that moment how much he'd been missing hearing Alexa laugh.

That sense of fun would be a good trait once Jericho was a teacher. He'd probably be the one who ran the drama club, dressed up in funny costumes on school spirit days, and would always laugh alongside the kids when he did something ridiculous so they'd be laughing *with* and not *at* him. He'd encourage his students to think outside the box, that making mistakes was okay, that failure can be part of the learning process too. In short, he had all the hallmarks of being one of those amazing educators his kids would remember fondly decades down the road. *Yeah, okay*—hiring him was definitely the better choice.

Ellen smiled at nobody in particular and sighed. "Must be nice having an artistic type around again," she mused. "I wonder if he does more than face paint? I know he's probably got his hands full watching your kid, but you should ask if he paints actual pictures. Proper art. And if he's any good."

Irene made an excited noise and had to cover her mouth momentarily to finish her bite. "Oh, believe me," she interjected, "he is! He took some art class while Chris and I were together, and for a semester he had drawings up all over their kitchen. All kinds of things—faces, bowls of fruit, the ocean. He did one of Chris snoring on the couch and I swear to God it was one hundred percent accurate, down to the way Chris wrinkled up his nose right before rolling over. He let me keep it after the class was over. Doctor, do you think maybe he'd want to do those paintings for the waiting room, the ones Dana never finished?"

Her eyes went wide at her slip, and she and Ellen both froze. Everyone still did, whenever Sterling was in the room and Dana's name came up, so he was careful not to let any reaction show in his expression. It was true that Dana had been thinking about painting a set of three canvasses for the practice's rather drab waiting room. She died before doing any more than conceptual sketches, though, and it felt decidedly odd to realize this was the first time anyone brought those paintings up again.

Two years. It's been two whole years. It was supposed to be okay not to feel the same immediate, visceral reaction he'd waded through in the months immediately after Dana's death whenever someone mentioned her. The ever-present ache was still there, the guilt over everything they'd not yet resolved between the two of them and everything their marriage was never going to be, but it wasn't as raw. And yet…this was probably the first time he'd thought about those aborted sketches since she died. As far as he could remember, they were still in the upstairs storage closet.

"I'll have to ask Jericho about that," Sterling answered smoothly. Like invoking Dana's name didn't always inspire a moment of embarrassed silence in the office. "He hasn't mentioned he's an artist, but I'm sure Alexa would be fascinated if he were. When she was a toddler, she used to lie on her blanket in her doorway during naptime and watch Dana paint. She loved putting on a smock and 'helping.' Nowadays she's drawing more diagrams and animal pictures—still on her dental zoology kick—but whatever artistic talent she has, she definitely didn't get from me."

Ellen snorted. "Let me guess—you were more interested in math and science. You sound like the type."

Oh yeah. No contest there. "Math, science, statistics, economics. Tried computer programming, even though I was never any good at it. I'll have you know, though, that I was the Florida state math bowl champion in high school. Three years running. You can imagine what a huge circle of friends I had—especially since I was a year younger than everyone else and I'd been homeschooled for the previous several years."

"I can easily believe you were a child genius," Dr. McClellan commented, squeezing past Sterling to get his lunch out of the break room fridge. "I'm imagining you looked just like Oscar, only with glasses on. And carrying a big stack of textbooks."

"You're not too far off," Sterling admitted. "Although I didn't get these square rims until college. I was a child of the '90s—think giant Coke-bottle lenses in an ugly plastic frame."

Dr. McClellan staggered theatrically and clutched the edge of the table. "Good Lord, you make me feel old. I'd already been in practice for a decade by 1990. Which means I probably started before you were born."

Ellen coughed discreetly. "And some of us were already here when you were an eager-eyed new partner joining Dr. Allen, Doctor."

"Speak for yourself," Irene interjected, chuckling. "Dr. Harper, someday you'll be the one talking about 'way back when' and I'll be the cranky old battle axe who's been here with you the whole time. Well, if global warming doesn't put our whole state underwater first." She stood and tossed the last little bit of her lunch in the trash. "And on that note, I ought to get back to work. My bosses might notice if I stretched out my lunch break sitting around here." She winked at them. "I'm glad Jericho is working out for you and Alexa, though!"

Ellen followed suit, which left Sterling to finally attend to his cooling corn casserole and the messy barbecue ribs. Dr. McClellan took the seat opposite and they both ate quickly but silently for the next several minutes. Technically the office closed from noon to one, but the staff all had a flexible half-hour lunch because there were inevitably still patients there from morning appointments running late and early birds who showed up forty-five minutes before their scheduled afternoon cleanings. Sterling was running on time for once, which was a novelty, and apparently so was Dr. McClellan. This was their brief calm in the eye of the storm.

"I don't intend to be here another forty years," Dr. McClellan declared suddenly, as if the earlier conversation had never stopped. "Have you decided on a timeline yet for when you want to kick me out of my office? I know we haven't talked about it for a few months, but…well, retirement's a process. Wanda's been chomping at the bit for me to cut back my hours even more. Be around the house more often, have the chance to go visit the kids for more than a long weekend. I don't want to leave you with more patients than you can handle, though, and Lord knows you've got plenty of work on your plate already."

Christ. Sterling was *so* not ready to deal with this question again—had it really been multiple months since the last time Dr. McClellan brought it up?—but he shook his head and plastered on a polite smile anyway. "Buying you out is a big step," he explained. *A huge financial gamble and a long-term commitment to staying in Willow Heights.* Dr. McClellan had made it clear right from when Sterling accepted his offer of partnership, three years ago, that he was looking to retire in the near future and wanted Sterling to take over running the practice. The contract he signed when he first started gave him the option—but strongly hinted that it was all but decided—to buy Dr. McClellan out within the next few years and inherit the name, staff, machines, and office all in one go.

The idea of owning a solo practice had seemed like an impossible dream back when Sterling was studying for his NBDEs at the end of dental school. Partly because running a dental practice requires a lot more business sense than merely being a dentist, but also because the outlay of money required was significant. He and Dana talked about it all the time that first year. Her parents were friends with Dr. and Mrs. McClellan through church, which was what had gotten Sterling the interview and the partnership offer in the first place, but it was obvious the *real* reason her parents pushed so hard for Sterling to accept it was because they wanted Dana permanently back in Willow Heights. They loved seeing Oscar and tolerated Sterling, but they still weren't ready to let Dana go.

She'd missed being near her parents too, though, and it was a darned good offer. An independent schedule, no faceless medical conglomerate determining salary and how long Sterling was allowed to spend with each patient, and the non-binding clause in the contract about the buy-out. It allowed him to start paying everything off faster if he scheduled himself for more patients, though, and Willow Heights *was* a nice town. Rich and snobby and elitist, but good schools and beautiful public spaces. It wasn't the worst place to raise a child.

Dr. McClellan was still sitting there watching him, his intense gaze giving Sterling the odd impression he was being looked *through* him instead of looked *at*. "I know you wanted time to settle in," Dr. McClellan said after it became obvious Sterling wasn't going to elaborate, "but I think it's obvious by now that both the staff and the patients love you. You've put down roots here. I know it's not the same after…after losing someone who has passed…but surely finances aren't the issue?"

They weren't. Between the six-figure income and the life insurance policy Sterling hadn't even known Dana possessed, he could probably have taken over for Dr. McClellan outright and still had enough left to comfortably pay Jericho to be there when Alexa got home every day for the rest of the year. *Not Jericho specifically*, he reminded himself. This arrangement was a temporary one and Jericho had bigger and better plans. It would be enough money to pay a theoretical future someone, though.

No, the issue was him. Sterling shook his head. "It's not that. I know three years is a long time to still be 'settling in,' but I…"

Dr. McClellan smiled sadly. "You're still missing your wife," he pronounced. "It doesn't feel right to make big decisions without her input, does it? I went through the same thing, after Rose. It does get better after a while."

Out of everyone in Sterling's limited social circle, Dr. McClellan was the only one who'd experienced something even remotely similar to Dana's sudden death: his first wife had been seriously injured in a car crash when they were both much younger, and she died at the hospital a few weeks later. By all accounts, Dr. McClellan threw himself into his work and had never looked back. His current wife had children from a previous marriage, some of whom had been occasional playdates for Dana when she was smaller, but they all lived elsewhere by the time Sterling and Dana moved back to

Willow Heights. Dr. McClellan rarely mentioned Rose, but when he did, it was always with that same wistful expression.

Did the sick nostalgia feeling ever truly go away? Sterling nodded a silent thanks at Dr. McClellan's understanding and stood to put his lunch bag back in the break room fridge. Someday, maybe, he and Alexa would have someone else in their lives like Dr. McClellan had his second wife and his stepchildren. Maybe Dana's memory would be reduced to the occasional wistful smile.

Sterling tried very hard to ignore the fact that the "someone" in his mind looked an awful lot like Jericho.

Chapter 7

"Did she like it? Did she like it?" Alexa barely let her father get through the door before she was literally tugging on his arm and bouncing up and down. "Did you give her my card too? I used my best handwriting and everything!"

Sterling hung his keys on the hook next to the door, then leaned down and swooped Alexa up into a hug. Jericho stood back and let them have their moment. Alexa wasn't particularly good at waiting, he was learning. As if that was a huge surprise for a ten-year-old. The enthusiasm was cute, usually, but the attack hugs were something Sterling probably was wishing she'd grow out of.

"She loved it, Pup." Sterling set Alexa back down again and ruffled her hair. "Miss Irene thinks you're both *amazing* artists, and she said she'd be honored to hang your painting up at her house. She's got the perfect spot on the wall picked out and everything. She said she'll keep the card with it too, to prove she knew the painters. Then if you're famous someday, she can brag about having an original piece."

"Did you hear that, Mr. J?" Alexa leaned on her father and beamed up at Jericho, eyes wide. "We're real artists now. Just like Mama was."

Something complicated passed over Sterling's face. "Just like," he echoed quietly.

Alexa was oblivious, though, already plowing on. "In the card I told her how we did it. We worked together to make a sketch on paper, then Mr. J helped me transfer that onto the poster board in pencil. Really light so you couldn't see it after. He fixed some of the places the lines got lumpy or didn't look right, but I did all the painting myself."

"Amazing," Sterling murmured, and headed for the living room. He looked exhausted. Jericho was used to seeing him come home a bit worn after a longer-than-usual day, but now he looked ready to drop.

Alexa trailed after him. "I picked what all the colors would be, but Mr. J helped mix them so they'd come out right. Dad, did you know you can make *every* color from combining the normal rainbow colors of paint? I knew about red and yellow make orange and blue and red make purple and red and white make pink and all of those, but Mr. J can make brown and tan and the peachy-pink color like the walls at your office—"

"Alexa," Jericho chided gently, "I think your dad is really tired right now. I bet he'd really like to sit down for a minute and have us all be quiet. Maybe you could get him a glass of ice water? And then, once he's had a chance to sit down after spending the last nine hours looking at people's mouths, maybe you could tell him about what we did today."

Sterling shot him a grateful look and collapsed into what Jericho was coming to consider his "usual" armchair. There were two, one on each side of the sofa, but Sterling almost always ended up relaxing into the right-hand one at the end of the night. The last few evenings, Jericho and Sterling had watched a TV show or two together and chatted a bit before turning in. When Sterling dozed off halfway through *Criminal Minds* a few days earlier, Jericho had ended up turning off the show and watching his employer instead. Sterling wasn't square-jawed and macho, like so many men wished they could be, but in that moment there was a softness about him that made Jericho feel weirdly protective of him. Of the two of them, of that quiet moment in the half-dark where he now knew Sterling—consciously or not—felt comfortable enough around him to fall asleep. They'd only known each other a week, and yet.

And yet.

Jericho took the other chair and they both sat in silence for moment.

"I love you, Dad. Really, really a lot." Alexa handed him a glass of water and climbed sideways onto his lap. Jericho felt a momentary pang of jealousy, and wasn't that ridiculous? Sterling was snuggling his ten-year-old daughter the way a father should. He didn't need Jericho's shoulder to lean on.

Alexa gave him a loud peck on the cheek. "Today Mr. J and I went to the library," she declared, alarmingly close to Sterling's ear given the volume of her voice. "We looked at books for a while in the kids' section but I'd read all the zoology ones there already so Mr. J found a librarian and she took us to the grown-up zoology books so now I have three new ones up in my room. The one about cats even has a bumpy page so you can feel their skeleton! There's a horse book too, and it mostly shows different breeds but also has a part about how a horse's body works. The third one is about the circulatory system which isn't really zoology, since it's about people, but Mr. J said understanding how an animal's circulation works is probably important when you're fixing their gums so I think it's good for me to learn."

The library had been a random suggestion for how they should entertain themselves for the day, one Alexa had been immediately enthusiastic about. It was encouraging to see her so positive about it even after the fact. "She really impressed the librarian," Jericho told Sterling. "The two of them had a talk about animal physiology in general and dental zoology in particular."

"Of course they did." Sterling hid a smile in the back of Alexa's hair, where she wouldn't see it. "I'm glad you had fun."

Apparently Alexa had shared all the news she planned to share, because she climbed back out of Sterling's lap and looked back and forth between the two of them. "So. What's for dinner? Dad, the chart on the fridge says it's your turn. Can we have milkshakes?"

Sterling huffed out a half laugh. "Milkshakes aren't really a dinner food. And honestly, I'm not up to cooking anything complicated tonight."

Only a blind person would fail to notice the exhaustion on Sterling's face. A blind person or Alexa, maybe, as she showed absolutely no awareness of it. *Chalk one up for ASD.* "I don't mind putting something together," Jericho volunteered. It was only a little bit of a lie. "I think we've got some chicken already cooked—"

"Actually," Sterling cut in, "I was thinking about getting pizza. If that sounds good to you two?"

Alexa wrinkled her nose, but conceded when Sterling promised they'd order a small pizza that was only cheese and she could have it all to herself. Jericho sat back and let the two of them sort out where to order from and what else to get, only dropping opinions into the mix when Sterling asked him directly. They eventually settled on one cheese and one "all the meat (plus onions)" pizza, from a local pizzeria, and Alexa could have soda with her pizza only if she ate something from the vegetable drawer in the fridge first. The lady on the phone at the pizzeria said it might be up to an hour for delivery, though, and Jericho wasn't sure his stomach would last that long.

"I'll go pick it up," he offered. "Alexa can grab a carrot and come with me."

"Are you sure?" Sterling made a visible effort to sit up straighter and not look quite so exhausted and relieved at the suggestion. "You've been on the clock just as long as I have."

Alexa had been reasonably stress-free all day—mostly due to the library and the fact that she'd immediately stuck her face into a book once they got home—but it was reassuring to hear that Sterling realized and acknowledged that Jericho shepherding Alexa around actually was "work." Yes, Jericho was being paid, but it would have been easy for Sterling to mentally stretch "nanny" into "housekeeper/cook/gardener/caregiver for Alexa whenever she gets cranky," and any number of other household chores.

Clearly the one who needed care, right now, was Sterling. "I'm sure," Jericho said. *You look like you're about to fall over, and Alexa's brand of help really isn't helpful.* "Gives me another chance to drive that new car," he added. It was a flimsy excuse, but Sterling didn't fight too hard. Boss or not, some part of Jericho wanted to wrap Sterling in a nice warm blanket and put him to bed. Letting him have a bit of silent solitude was the second-best solution.

Alexa did choose a carrot—Sterling assured Jericho when he first moved in that Alexa would theoretically eat other vegetables, but so far she'd turned her nose up at most of them—and Jericho waved her out to the garage. He turned the dimmer lights in the living room down by half on the way out.

"Thanks," Sterling said with a sleepy smile that warmed Jericho to his toes. "I don't usually let myself run this late getting home, but surgery this afternoon went *so* ridiculously long it threw off my whole schedule. I'm sorry you had Alexa longer than usual."

Yeah, wrapping Sterling up and putting him in bed definitely sounded good. A sudden vision of the two of them cuddling together flashed into Jericho's mind. He'd have to be the big spoon due to their height difference, obviously, but hopefully Sterling wouldn't mind. And dammit, he had no business even *thinking* like that about his boss, much less hoping for anything.

Jericho let Alexa's chatter wash over him during the drive. She rarely required any input from her audience, and he found himself coming again and again back to the memory of Sterling's sleepy little smile. It would be nice to earn more of those. And other, mostly platonic things—Jericho was steadfastly trying not to think about Sterling in a sexual sense because if Sterling ever guessed what was going through his nanny's head, the next two months would become hella awkward. The man was probably straight anyway. Even if he were a little bit bi and interested in Jericho and if they ignored the awkward employer/employee dynamic, Sterling had still been married to a woman for…Jericho did the math. Ten years? Eleven years? They'd have to hide their hookups from Alexa, Sterling's coworkers, his in-laws, everybody. Three years of careful internet history and not being able to confide in another soul at TeachUniversal cured Jericho pretty damn quick of ever allowing himself to be jammed into the closet again.

"Mr. J?" Alexa's insistent tone snapped Jericho out of his daydream.

"Sorry, what was that?"

"I asked if you knew any transgender grown-ups, and what they're like. Weren't you listening?"

"Sorry," he said again, instead of a more truthful *no, you were rambling.* "And yes, I know a few. Trans adults are just like any other group of people—you know that, right? Some are cheerful and some are grumpy and some are loud and some are shy and some have boyfriends and some have girlfriends and some don't identify as male or female at all. There are as many flavors of trans people in this world as there are cis. Err, non-transgender."

"Oh." She sounded disappointed. "I guess that makes sense. I was kinda hoping you knew something about grown-ups who transitioned when they were kids. I don't know anyone else in my school like me—is it going to be like this forever? Do you think I'll meet someone else like me someday?"

Christ. Jericho was really not the best one to deliver this particular "birds and bees" talk, especially given the political and social issues surrounding being transgender in public. An idea, though… "Alexa, would you like to meet a friend of mine? Her name is Regina and she's the same age as me. She lives a ways away up in central Georgia, but I haven't seen her in a while and I'd like to."

Alexa nodded slowly. "Okay, I guess. Is she trans?"

"Yes, and she doesn't get embarrassed by anything." Like, *anything.* This might be the one time Regina's lack of a TMI filter could be helpful, though. "If you've got any questions about transitioning or anything else, she'll be an excellent one to ask. Even for stuff you don't feel comfortable asking me or your dad."

No question Regina would love to meet Alexa, either. Truthfully, from what Jericho had heard second-hand, she'd been a maternal figure to half the newly transitioned women in Atlanta. Maybe whatever the trans equivalent of a drag mother would be? Somewhere between a peer and an accepting surrogate parent, perhaps. He and Regina hadn't seen each other in years, but they still emailed back and forth a few times a week. Usually to share funny internet articles and to gripe about politics together. Her fashion sense was legendary throughout Georgia—if she said a special look worked for you, you didn't argue. She charged big bucks for the movie companies to get her expertise and opinions, and she got a lot of repeat business from all her happy clients.

"I did tell your dad I'd take you shopping one of these days," Jericho added. "Miss Regina is *amazing* at finding things that look good no matter what your body shape is. It's literally her job to find clothes for movie stars. I'll have to work out when she's free, but I'm sure she'd be excited to meet you." Especially because it was becoming obvious that when Sterling said Alexa could spend whatever she wanted on her wardrobe, he truly meant it. Regina would help Alexa find a style, answer her questions, and happily help her buy all the clothes she liked. She'd probably do it for free since it was Jericho asking too, but if Sterling was going to pay stupid amounts of money for clothes anyway…

Regina's answer to "do you want to take a newly trans girl shopping with an unlimited budget?" was probably going to be a squeal audible even through a text.

There was a rustling from the back seat, one that sounded like Alexa sitting up straighter and wriggling a bit. "I'm gonna make a list of questions when we get home," she declared. "Because I've got lots and lots, and Dad won't let me look them all up on Google because he said some of the things I'd find aren't suitable for kids."

"He's probably right." Jericho flashed Alexa a smile in the mirror. "Regina's not always suitable for kids either, but I think you two will get along fine. She's pretty, she's funny, and she'll help find the best clothes on the planet for you."

Sterling had better say yes.

Chapter 8

Sterling did say yes, without having to think about it. He even let Alexa talk him into coming along. She was more excited about this shopping trip than he'd seen her in forever, and Jericho seemed cautiously eager too.

"I haven't actually seen Regina in person for years," Jericho confessed on the two-hour drive up the coast. "She was one of the first people I met at Georgia State my freshman year, though, and you both are going to love her. Regina is…well, she's one of the handful I kept in close touch with while I was in Haiti. It was her, my roommate's circle of friends, and my family. That's really about it. I did eventually learn enough of the language to function socially down there"—he flashed Sterling a quick smile—"but that was hard at first. Haitian Creole is a lot further from either French or Louisiana Creole than I expected, and the language barrier makes things difficult."

"There weren't other Americans at your school with you?"

Jericho shook his head. "One lady from Switzerland, one from the Philippines, a guy from Canada, and Pére Michel, who started the school in the first place. I think he grew up in Australia once upon a time, but he's lived in Haiti for so long it wasn't the same. His accent was more Haitian than Australian, anyway. We foreigners did talk in English most of the time when we were all together, since it's the one language we all shared, but the point of being there was to train local teachers with the skills to better handle children's needs in the classroom when they went back to their own schools. A few of them knew some English or French, but…yeah."

"Sounds lonely."

Jericho shrugged. "I survived. Anyway, Regina is delightful and she's a pretty famous wardrobe consultant in the movie world. The Atlanta contingent, anyway. If anyone can find Alexa the perfect look, it's her."

"Hear that, Pup?" Sterling peeked in the rearview mirror to catch Alexa's reaction, but she was sound asleep. "Oh." *Oops, better keep our voices down.* She needed the nap.

Jericho twisted around to check on her, then straightened with a grin. "She looks so innocent when she sleeps, doesn't she? You'd never guess what she's really like."

* * * *

Regina was stunning. Not in a "man who looks feminine" sense, or even "that woman is hot"—Sterling's first impression of her was more akin to *damn, that is a gorgeous human being.* Suddenly the concept of anyone being able to command such a high fee for a few hours of personal shopping didn't seem so ridiculous anymore. True, she was built like a model, tall and thin, but something about the way she carried herself made her bright-patterned dress stylish instead of jarring. Long, wavy hair, frighteningly pink high heels, and a genuinely warm smile for the three of them as they approached the entrance to the mall, and Sterling was already starting to feel more optimistic on Alexa's behalf.

Jericho ran the last few yards and enfolded Regina in a bear hug before she could actually say hello. There was quite a bit of excited chatter and "I've missed you so much," before Jericho finally stepped back and put a hand on Alexa's shoulder. "This is the girl of the hour, by the way," he declared. "Alexa, meet my friend Miss Regina. Regina, this is Alexa Harper and her dad, Sterling. Alexa is ten this year and will be going to school presenting as female for the first time this fall. I promised you'd be able to help her find something suitable."

"You're really pretty," Alexa pronounced.

"Aww, thank you." Regina shook Sterling's hand, then leaned down so she could offer the same courtesy to Alexa. "I think you're really pretty too. Are you looking for some specific clothes today, or should we just browse and see if I can help you find something you like?"

Alexa glanced up at Sterling. "I'd really like to find a sundress," she said, "but browsing is good. Most of my clothes… I have a lot of jeans, and Dad let me order some new shirts and a few dresses, but he's not so good at fashion—"

"Hey!" Sterling interjected.

"—so I don't know what I'm missing, only that it feels like I am. Missing something."

Regina's face softened into a much more organic smile. "Been there, sister," she declared. "We'll start with a few stores I think might be the most promising and we can go from there, okay? I love your haircut, by the way—the edgy, spiky look gives you a lot of style options. When school starts, you'll be looking so fabulous nobody will remember what you wore last spring."

Alexa looked down. "That'd be nice," she said quietly. "I wore a skirt on the last day of school this spring, and told everyone my new name. Nobody understood, and some of the kids were really mean about me dressing like a girl. I'm hoping maybe by the time summer is over it won't seem so weird to everyone anymore."

"You are a girl, and don't let anyone make you doubt that." Regina led them unerringly down the crowded central walkway of the open-air mall, managing to keep up a conversation with Alexa and Jericho despite having to dodge so many slow-moving people. Sterling counted two balloon animal artists, a handful of street musicians, at least one birthday party in progress, and an impressive number of tipsy adults given that it was barely noon on a Saturday. A peek through the window as they passed a pub-style restaurant revealed a soccer match on the TV—one mystery solved, then.

The first store Regina showed them was a cute little boutique brimming with pink and glitter on everything. Alexa loved it. Sterling suspected the only thing saving him from sticker shock was the fact that he could barely stand to shop for his own new clothes, much less anyone else's, and he had absolutely no idea how much a "good deal" would be. $40 for a tank top? Certainly more than something cheap from Walmart, maybe, but he didn't see any sale signs at all in the store. Maybe that's not something girls' clothing stores did.

"Holding up okay?"

Sterling startled from a half daydream to find Jericho at his elbow. "Was just thinking I'm terribly out of my depth with all this," he admitted. "And if she's this clothes-happy when she's ten..."

Jericho snorted. "Give her some time to revel in it—if all I'd ever owned was frilly dresses, I'd probably feel the same way about buying my first pair of jeans."

"God, now I'm picturing you in a frilly dress."

"You'll never get confirmation. A few years ago I talked my oldest sister into burning the one picture Mom and Dad have of her and me playing princess dress-up together."

"When you were younger and more open-minded?"

"Ha ha. I'll have you know I look fabulous in a tiara…or I did before I started shaving my head. Don't tell Alexa; she'll be jealous."

Alexa chose that moment to pop out of the small dressing room and model a frilly hot pink shawl-type thing over a much less garish knee-length dress. Regina *hmm*ed and indicated for her to twirl around.

"How's it feel?"

Alexa's glow nearly outshone the neon of her shawl-shrug-whatever. "Like I'm pretty," she said, her eyes never leaving her reflection in the mirror.

"You're the best daughter a dad could ever hope for," Sterling said, and pressed a kiss to the top of her head as soon as she held still long enough. "I'm happy for you to feel pretty, Pup, but no matter what you look like you'll still be you. And I love you more than I can ever say."

Jericho was looking at him like he'd done something impressive. Sterling raised an eyebrow, silently inviting an explanation, but Jericho only shook his head and kept smiling.

Chapter 9

Jericho's twenty-sixth birthday fell on a Saturday. Alexa had been meticulously planning a party for him for weeks. There was no way he hadn't noticed *something* was up—subtlety was not one of Alexa's strong suits—but Jericho seemed suitably surprised when Sterling pulled into the beach parking lot and unloaded a blanket, umbrella, and a picnic basket.

"You two did this for me?" Jericho smile threatened to wrap all the way around his head. "I can't believe it—it's been ages since I last had a birthday party. Y'all are both amazing."

"We packed swimsuits too," Alexa announced. "I have mine on under my clothes already. It's the one Miss Regina helped pick out and I love it!"

"I remember." It was hard not to. The find had been the golden moment of their shopping trip—a purple and silver one-piece, with a gauzy skirt which ought to prevent any potential double-takes. Alexa had every right to be giddy about getting to wear a "girl" suit out in public for the first time.

The look on Jericho's face suggested he understood the significance too. "Are you planning for us all to swim? I've never been swimming in the ocean."

"Alexa is," Sterling hedged. "I'll probably opt out of the full aquatic experience, but a bit of wading and splashing would be fun." He'd always been too much of a nerd and an introvert to enjoy hanging out at the beach, even though Key West wasn't *that* big and there wasn't much else to do when you're sixteen. Alexa was already a stronger swimmer than he was and she was only ten. He cleared his throat. "Let's get our picnic lunch set up first. Mind carrying the umbrella? I can't juggle everything at the same time."

Together they found a relatively uncrowded patch of sand to stake their claim on. Sterling could have sworn he and Dana had done the occasional picnic before, when they were still living in Tallahassee and too broke for anything else, but a discreet rummage through all the likely storage areas in the house didn't turn up anything except the wicker basket. Ultimately he'd had to grab the spare blanket for his own bed and pray that the sand washed out later. The umbrella had been Dana's, though, from when she sat on the balcony to paint. It looked more like patio furniture than a beach umbrella, but it was portable and—more importantly—large. He, Jericho, and Alexa all fit in the shade once they squashed into a loose huddle around the picnic basket.

Sterling opened it up and pulled out sunscreen, Jericho's swim trunks, and an assortment of sandwiches and fruit. Probably too many, but that was better than not enough. Alexa had been helpfully keeping Jericho distracted upstairs while Sterling threw the lunch together, so he'd been more focused on having enough food than editing his plans. The selection worked, though—even Alexa put back a reasonable number of calories. By the time they were all done eating she was nearly vibrating with sugar and repressed energy.

"Go on," Sterling declared, waving her down toward the water's edge. "You've got your sunscreen all the way on already, right? Including your face?"

She nodded. "I finished it in the car while you and Mr. J were talking."

"You can go introduce yourself to those girls down there if you want to, then." Sterling indicated toward a giggly trio walking together in the wet sand. One looked a bit older than Alexa, the other two definitely younger. All three were walking side by side with their heads down, probably searching for seashells.

Alexa grinned at him and charged off to meet her new friends.

"Not shy, is she?" Jericho leaned back on his elbows and sighed. "I know I said it before, but thank you for this. It's a beautiful day for it, and a beautiful beach."

"Willow Heights is pretty good about enforcing their 'no littering' rules and keeping the restrooms clean." Dana had some fantastic anecdotes about playing on this particular stretch when she was growing up. "Speaking of which, do you want to get your suit on? Restrooms are down there." He pointed out a squat building back near the parking lot and the paved trail. "I'm going to keep an eye on Alexa while she's near the water, but if you want to go change, we can swap out after."

"Sure, that works." Jericho picked up his suit and trotted off. Sterling put the rest of the food away, shook the sand off the blanket where it had already accumulated in little swirls, and dug out his own swim trunks. He nearly dropped them again when he looked up to see Jericho loping back toward him, wearing his dark orange shorts and absolutely nothing else.

It was all Sterling could do not to drool. Jericho had a long, lean build—he'd damn well noticed *that* the first time he met the man—but now it was painfully obvious Jericho looked even better without his shirt. Faintly defined abs, more muscle than Sterling would have expected, a bit of fuzz on his pecs but not enough to obscure his nipples… Jericho's body was a gorgeous vista of smooth, dark skin topped off with a dangerously tempting smile. One which held a bit of amusement, like he knew Sterling was ogling—

Crap. Sterling quickly scrambled to his feet and hugged his swim trunks to his chest. "I'll, um. I'll be back in a sec," he stammered. "Alexa's still playing with those girls. Building a sandcastle, I think? I can't tell who's the architect and who's the grunt labor, but they all seem to be having fun."

"I'll keep an eye on her," Jericho assured him. He tilted his head back toward the restroom. "Go change."

Sterling did. He took a minute to splash some cold water on his face, double-check he didn't have any strawberry seeds stuck in his teeth, and repeat over and over in his head that they were at the beach to have *fun*. Not so he could ogle his daughter's nanny. It was so, so tempting to start thinking about Jericho in that way, but if he let himself fantasize, it would set them both up for awkwardness further down the road. He'd probably give it away somehow and creep Jericho out. Or, if by some miracle he managed to keep his daydreams a secret, he'd pine all summer and all he'd accomplish would be to make himself miserable. Sterling purposely kept his eyes on Alexa, the water, and the sky as he walked back to their little beach homestead. Maybe he wouldn't make a complete and total idiot of himself if he just didn't look at Jericho while the dude was only half-dressed.

"Navy looks good on you," Jericho called once Sterling was close enough to hear him over the sound of the waves. "What happened to the sunscreen? Thought I saw it in here somewhere."

Sterling dug it out from the picnic basket and set it on the blanket between the two of them. "Go ahead. I need to slather myself with it too."

"No surprised comment about me needing it in the first place?" Jericho's amused huff let Sterling know he was kidding. "In my experience, white people tend to assume anyone with dark skin has magical sun-repelling powers."

The question had popped up in Sterling's mind, but he knew better than to ask. "Skin cancer's no joke," he said instead.

"That and I sunburned the top of my head once, when I first started shaving it. That freaking *hurt.*"

They sat together in silence for a few minutes, trading the tube of sunscreen back and forth. Sterling kept an eye on Alexa and her new friends—they weren't *that* close to the water, but accidents do happen. The beach only had one lifeguard, down near where the restrooms were, and she obviously couldn't keep an eye on everyone at once. The relatively mild Saturday, for June, had apparently drawn everyone in a fifty-mile radius to the beach.

The other advantage of focusing so closely on Alexa, of course, was that Sterling couldn't do that and drool over Jericho at the same time. Not as obviously, anyway. Even though Jericho was revealing new information with every twist and turn as he worked sunscreen into his back, his legs, his shoulders. It was hard not to be self-conscious of his own more thoroughly average proportions in comparison.

"You're staring," Jericho said.

Sterling's breath caught in his throat. *Crap.* "I, um. I apologize if I gave you an unprofessional impression—"

"Not just an impression." Jericho's voice had an odd humorous note to it. "And not just today either."

Crap crap crap. Sterling buried his face in his hands so Jericho wouldn't see the vivid crimson that had to be climbing up his cheeks. Not that hiding his face would help much, since the blush probably showed up on his neck and shoulders too. No way Jericho wouldn't know exactly what Sterling's embarrassment meant. Maybe he could try to pass it off as sunburn and they could both pretend...

"Hey," Jericho said quietly, tugging Sterling's arm back down and away from his face. When Sterling opened his eyes, Jericho was hunched down low so his face was in Sterling's field of view. "It's not only you," he said. "You know that, right? If you haven't noticed me doing the exact same thing, I must be more subtle than I thought. Or did I read this all wrong? You've never outright said you were bi, but..."

There were *so* many reasons to take the high road. Sterling blamed Jericho's mostly undressed state for the fact that he was having a hard time remembering any of them. *Christ.* "You're not wrong," he admitted. "I've been trying to be discreet, but...well, have you *seen* you? You're hard not to appreciate."

Jericho's response was a soft chuckle. "Yeah?" His smile was contagious. "Why the embarrassment, then?"

Lord, that was a *very* long answer. One Sterling wasn't in any state to explain clearly at the moment. The crux of it, though… "I'm your employer, strictly speaking. I don't want you to feel uncomfortable—especially since you're living with us right now. I'd be taking advantage of you."

Jericho sat back up and laughed. Straight-up belly laugh. Sterling sat a bit straighter too, now that he had to look *up* to see Jericho's face. Dude didn't look uncomfortable or offended in the least.

"I'm trying to find the best way to say this," Jericho said once he got his breath back and saw how Sterling wasn't laughing along, "but basically that's all bullshit. Pardon my French. Yes, you're technically my boss, but living together kind of blurs those lines, don't you think? And the money issue… Look, you're being more than generous with what you're paying me to hang out and goof off with Alexa, but I could go to Uncle René and Tante Brielle and they'd welcome me back at Camp Ladybug in a heartbeat. That's a direct quote. I'm here because I'm loving the job, I'm having a blast with Alexa, and I like being around *you.* I've done my own 'appreciating' too. You look dead sexy when you come home from work and undo the top buttons of your shirt—makes me want to tear open a few more."

"Oh." Sterling's thoughts were swirling faster than he could put words to them, so apparently "oh" was the only thing that remained. He'd known he was offering an unusually high salary for live-in childcare, especially since Alexa wasn't a baby who required feedings and diaper changes, but it was only for two months and Alexa *needed* someone. Someone like Jericho. Who somehow found Sterling attractive, average body and all. That part still didn't compute. Jericho had said he was gay the one time and they never talked about it again. Sterling took it as license to look but not touch, but that was based on the assumption that Jericho would be getting his needs met elsewhere. Gay bars on his nights off? Clubbing? Not asking meant not having to know what Jericho was like when he focused all that incredible magnetism on another man with the intent of getting laid.

"You're awfully quiet," Jericho said, breaking into Sterling's spiraling self-doubt. He dropped a hand down on top of Sterling's bare foot—not squeezing, just skin-to-skin contact. "Do you want to pretend this never happened and go back to how we were? I can't promise I'll never think about you like that, but I'll do my best to keep our relationship professional if I drastically misread what you want."

Sterling licked his lips. The maelstrom in his brain condensed down to a single thought. "So…what if I do want it? That?"

Jericho's eyes sparkled. "If you do," he murmured, leaning closer and letting his hand travel higher up to curl around Sterling's ankle, "then we go splash around with Alexa for a while. Enjoy the beach. Maybe Alexa and I try to bury you in the sand, and I get an excuse to put my hands all over your body while we're both pretending nothing has changed. We'll each catch the other ogling when Alexa's not watching. We'll all go home, take our showers, eat dinner…and then take I'll Alexa to the Summer Nights at the Y event she and I saw a flyer for at the library the other day. Costs thirty bucks to drop her off between five and six and pick her up at ten and she'll have a blast. While she's there, though, we'll get the house to ourselves. And I'll finally get to touch you the way I've been wanting to ever since that interview at the coffee shop. Sound good?"

Sounds damned amazing. "That does," Sterling squeaked. "Sound good, I mean. So we can…yes. Do that. If Alexa's willing to go."

"She was asking about it in the car on the way home after I pointed it out." Jericho rose to his feet in one graceful movement and offered Sterling a hand up. "So with that settled," he said, "race you to the water?"

* * * *

It was the second-best birthday Jericho could remember ever having. The best was still his seventh, because that was the day Malachi had been born and getting a *brother* for his birthday—after being outnumbered five to two by sisters—was the absolute best thing ever, but flirting with Sterling on the beach was definitely a close contender. Jericho made a point of calling Malachi after they got home, to say happy shared birthday and to gloat about Sterling and Alexa having thrown him a sort-of party. Sterling leaned against the refrigerator, looking sexy as always, listening in to Jericho's side of the conversation and laughing silently as Jericho teased Malachi in the way only older brothers can. This year Malachi was turning eighteen and in the middle of obsessively packing in preparation for starting his freshman year at Louisiana Tech. His girlfriend just so happened to live in Monroe, half an hour east of his new school, which Malachi insisted hadn't affected his choice of school in any way. Jericho found a dozen ways to teasingly call bullshit on him and rag him a bit, but Malachi was the baby of the family and college was going to be a culture shock.

"I've got to admit I'm a bit jealous," Sterling said once Jericho stuck his phone back in his pocket. "Do you get along with all your siblings that well?"

"Mostly, yeah." Jericho ticked them off on his fingers as he counted. "Naomi's nine years older than me, so she was in high school right when I was at the perfect annoying little brother age. Aaron's ahead of me five years—he's an investment banker now. Hannah's two years older, but she was always more of a peacemaker than a pest. I'd say I only really fought with Abby—a year and a half younger than I am—but we get along fine now. Then Leah and Tamara are next, three years after Abby. They're twins and were always into girly stuff I didn't care about. Leah's in school for fashion design now, which was a surprise to absolutely nobody. Nor was me going into teaching, or so I'm told. Malachi and I had a lot of shared birthday parties, though, and honestly I think he's the one I got closest to even though we're so far apart in age. He's starting college this year, halfway across the state." *God, Mom and Dad aren't going to know what to do with a quiet house.* He made a mental note to try and schedule a visit next time he had a school break—they'd be eager to come see him in Georgia once he had a semi-permanent job, but getting Jericho back in the house would probably be even better.

"Let me guess," Sterling said. "Malachi looked up to you and thought you could do no wrong?"

Oh, God yes. Jericho grinned. "Pretty much. My sisters all knew better. I tried not to abuse my power too much, though."

Sterling got a faraway look in his eyes. "I had one really good best friend growing up," he said softly. "He's got a little brother. Two years younger. His brother got sick—really sick for about eight months, I think it was a kidney thing—and even though I obviously wouldn't wish a potentially fatal medical problem on anyone, I was so jealous of all the family closeness. For a long time I was secretly mad at my mom for our family being just me and her. I was weird and nerdy and awkward and probably wouldn't have connected well with a brother anyway, but I wanted so badly not to be an only child."

And now he was raising an only child of his own, despite his best efforts to protect and support his little family. *Damn.* Jericho glanced over toward the sofa, where Alexa had collapsed to watch a cartoon right after they got home. She was curled up on her side and sound asleep.

"Yes, I've noticed the irony," Sterling said, following Jericho's gaze. "She doesn't seem to mind being an only, though. Alexa is more easygoing than I ever was."

"I have a hard time imagining you as a difficult kid."

Sterling snorted. "My mother would argue otherwise." He strode to the sofa and gently shook Alexa's shoulder. "Hey, Pup," he said. "You still want to go to the Y tonight?"

Alexa blinked awake slowly and met her dad's gaze with a small smile. "Was I asleep?"

"For a little while."

"Oh." She yawned, then leaned over and immediately began putting her shoes back on. "Yeah, I want to go. I'm not as tired now."

"I'm not surprised you needed a nap after all that swimming you two did," Jericho chimed in. "And then all the running around with those girls. What do you say we make you a snack-type dinner before we go? Your dad and I are going to have the leftover mushroom tortellini"—Alexa made a face—"but I'm guessing you'd rather have a sandwich. Peanut butter?"

"Nutella?"

"Deal." He'd finally been in the house long enough that the Nutella jar appeared in his hand without him consciously having to remember which cupboard it was kept in. Which was good, because thoughts of Sterling and the evening ahead were damn well keeping Jericho's mental capacity at half power. He quickly whipped up the sandwich and poured her a glass of milk, which Alexa downed with impressive speed. "We can go whenever you're ready," he added. "It'll be five by the time we get there."

The good dose of sugar had Alexa back to her usual chattery self by the time they got to the YMCA. It took a few minutes to do the paperwork, since Sterling and Alexa weren't members, but she'd been there for enough classes and programs already that her basic info was already in their system. The teenager manning the desk didn't even bat an eye when Jericho quietly explained why Alexa was previously in the computer as "Oscar."

"Not sure there's an official policy for it," she told him, "but doing a name change is simple enough. And it lets me edit the gender field too. I'm gonna put you in as Alexa Jean Harper, okay, hon? 'Jean' with one N, or J-E-A-N-N-E? Oh, and let me get a new picture of you too. Look up at the camera here."

Jericho didn't realize he'd been primed for a fight until there suddenly was no need. Alexa ran off to the youth room with all the other preteens, only one staff member knew she was transgender, and that staff member hadn't given either of them grief over it. Maybe someday Alexa would need to sort through how to find privacy in the locker room or the like, but for tonight she was just a girl making new friends and she seemed perfectly happy to dive in. He spent the drive home torn between being hopeful on her behalf and being hopeful on his own. Because Sterling was back at the house, they'd be alone, and maybe *finally*…

He was greeted at the door by the smell of mushroom tortellini. Sterling was already sitting at the table with a candle lit, the wine poured, and the pasta plated up like a dish from a fancy restaurant instead of merely day-old leftovers. He lifted his glass in a salute to Jericho and nodded. "Happy birthday. Come eat."

They talked about nothing in particular for a while, but Sterling *had* to have noticed the electric current flowing between them the closer they got to finishing their food. By the time Jericho had cleared his plate, it felt like they were liable to either combust or implode.

"Move on over to the sofa?" Sterling asked. He poured them each another half glass of wine and led the way. He reseated himself with a sigh and a genuine smile, which warmed Jericho more than the alcohol ever could. "Thanks." Sterling raised his glass in the air. "Happy birthday to you, Jericho Johnston. I'm glad you had fun this afternoon."

"I really, truly did." Jericho mirrored his toast and they both drank. "Three guesses as to my favorite part was?"

Sterling looked away and—as best as Jericho could tell in the half-dimmed lights he'd left on—he was blushing. Despite the blatant signals that *yes*, this was it. "Can I hope instead of guess?" he asked quietly.

"As long as you're hoping for the right thing." God, Jericho was hoping too, but Sterling was all curled up at the opposite end of the sofa. Although the fact that he was on the sofa instead of his armchair was promising. Still, it seemed best to play it casual. "So…you're bi, then?" Jericho asked. "And I'm assuming you're not out to everyone?"

"It's not the way you're probably thinking." Sterling grimaced. "I've never particularly been attracted to women, but I have next to zero experience with either gender so I can't really compare. More gay than bi, though."

That took a minute to process. "You were married," Jericho pointed out. Stupidly, because that wasn't exactly new information, but his brain kept getting stuck on it. "Were you and Dana not interested in each other like that?"

Sterling shook his head. "It's…well, I told you we got married young when we found out Dana was pregnant, right? There's more to the story."

"I'm not in a hurry."

"Okay. Good." Sterling fiddled with his glass, but Jericho kept his expression neutral and waited patiently for him to find the words. "So I don't remember if it's ever come up in conversation between us," Sterling finally continued, "but I was homeschooled for several years and then skipped a grade when I went to high school. I was the youngest in my year by a fair bit. Also shy, awkward, smarter than everyone else, and just beginning to realize I was never going to start liking girls. You can probably guess what my social life was like."

"Sparse?"

"That's one way to put it. 'Lonely' would be another." He flashed Jericho a sad smile. "Mom tried to help, she truly did, but I hadn't learned yet to keep my mouth shut when someone else was wrong about something. That didn't win me any friends."

"Abby had problems like that," Jericho told him. "We were two years apart in school, but I knew most of her friends and she knew mine. High schoolers can be vicious."

Sterling nodded. "Exactly. So anyway, I applied to colleges and got a fantastic scholarship to Florida State. When I started my freshman year, I was seventeen and didn't know a soul there. Dana was a junior. She and I met in the library one day, neither of us felt much like studying, and she sort of...adopted me, I guess. She was popular and fun and exciting and everyone liked her, and I could never figure out what she wanted *me* around for."

"Friendship?"

"I understood that eventually. She introduced me to her other friends, invited me along to parties, came to hang out in my room when we both had to cram for a test, that sort of thing. She was the first person I came out to, if you don't count my mom—with Mom it was more confirmation of what she suspected than any sort of big announcement."

"That you're gay?" Jericho could envision the other parts, could imagine Sterling as a shy, awkward genius who didn't connect with many of his peers, but "gay" and "married to a woman" still refused to logically mesh. "Was she supportive?"

"Mom, yes. And I guess Dana too. Well..." Sterling sighed. "I turned eighteen that spring of freshman year. Dana threw me a party. It was mostly her art friends—all upperclassmen, because I only had a few other freshmen I was close to and most of those weren't big on that sort of thing. Social events. I liked her friends well enough, though, and it was a nice idea. And an excuse for a party—she and her housemates had no shortage of those. She'd just turned twenty-one and brought a bunch of booze. I had tried alcohol before, but not in that quantity. Or all at once."

Oh, Jericho had a guess as to where this was going, and it didn't sound good. "Did you get sick? First blackout and hangover?"

"Some of Dana's friends did. But no, only a bit tipsy—I had two beers and decided that was plenty for my first try at partying. And she wasn't sloshed either, so I'm not blaming anything on that. Anyway, Dana and I ended up going up to her room to get away from the noise. We talked for a while and it eventually got to personal stuff. I told her I was gay. I don't remember exactly how the conversation went, but the end result was that she offered to sleep with me if I wanted to get my first time over with. You know, so I could be *sure* I didn't like women." He grimaced. "We did, it was nice but not the earth-shattering euphoria I was hoping for, and we both thought that was the end of it."

It didn't take a genius to connect the dots. "She got pregnant from that one time?"

"Yep. Found out right after classes ended for the semester. Her parents freaked out, no surprise there, but Dana was pretty calm about it. She wanted to keep the baby, be a mother. She'd always wanted to be a mom more than a graphic designer anyway. And I didn't…I didn't want to be an absent father in the kid's life. I've never met my own dad—Mom doesn't like to talk about him, although I gather it's with good reason—and I wasn't going to do that to another child if I could help it. Long story short, we ran off to the courthouse and got married right after finals week. Didn't let anyone in on the situation until after. I applied to the dental school program that summer because it was a combined undergrad-graduate thing and it meant my scholarship would cover the whole seven years. I figured when I was a dentist, I'd be able to earn enough to provide for a family. Also because I didn't know what the heck I wanted to do back then, other than 'something in science.' She moved out of the house she was sharing with her friends, I moved out of the dorms, and we got a crappy little apartment within walking distance of campus."

"What did your mother think?"

Sterling smiled at nothing in particular. "I hope you get to meet her sometime while you're here," he said. "My mom is wonderful. Came up and helped us settle in, got along great with Dana. I'm sure she wouldn't have chosen for me to get married at eighteen, obviously, but she was supportive of the choice we made. Always has been."

"You'd already told her you were gay, though."

"That's true." He shrugged. "Mom didn't pry, and we never did tell Dana's parents. They hated me already. Dana dropped out of college—she hadn't wanted to go anyway, that was all her dad's doing—but we both worked our butts off to get me through dental school and to support ourselves. I had classes all week and got a job at the law library on weekends where I could sometimes study at work. Dana even waited tables for a while. It was rough. She and I stayed best friends, and we got along well as spouses, but sex wasn't…"

"Not something you shared?" Jericho guessed.

"Not together, anyway. We—God, I can't believe I'm telling you this." Sterling pinched the bridge of his nose and sighed. "We had an agreement, of sorts. Separate computers, separate porn collections. She had a whole giant bookcase of romance novels. I think some are still up in the storage closet somewhere. We texted each other about things every once in a while, shared fantasies or she'd leave me an erotic sketch she'd done that she was particularly proud of, but never… We slept in the same bed, but that's it. We were basically good friends who happened to be raising a kid together."

"Mmmm." Even though it sounded like Sterling and Dana had made the best of an awkward situation, looking at someone's doodling wasn't anywhere near as good as the real thing. Jericho blinked. Ooh, now *there* was an idea. "How would you feel about trying it, then?" he asked.

Sterling gave him a blank look. "Trying what? Drawing erotic art?"

"Watching something together." Jericho put his empty glass down on the end table and leaned in, elbows on his knees. "I've probably got a few recommendations you'd like, and I'd *love* to see yours. If you think that sounds like a fun and interesting way to spend an evening."

That earned him a slow blink and an adorable crinkly line across Sterling's forehead. "You want to…watch porn with me?"

"Of course with you. Or was my come-on still too subtle?" He stood and offered Sterling a hand up. "Your room or mine?" *Please take it please take it please—*

"I've got a bigger bed," Sterling said. And then crinkled his forehead again. "I mean, um. Yes, let's do it. I've never done…that…with someone else before, but it sounds good. Fun."

Chapter 10

Yes! Sterling took the offered hand up, and he was smiling. Jericho vowed right there and then he was going to make a mental catalogue of all Sterling's smiles and collect as many of his favorites as he could. This, right here—palm to palm, Sterling looking up at him, all trusting and hopeful—this was something worth keeping forever.

The master bedroom was huge and had several framed pencil sketches on the walls. Jericho's brain didn't get much past those two observations, though, because there were more important things to focus on. The little hesitation before Sterling let go of Jericho's hand, for example, or the way he sat on the near side of the bed but had to flop backward the full width of the mattress to reach his laptop on the nightstand. The movement made his shirt ride up, exposing a sliver of pale skin. Lickable. Touchable. Jericho stuck his hands in his jeans pockets so he wouldn't scare Sterling off this experience, whatever it was shaping up to be.

Sterling sat back up and scooted over subtly, making space for Jericho on the bed next to him even though there was already plenty of room. Jericho sat cross-legged and kept his hands in his lap.

"So should I just pick something?" Sterling hovered the mouse over the address bar. "Sorry, I don't really know…"

God, he was adorable while nervous, which was not at all a surprise. "Want me to pull up something first?" Jericho tugged the laptop from Sterling's unresisting grip and turned it toward himself to do a quick search. *What to start with?* Something nonthreatening, definitely. At least mostly vanilla. Ought to be two men for obvious reasons. And sexy, that was the number one requirement. It'd be incredibly disappointing if this evening didn't end up in both of them getting off.

A vague memory of an old favorite flashed through Jericho's mind—a short scene with two buff guys trading blowjobs. The recording was amateur, probably self-taped with a camera on a tripod, but the men were hot and the sex was steamy and obviously real. Jericho found it after only a minute of searching. "Here." He put the laptop down on the bed so they could both see the screen.

The video started off slowly. The smaller guy climbed into the bigger one's lap and the two started making out. Clothes disappeared quickly, but they only broke their lip-lock by necessity, when taking each other's shirts off. Jericho stole a glance at Sterling's lap. Sterling knelt there on the bed, completely unmoving, with his hands clenched tightly into fists at his sides. His eyes were glued on the screen. *Like, if he ignores me, we can both pretend this isn't gay as hell.*

"What do you think?" Jericho asked softly.

It took a few moments for Sterling to acknowledge the question. "I guess they seem to be enjoying themselves," he finally said. "Is this—have you done this before?"

"That?" Jericho nodded toward the screen. "Or watching porn with someone?"

The light from the single muted floor lamp in the corner combined with the laptop's glow made it hard to judge Sterling's color, but Jericho would have bet a hundred bucks he was blushing furiously right then. "Um…either?"

On the screen, the smaller man was gripping the back of the taller one's chair and leaning in with his eyes closed. The taller dude slumped down lower so he could get his mouth on his partner's cock. The video stayed fixed at the same constant distance, which—thankfully—meant no cheesy, slurpy close-ups. It also meant the shorter man's face was always in the shot. There was no missing his look of genuine pleasure. The taller partner's face wasn't as easy to see, but his fingers were splayed across the shorter dude's ass in a blatantly possessive hold. The main reason Jericho kept coming back to this video every so often over the last several years was that both participants really, truly looked like they wanted to be there. There was no terrible porn-star acting because they didn't need it. And there was absolutely no question the two of them were an actual couple, not actors or fuck buddies with a camera.

"I can vouch for the making out and blowjobs part being worth trying, definitely," Jericho said. If that admission was going to shock Sterling, too bad. "As for watching porn with someone else…only once. With a friend." He and Chris browsed a few videos together one late night, back during their first year living together. Chris's then-boyfriend had dumped him that afternoon after almost a month of dating, and Chris needed a final *fuck you* to the jackass, even if said jackass would never find out. It started out as Jericho comforting an emotional friend and ended with the two of them each huddled under their own covers, jacking off to the same mediocre video. Neither of them mentioned or acknowledged it the next day. They never actually saw each other's cocks. And Jericho sure as hell never had as many distracting, pervy thoughts about Chris over the course of four years living together as he'd had about Sterling in a matter of a few weeks. "We were in separate beds and it was a one-off thing, though," he clarified. "He's still a friend, but I never actually saw his dick and I never want to. You?"

"Ogle your friend's dick?" Sterling's bark of laughter escaped so quickly he started himself on a coughing fit. "Sorry," he gasped. "I know what you meant. It's just that other than some kissing and groping at the end of freshman year with my DiffEQ study partner, I've already confessed my entire history. It's…really sparse."

The couple on the screen started moaning louder, the taller man's grasp on his partner's ass shifting as he lost his coordination, until he abruptly stiffened, moaned, and then slid off the chair to lie face-up on the floor so the shorter man could come all over his face. Jericho cleared his throat and paused the video. "Bit artificial, that ending, but I love this one because they both seem so into it. And into each other. Show me your favorite?"

Sterling hesitated, then opened something in his bookmarks folder and clicked through whatever ads popped up. "I can't believe I'm showing you this," he mumbled.

"Is it really more outrageous than the rest of our conversation tonight? Or how much we've both been eying each other whenever we thought we could get away with it?" Jericho smiled to show he was teasing. "You've got me curious now." Curious, cautious, and even more determined to get them both off. If Sterling wanted a gentle introduction, Jericho was more than happy to volunteer.

"Oh, fine." Sterling let the video start playing and replaced the laptop where they could both see it. It opened on a scene in which a pizza-delivering twink in a generic uniform was being talked into earning an "extra tip" by the overly muscled homeowner. "Sorry," Sterling mumbled over the barely plausible dialogue. "It's not—I don't have a pizza kink or anything, I just like this next part."

"It's promising so far," Jericho assured him.

Sterling was still kneeling straight-backed with his eyes locked firmly on the screen. Jericho was up for anything, even if all Sterling wanted was this side-by-side situation, but maybe… Jericho shifted his hand toward his zip one slow inch at a time. Sterling's head turned minutely—watching in his peripheral vision? Jericho rubbed himself lightly over the denim of his jeans and let out a tiny, itty-bitty hint of a moan. Sterling shifted his weight and snuck a slightly longer look. *Gotcha.*

"Okay if I…?" Jericho gestured toward his own hard-on. Like he didn't already know Sterling was watching him tease himself, was merely asking to be polite. If there even was a "polite" in this situation. *That would take one hell of a thorough etiquette guide…*

Sterling shrugged. "I guess that's kind of the point." Despite what had to be a valiant attempt to pretend otherwise, his uncertainty came through in his voice.

"Oh, it's definitely part of it." Jericho palmed himself again—with a bit of an involuntary hip thrust—and then unbuttoned his fly and slipped his hand inside. Nothing Sterling could see, not yet, but if he was interested it would be a good first step. And… *Bingo.* Sterling focused back on the video, but he subtly adjusted his own cock and left his hand there. *Perfect.* Jericho was barely even cupping himself and he was already half-hard. That had a lot more to do with Sterling than with anything happening on the screen.

More terrible dialogue, and the bigger dude pinning Pizza Twink up against the wall. Jericho was already tuning out the details in favor of watching Sterling's face. When someone in the video moaned and Sterling let out a startled squeak, Jericho slipped his hand inside his boxers and gave himself a couple of firm but slow strokes.

"You like that?" he asked Sterling in a low voice. "Being pinned up against a wall? Or do you visualize yourself as the one doing the pinning?"

Sterling's breath faltered for a second, then he let out a long, controlled sigh. "I like the…the thing they do next. This." On the screen, the two guys were stripping and then frotting together, moaning loudly. Their moans sounded a hell of a lot more real than their dialogue had been.

"Ooh, damn," Jericho whispered for Sterling's benefit. "That's hot." He sped up his strokes—now there was zero ambiguity about the fact that he was jerking himself off. His wrist and the open flap of his jeans had to be blocking Sterling's view, but that didn't seem to matter much. Sterling kept up his unaffected statue act for only a few seconds longer before finally giving in and rubbing his hard-on through his khakis. He had to be *aching.* "Come on," Jericho urged. "You know you want to unzip and get your hand on yourself for real. Don't be shy for me."

Beside him, Sterling stilled.

You know what? Fuck it. Jericho peeled off his t-shirt and tossed it aside. Now if Sterling turned to look, he'd see the head of Jericho's cock as it peeked in and out of his fist. He didn't have to look if he didn't want to, he could plead fatigue or ignore or—

Sterling looked. He saw that Jericho noticed him looking, but didn't immediately tear his eyes away. *Oh hell yes.* Jericho threw in a few slower, tighter strokes so Sterling could see every single moment of how Jericho's cockhead stretched and was already leaking a bit.

"Go on," Jericho urged him, almost in a whisper. "I showed you mine..."

Sterling flashed him a small smile, shy but determined, then sat up straighter and pulled his own shirt off. His khakis offered more room to maneuver with the fly open than Jericho's jeans did, so Jericho got a mouth-watering eyeful of Sterling's light blue boxer-briefs underneath as he quickly tugged the waistband down and let his erection pop free.

Jericho didn't even pretend to be watching the video anymore. He'd had all afternoon to ogle Sterling's bare chest, of course, but topless at the beach surrounded by people was completely different than seeing him in muted lamplight while both of them were openly displaying matching hard-ons. Sterling's cock was cut, with a lovely thick head and a bit of an upward curve to it. Jericho wanted to grab him by the hips, tug him closer, and map the veins with his tongue. He used the sudden rush of precome to slick up his own dick instead. "Fuck," he breathed. "You're gorgeous. Wanna see how you do it, all these times you get off alone. Let me watch you. You want me to see?"

Sterling bit his lip, muffling his moan, and nodded. He liked to tease himself, Jericho learned—a few gentle strokes with his fingertips, a few firmer ones, only the head for a bit. Reaching down and fondling his sac when the feeling got too intense. The actors on the video were now making wet, sucking sounds—blowjob, rimming, or really bad kissers?—but Jericho had no interest in being distracted by what they were doing so he angled his body away from the screen. Only watching Sterling, now. With a jolt, he realized he was unconsciously copying Sterling's rhythm.

"Yours is nice too," Sterling murmured, ignoring the porn in entirely the same way. He kept greedily eying Jericho's cock, wrenching his gaze away, eventually looking down at his own, and slowly working up the courage to look at Jericho again. Jericho started letting his hips get in on the action. Only a little bit, only a hint of movement, but it felt *amazing.*

"You want to touch?" Jericho was aiming for friendly, nonchalant, but he had a feeling he only half succeeded. Surely the *want* suffusing every cell of his body had come through in his voice as well. "Watching you like this is so hot, *fuck*, but if you want to touch me…or I could touch you?"

Sterling's hand froze for a moment. "I've never…"

"Me either, not like this. But I want to—God, I want to. Your hand on me or my hand on you, either or both or whatever else you want. You're so gorgeous…I mean, *damn*."

Several more silent moments, then Sterling finally sucked in a long breath. "That would be…yeah. You'll have to tell me if I'm doing it wrong, though."

Ha. "Not a chance of that," Jericho assured him. "Here, maybe this way?" He knee-walked around to behind Sterling and sat back down on his feet, so he was cradling Sterling between his thighs and could press his chest up against Sterling's back. The couple extra inches of height meant he could see comfortably over Sterling's shoulder. He slid an arm around under Sterling's and kneaded Sterling's clothed thigh gently. "You can keep watching the video, if you want, but I think I'd rather focus on touching you for a while. Feel free to pretend I'm not here."

Sterling panted out a strangled laugh. "Not a chance of that either. Oh, Christ." He slowly, so slowly, took his slightly damp hand off his cock and ran it up and down Jericho's forearm. Jericho kept up the gentle massage until Sterling finally groaned and tugged Jericho's hand inward to land on that lush, tempting cock. "Damn, that feels good. I've got to be dreaming. Am I?"

"Depends," Jericho murmured in his ear. He punctuated it with a playful tug on Sterling's earlobe, then soothed the nip with his lips. "How vivid is your imagination? Because this"—he closed a fist around Sterling's prick and gave him a gentle stroke—"is way hotter than anything I could have come up with. Look at the contrast. Lock this image in your brain." *I sure as hell plan to.* "My long fingers, wrapped around your dick, jerking you off the way you like it." He attempted to match Sterling's pattern from earlier. Gentle, firm, just the tip. Slow stroke down, play with his sac for a bit, repeat. "It's not even black and white, is it? The contrast of my skin against yours? It's more like black and nearly purple, you're so hard. And we're not even all the way naked. What does your imagination tell you we'd want to do if we *really* decided to make a night of it?"

Sterling's heartbeat felt like a metronome against Jericho's chest, a physical pulse he could lean into and inhale and become a part of. His own cock was aching. It would be easy to lift up a bit more and grind against Sterling's lower back—he didn't, but he *could*. Learning what turned Sterling on felt more important than dealing with his own hard-on at the moment, though. It would wait. Jericho wrapped his left arm around Sterling's torso and circled the base of his erection, then slipped his hand down to play with Sterling's balls while he kept up the relentless rhythm with his right.

"Let me see you come," he whispered, and Sterling's heartbeat went crazy for a second before he *was.* Warm and wet all over Jericho's fingers, the back of his hand. It was beautiful. Jericho had slid forward and was running his own dick up and down Sterling's lower spine before he realized what he was doing—and even after, he couldn't stop. Not with Sterling's cock still leaking and shivering with aftershocks, the smears of come only visible when Jericho tilted his hand at the perfect angle and the lamplight reflected off the wetness. Sterling groaned and let his head sag back onto Jericho's shoulder.

"Holy hell," he panted. The awe in his voice was something Jericho wanted to cherish forever. "I don't know what I expected, but it definitely wasn't that."

"A handjob?"

"The hottest damn moment in my entire *life.*" He rolled his head to the side and nuzzled the side of Jericho's neck. "God, you're still hard, aren't you? I can feel it against my back. *Christ.* Hang on; I want to watch."

Jericho had to squeeze himself, hard, to keep from coming right there and then. Sterling flopped over onto his side, propping his head up on one hand and cupping his now-flaccid cock in the other. Not particularly stroking…in sympathy with Jericho's aching dick, maybe?

"This is so much better than watching a stranger on a screen," he added.

There was a liquidity in his voice that Jericho had never heard from anyone apart from dudes whose higher processing functions had recently leaked out their dick. He usually felt a little smug hearing it, knowing that they probably rated sex with him as a neat five stars in their mental black book. "Smug" didn't begin to describe what Sterling's lazy drawl and languid stroking were doing to Jericho's brain, though. Pride was only a small part. Sterling's voice made Jericho's dick twitch, but it had been doing that off and on for the last week. The look too. It was the combination, though—Sterling's sated smile, the voice, the compliment, the smell of sex in the air, and the knowledge that most of what was on his hand and lubing up his aching cock was Sterling's come. Jericho twisted his hips at the last possible second so he spurted all over Sterling's blanket instead of on Sterling himself. *Holy fuck.*

They probably could have stayed there like that all night, naked and messy, but Alexa needed to be picked up by ten. Jericho groaned and levered himself back up to sitting. "Not bad for our first time," he teased. And then, more earnestly so Sterling could tell he was serious, he took Sterling's messy hand in his own and squeezed it. "Really, that was incredible. And hot."

"It…yeah, it was." Sterling squeezed back.

Shit. Get ahold of yourself, dude. He was lying in bed with Sterling, holding hands and probably grinning like an idiot. That was way more than the casual let's-watch-porn-together they'd agreed on. He'd be in over his head, and fast, if he wasn't careful. And if he went all-in but Sterling didn't feel the same way… Yeah, that would seriously suck.

Jericho let go and levered himself back up to a sitting position. "Guess I've been doing it wrong the last ten or twelve years," he deadpanned, "because having you here is a hell of a lot better than watching anything solo. You have Kleenex around somewhere, or…? Oh, I see it. Never mind." He grabbed the box off the nightstand, pulled out a few to wipe himself off with, and tossed it on Sterling's side of the bed. Most of the come had ended up on the blanket and/or on Sterling.

"Definitely not what I expected today to bring," Sterling replied. Jericho couldn't read his tone and didn't dare look at his face. "I haven't come that hard in forever. Dang, this wet spot's a bit obvious, isn't it?" Sterling dabbed gingerly at his damp stomach, then got up to go retrieve his shirt. There was a square set to his shoulders that said all Jericho needed to hear about whether Sterling was feeling snuggly and sappy too. He'd thought Sterling seemed like the kind of guy who'd like to stay close and enjoy the afterglow for a while, but maybe not.

The mess wasn't *too* terrible, truthfully, but fine. They could both focus on the practical stuff. Jericho closed the laptop—it was one good bump from ending up on the floor—and found his shirt stuck between the bed and the nightstand. They finished cleaning up in silence. Jericho helped Sterling put a new blanket on the bed and the old one in the laundry, threw the tissues in the trash, then stood around feeling adrift while Sterling kept buzzing around and touching things even though all evidence of their mind-blowing side-by-side orgasms was gone.

"I guess I'll head back to my room until it's time to pick up Alexa," Jericho said. The words felt strange. Usually he had no problem parting with his hookups on casual terms—they fucked, sometimes cuddled, occasionally slept a bit…then kissed a quick thank-you-and-goodbye and that was it. For the first time in ages, Jericho didn't want to leave. Sterling was the one acting chill and Jericho left off-balance.

Is he having regrets? Jericho hoped like hell Sterling was being so casual because he enjoyed himself. Or maybe he was out of his usual comfort zone and covering it up? Either way, they had another month and a half together. This was going to either be the best or the most awkward summer ever.

* * * *

Sterling awoke with a start the next morning, following a sheet-twisting erotic dream featuring a tall, dark man groping him from behind. In the dream, the man was pounding Sterling's ass while he held Sterling's hips in an iron grip. The figure may have started off as Jericho at some earlier point in the dream, but by the time Sterling startled awake it had somehow changed to someone different. A stranger. Sterling had both wanted and not wanted it—the cock pistoning in and out of him felt good, overwhelming, but at the same time Sterling-in-the-dream was painfully aware the stranger wasn't Jericho. The stranger didn't talk, didn't nip at Sterling's earlobe the way Jericho had, just…took.

He shivered. It didn't take a genius to figure out what his subconscious was dwelling on, obviously. Sterling glanced at his phone—not quite six thirty. A bit earlier than he usually got up, especially for a Sunday, but not unreasonably so. And since there was no way in hell he'd be getting back to sleep…

Jericho was the next to emerge, about an hour later. His bedroom was closer to the kitchen than Alexa's was, so he probably smelled the bacon Sterling had pulled out of the oven where it had been warming. Sterling wasn't a *complete* mess in the kitchen, thankyouverymuch, and sometimes cooking was exactly what he needed to help him settle when his thoughts wouldn't stop churning. He'd cooked a lot after Dana's death. Buttermilk waffles from scratch were pushing him past his comfort zone—thank goodness for the little handwritten deck of recipes his mom gave him when he left for college—but his poor, dream-abused brain had decided they sounded heavenly so homemade waffles it was. Jericho ambled out of his room in flannel pajama bottoms and a plain gray t-shirt, leaned on the kitchen counter, and yawned.

"You're up early," he mumbled. And immediately had to cover another yawn. "Sorry, still not all the way awake. Smells delicious, though. Need any help?"

"I don't think you're functional enough to help yet," Sterling countered. "Coffee?"

"*God* yes."

Sterling put a full-strength pod in the Keurig and pulled a mug out of the clean-but-not-unloaded-yet dishwasher. "You're usually the morning person," he said. "Or is that an act to make Alexa more willing to get out of bed?"

"Most of the time I am," Jericho admitted. "Didn't get a lot of sleep last night, though. I kept thinking about this *amazingly* sexy guy I saw yesterday. Maybe you know him? He's a gorgeous white dude with brown hair and blue eyes, total genius, and he makes the most incredible noises when he comes. I got off again at about two in the morning, just remembering what he sounded like. And I'm maybe…hoping to hear it again sometime?"

Jericho's body language was still lethargic from drowsiness, but there was no mistaking the desire in his tone. Sterling sucked in a deep breath and busied himself with the waffle iron. "I'm not sure that's a good idea," he said softly. "I was thinking too, and—well, I do appreciate you sharing that with me and it was way better than I expected, but…"

"But what?"

"But I'm paying you." He forced himself to look up, to meet Jericho's eye. "Traditional 'nanny' or not, you're technically my employee until August. It would be wrong of me to take advantage of our relative positions and start a sexual relationship. Plus, with Alexa…"

Jericho licked his lips and nodded seriously. "Okay," he said. "If you really and truly want last night to have been a one-off, I'll respect that. We can call it one hell of a birthday present and be strictly professional from now on. However, if I may make a counterargument?"

The Keurig dispensed an aromatic stream of coffee into the waiting mug. Sterling grabbed it and passed it across the counter to Jericho. Part of him was resigned to the reality of their situation, but another part—the greedy, lustful part—was desperately hoping Jericho's counterargument was going to be a worthwhile excuse for what he really wanted to do anyway. Which was to feel Jericho's hands on him, cock *in* him, for real. Sterling folded his hands on the counter in a polite "I'm listening" pose and waited.

"I really enjoyed last night," Jericho said, visibly choosing his words with care. "Not only because I was aching for it after three years of celibacy, but also because seeing you, feeling you come, was really damn sexy. Seriously. You're… Hell, I don't even know how to describe it. You're exactly what I want right now, and I hope I'm not flattering myself too much when I say I think I'm what you want right now too. It's not like we picked each other out at a club and are only using each other for anonymous sex, right? I'm happy to go as slow as you want, whatever you're comfortable with, as long as I get to be in the room when it happens. No pressure, no expectations. Although I won't promise not to tempt you sometimes." He flashed Sterling a wicked little smile, which looked a hell of a lot more confident than his voice made him sound.

Still, though… "I'd be taking advantage of our business relationship. It would make things awkward for both of us if something happened to ruin it."

Jericho managed to give the impression of rolling his eyes without actually moving a muscle. "We went over this already," he said. "You need me a hell of a lot more than I need you. Job at Camp Ladybug waiting for me, no questions asked, remember? I'd still have somewhere to live and some income to save up until I move to Brunswick at the end of August. You, on the other hand… Deny it or not, I know you'd be in a tough spot if I left. Hard to find someone at the last minute, as I'm sure you discovered when you first hired me." He twisted his coffee around and around on the counter, large hands and long fingers encircling most of the mug. "I'm right, aren't I?"

Sterling had to concede the point. Losing Jericho a month into summer break would be difficult at best—and if that happened, Sterling and Alexa wouldn't have a lot of options. Dana's parents would volunteer, probably, but they weren't getting near Alexa alone no matter how much they tried to guilt-trip him. He could probably cut back to half days at the office and leave Alexa home alone in the mornings, if he had to. It would be a financial blow, but there weren't a lot of other options. Even working part-time would depend on Dr. McClellan to pick up some of his patients for several weeks, which would be a huge favor to ask. *Crap.* "You are," Sterling admitted. "We could deal, but it would be hard. And complicated."

Jericho tried to hide his smug smile behind the rim of his mug, but it still showed in his eyes. "By your logic," he concluded, "that makes me the one taking advantage of you. Room and board, excellent pay—I'm sure you know most other childcare options are a hell of a lot cheaper than having a live-in elementary school teacher—and I get to discreetly ogle you whenever I want. Surely taking that a bit further wouldn't totally ruin everything?"

"I…" *Damn it.* Sterling sighed. "I can't tell whether I'm backing down because you have a valid argument or because I'm really hoping to be convinced." The way Jericho was casually leaning against the counter in his slightly-too-small t-shirt was a factor too, in the sense that Sterling's dick was chipping in with an insistent chorus of *hell yes look at him look at those muscles I bet if you get the perfect angle you can see the shape of his nipples even though the fabric those fuzzy pajama pants shouldn't look so sexy they'd feel amazing against your skin if he was wearing them and you were already naked and he lay over you and took his time sliding his body over yours...* Sterling didn't have to look down to know his cock was half-hard just from Jericho standing there and being himself. "Hopeful" was essentially its default state now. "I do want this," Sterling admitted, "but only as long as we can keep it under the radar."

Jericho's eyebrows leapt upward in surprise. "From Alexa, or from everyone? Are you worried what people would think? I know you said you never told your wife's parents, but I thought you said it wasn't an issue of still being in the closet."

Damn it, he *would* have to pick up on that. "Dana knew, obviously," Sterling admitted, "and I'm pretty sure Lawrence and Vivian have figured it out but are pretending the LGBT world doesn't exist. I couldn't really go around announcing I'm gay while Dana and I were married, though, and it's a bit late to come out now."

"So you're planning to stay celibate for the rest of your life?"

"At least until Alexa is off to college and not in danger of Lawrence and Vivian trying to take her away in a custody battle, yes." Sterling mostly dealt with that eventuality by ignoring it and reminding himself he'd gotten through eleven nonsexual years with Dana. "The rest of your life" was just eleven years after eleven years after eleven years, right? He'd already managed a third of his life keeping his dick out of his social relationships. Two-thirds, if you only counted the years since puberty. Lonely masturbation for the next several years was a depressing thought, especially after last night, but it was possible. For Alexa's sake.

"It's not you, it's me," he joked, and pretended not to notice Jericho's wince. "Is that the phrase?"

"I...yeah, I guess." Jericho grimaced. "I was hoping you'd have a stupid reason so I could tell you it was stupid, but I do understand. Alexa's told me some things about her grandparents—she's got really conflicted feelings about them—but you're having to play a part, aren't you? You're the upstanding, heterosexual widower, who doesn't date anyone and devotes himself to his child and...I don't know. Learns knitting, maybe. Bonsai. Spends every day pining over your late wife's memory. You're worried that if you stop pretending, someone's going to see that you aren't actually the dad equivalent of June Cleaver, and it's all going to come crashing down."

"Something like that." Something *frighteningly* like that. It sounded worse when said aloud.

Jericho tilted his head and studied Sterling's face intently. "In theory, though, you'd be up for some after-hours fun? As long as nobody finds out?" He held his arms out wide in a "here I am" gesture. "You realize I don't always read as straight, right? I guarantee you someone's already been wondering. About me personally or the two of us together. Hell, the fact that we're two men living under the same roof is proof enough for some people. Alexa might not pick up on it, but others will."

That issue was a lot easier to explain away, partly because Sterling had turned the question over and over in his head for days before calling Jericho back and offering him the job. "You read as 'cool,'" he admitted. "The shaved head and the perma-smile and the sexy clothes you wear and your willingness to do things like splash around at the beach with a ten-year-old for an hour with no dignity whatsoever simply because she asked you to. I think the overall impression is 'unexpected' instead of 'definitely gay.' Willow Heights is ninety percent stupidly rich, straight white people, so..." *So damn, now I'm acting like one of them.* It had to be weird for Jericho to be out and about with Alexa in such a snooty, homogeneous area. Sterling had never particularly had to think about his skin tone before—and that was the definition of white privilege, wasn't it? At least being queer was invisible if he wanted it to be.

"I'm used to it," Jericho said, like he was reading Sterling's mind. Maybe he was. "Can you come around to this side of the counter for a minute, please?"

He'd set his nearly empty mug down and was leaning sideways against the countertop, loose-limbed and gorgeous. Sterling slowly rounded the end of it and stopped a few feet away. Jericho snorted, took two quick steps forward, and bent down to press a warm kiss onto Sterling's lips.

Oh, this was *definitely* something worth pining for. Jericho didn't press for more, just kept up the slow tease-and-retreat until Sterling found himself literally standing on tiptoe to chase Jericho's agile tongue when Jericho finally pulled back.

"I think we both needed that," Jericho declared with a little smirk. "Should have done it last night. And now that our ongoing torrid affair has been defined and decided on and mulled over and second-guessed and discussed again and finally accepted, can we get to the step where we all get to eat waffles?"

"I didn't say..."

Jericho ducked and kissed him again. "Yes, you did," he murmured. "I can speak Sterling. You're curious, aren't you? You want to see what all I can teach you. As long as we hide everything and I don't raise too many eyebrows flouncing around being all fabulous while living here, you can get what you want. We both can. Question is, are you brave enough to come get it?"

He wanted to be. Lord, he wanted to be. "Yes?"

"Good."

Chapter 11

The next weekend was hot, stormy, and miserable. Sterling and Alexa were both skulking around the house being grumpy at nothing in particular, aggressively flipping through Netflix menus and generally being annoying to live with. Jericho was ready to be done with it by mid-Saturday morning. Technically he was off the clock during the weekend, but the idea of driving through the pounding rain to go visit Uncle René and Tante Brielle only to sit around in *their* house feeling hemmed in was no more appealing. In an ideal world, he and Sterling would be spending the day naked in bed.

Alexa snapped something at Sterling's back and stomped upstairs. *Ten going on sixteen*, the way Sterling said it. Jericho didn't have to work particularly hard to imagine Alexa as a high-schooler, with the long hair she kept lusting for and an addiction to makeup and maybe a best friend she'd text constantly even though her dad told her not to. Her high school years probably wouldn't be the same as a cisgender teenager's experience, unfortunately, but with the right peer group she could get pretty close.

Sterling sighed and pinched the bridge of his nose, something Jericho had noticed him doing a lot recently. "We need to *do* something," he grumbled. "I finally get a full weekend to spend with my daughter—and with you—and all I can do is sit around and snap at her. How the hell do parents with a dozen kids cope?"

"Family support and a high tolerance for chaos," Jericho answered. It was probably supposed to be a rhetorical question, but fuck it. "We had a morning routine when I was a kid: Dad woke us all up while he waited for the coffee to kick in, Mom dealt with the diaper and potty chair issues, and Naomi would set out some sort of breakfast for everyone. Tante Delphine lived with us for a while, and she basically planted herself down on the stairs and helped with snaps and zippers and tying shoes. She and Naomi aren't all that far apart in age—nine or ten years, I think—so they've always acted more like sisters or best friends rather than aunt and niece. I was smack dab in the middle of the lineup, so I didn't get a special job. Getting myself fed, dressed, and ready to go in the mornings counted as my share of the work."

Sterling blinked. "I forgot you were one of eight," he admitted.

"It's not something you forget while you're living it." Christ, *how* could he be feeling so cooped up in Sterling's huge house when compared to the chaos back at home? "You get used to having no personal space and almost no alone time. There's always a lot to do, so you do it."

"Did you have to share a room?"

"Yeah, for *ages,* with my brother Aaron. He's always been obsessed with basketball, so his side of the room was basically a shrine to various NBA players. We had it better than my younger sisters, though—Abby, Leah, and Tamara all got the bedroom in the attic together until Tante Delphine moved out. It was big enough, but still. Six bedrooms with eleven people—someone's got to double up."

"What was your side of the room, then? If Aaron's was all basketball?"

"Promise you won't laugh?"

Sterling pretended to make a big show of thinking about it, then nodded seriously. "Can't have been uglier than mine," he said. "It was originally supposed to be a laundry room, but we didn't have a washer or dryer so Mom let me have it for my own space instead. I hung stuff from the ends of the pipe hookups sometimes. And I had a poster of Alan Turing over my bed. You know how it is—some kids put up pictures of bands or movie stars; I had a gay cryptologist."

Jericho immediately got a vision of a younger, scrawnier Sterling, sitting on a bed in a small yellowed room with a peeling linoleum floor, poring over a complicated math textbook. The little clues he'd let drop so far made it sound like he grew up, if not in the projects, something awfully close to it. "Nothing like that," he clarified, "but it's embarrassing."

"Shoot."

"My side was dinosaurs. Lots and lots of dinosaurs." *God, why am I admitting this?* "My parents live a ways out from New Orleans proper, in this ridiculous Victorian-esque house. Apparently the original builder wanted it to look old and fancy but went bankrupt before he finished? Anyway, Aaron and I had the back bedroom. It's kind of a weird shape, with one slanty corner that was on my side. I was four or five when Mom and Dad went through a big renovation kick and let us all pick a color paint and if we wanted a wallpaper border. Aaron had a sports one and I chose dinosaurs because I was *obsessed* with dinosaurs for about six years. Seriously, quiz me. You'd be amazed at how much sticks." He allowed himself a flirtatious wink, solely in the hopes of eliciting one of Sterling's adorable nose-crinkle reactions.

Sterling merely sat and looked pensive, though. "It's been a long time since I've tried my hand at painting," he said slowly, "but we did want something to do this weekend. And Alexa has been lamenting the 'boy' colors in her room for ages. Maybe we could—I mean, you don't have to, of course—"

"Would I like to help you paint Alexa's room pink and purple with glitter rainbows and sparkly unicorns?"

Sterling winced. "God, I hope not. I know she's been thinking about what she'd do for a while, though, and I wouldn't be surprised if she already had a color in mind. If she's open to something not too ridiculous…"

The only reason Jericho didn't say yes immediately was because his stint helping paint several of the newly built classrooms in Haiti was still all too recent in his mind. Specifically the memory of how his back ached for ages afterward. On the other hand, though, it was an excuse to hang out with Sterling while not on Alexa-minding duty. The thought was tempting even though it wouldn't exactly be conducive to flirting. And if Sterling had never painted a room before, there was something appealing about the idea of showing off as the expert. "Sure, I can help," he decided. "I didn't have other plans—at least, not other plans Alexa's invited for."

Sterling did laugh at Jericho's exaggerated eyebrow waggle this time. "Let's go see what Alexa thinks?" he suggested. "She's probably over her snit by now."

As it turned out, Alexa thought repainting her room was an excellent idea. All traces of her earlier grumpiness were gone and everything was forgiven. She squeezed Sterling and Jericho both in a tight hug, then dug a notebook out of her desk. The first page was a full-on mural, all sketched out and ready to go. *Ambitious* would have been an understatement—the page wouldn't have been out of place in a zoo brochure.

"One and only one color," Sterling decreed. Clearly he was having the same thought. "If you want to paint a mural on your wall later, we can talk about it, but right now Mr. Jericho and I are just offering to help with the base coat." He smiled and kissed the top of her head. "Besides," he added, "all your art genius came from your mother. There's no telling what horrors I'd end up inflicting on your nightmares if I tried to draw all those animals."

Jericho had never seen Sterling's self-professed terrible drawing skills, but it was easy to believe Alexa was the better artist. The picture would have been impressive even for an adult. A remarkable number of exotic animals crowded each other out for room on the page, each one carefully colored and shaded. The fact that he couldn't identify half of them had more to do with Alexa's single-minded zoological reading material rather than her art skills. Actually painting them all on the wall would take months—and that was for someone who knew what they were doing, which Jericho and Sterling decidedly did not.

Alexa sighed. "Dad, Mr. J…can we do two colors, then?" She flipped a page to show another full-color drawing, this one of her bed and the wall behind it. "If we put up a border here in the middle of the wall, we can hide the seam and it would look okay even if you mess it up a bit."

"If *I* mess it up?" Sterling raised one eyebrow. "You're going to be working on this too, young lady. It's your room."

Alexa grinned. She definitely knew how to read her father—and Jericho did notice the question had moved from "if" there were two colors to "which ones"? The drawing showed white on top and a lurid purple on the bottom, with something pink and silver in between. It might look like Lisa Frank threw up all over the wall, but Alexa's room would certainly be unique.

Jericho volunteered to stay behind while Sterling and Alexa braved the rain to go haggle over which shades of purple would and would not be allowed. He needed a shower and a shave, for one thing, and the whole painting experience would be a lot easier if Alexa's room had about half as much furniture in it. By the time Sterling and Alexa got back, he had the bed, desk, and dresser pulled to the middle of the room and everything else out on the landing.

"Perfect," Sterling pronounced. "We bought tarps and brushes and rollers and… Well, I'm not really sure how much of all this we'll need, but I figured it was better to buy something and not use it rather than skip it and find out later it was important. Alexa, can you help Mr. Jericho get the big tarp over your stuff in the middle and then the clear plastic ones along the walls? You don't need paint on your carpet."

Alexa obeyed immediately. Usually she tended to be all-in or all-out, either enthusiastically participating in whatever Jericho had suggested they do that day or totally against the idea and anything like it. Painting was apparently an all-in endeavor.

Finally everything got removed, draped, taped, covered, dusted, and whatever else Sterling deemed was necessary for them to be "ready." Jericho, by virtue of being "really, really tall" as Alexa put it, got to start on the upper part of the wall with a nice cream color. Alexa and Sterling started on the bottom half on the opposite side of the room with what turned out to be a much-less-lurid-than-expected lavender. She'd picked a beautiful silver scrollwork border for in between.

Working on Alexa's bedroom was a lot more fun than painting cinder-block classroom walls in Haiti. It was air-conditioned, for one thing. For another, he and Sterling and Alexa all spoke the same language and were able to joke around over the course of the afternoon. The group in Haiti had been a mix of locals with building experience but no English, mostly American teachers with next-to-no Creole fluency, and the three TeachUniversal staff—one of whom was Jericho, who had been there two years at that point and was able to translate. A lot of humor didn't cross over from English to Creole and vice versa, they'd found. Alexa's smooth walls were also much easier to paint than handmade cinder blocks.

"Ugh." Sterling stood and stretched, cracking his back and flashing a glimpse of hip under his shifting t-shirt. Jericho stretched the soreness out of his arms too, and belatedly realized they were almost half done.

"Progress, I guess? It's looking more colorful in here."

"Oh, definitely." Sterling nodded. "Let's get something to eat and take a break for a bit. Give the room a chance to air out. When we get back, Alexa and I can do the bottom half of your side and you can do the top half of ours, and we'll have the first coat down."

Sterling had a big patch of lavender on his knee and a faint smear of it across one cheekbone. Jericho fought the irrational urge to wipe it off with his thumb and then follow that up with a kiss. *Not the time, dammit.* Sterling was totally oblivious, which only made that odd swath of color that much more adorable on him.

Jericho decided that taking a break—and putting something food-like in his mouth so he wouldn't be tempted to obsess about how else he could be filling it—was an excellent idea.

* * * *

They did get Alexa's walls fully painted by about an hour before her bedtime, to Sterling's great relief. He opened the doors to the balcony, across the second-floor landing, so the post-afternoon-shower breeze could clear out some of the paint smell. The walls still needed a touch-up, though, so he made the executive decision that Alexa should sleep in his own room instead.

"Are you sure?" Jericho asked. His raised eyebrow suggested the question was about more than simple concern about Sterling's quality of sleep. Sterling briefly considered trying to make up an excuse to share Jericho's bed—but no, Alexa would figure it out. Maybe not immediately, but sometime. And she'd wonder why her father and her nanny had to share the same queen-sized bed when there was a perfectly comfortable sofa in the living room between them.

"It's fine." Sterling forced a shrug and a little smile. "The couch isn't that bad, actually—I've slept out there before."

Jericho laughed. "Usually you fall asleep in your armchair, but okay. If that's what you want to do. Alexa, how about you go dig out your pajamas and get ready for bed? We all have enough time to watch one episode of something before you need to sleep, if you're fast."

She trotted obediently upstairs, which left Sterling and Jericho both standing in the middle of the kitchen and at least one of them not sure what to say next.

Or only one of them, apparently. Jericho stepped forward in two quick strides and wrapped his arms around Sterling's waist as soon as Alexa was out of sight up the stairs. "I really am happy to share," he murmured quietly into Sterling's ear. "We can wait until she's all the way asleep, and we both know my door has a lock. I haven't gotten to touch you for *ages*—since my birthday—and I damn well hope that wasn't a one-off. Or have you changed your mind?"

Hell. Sterling shook his head no, but didn't bother trying to pretend he didn't like the feeling of Jericho's arms trapping him against that warm chest. "I didn't mean for it to be that either," he mumbled back. His voice had to be garbled because he was mostly speaking downward into Jericho's chest, but Jericho squeezed him in answer so the idea must have come through okay. "It's not that I don't want to."

"Let me guess—you don't want to give Alexa cause for concern?" Jericho slipped a finger under Sterling's chin and tilted his face up, then dropped a gone-before-it-registered kiss onto his lips. "I get that. And it's okay. Can't blame me for being hopeful, though?"

God, his cheeky little grin was impossibly sexy. Sterling nuzzled upward and pressed a much wetter kiss against Jericho's carotid instead. "Hopeful's good. And maybe we can arrange for a repeat, somehow. I just—let me think about it, okay? I'm *really* not an exhibitionist. Especially in front of my ten-year-old daughter."

"Yeah, all right." Jericho took an exaggerated step back and let his arms drop to his sides. "I guess I won't try the whole 'yawn and stretch to put my arm around your shoulders' thing once Alexa gets back down here. I'll be thinking it, though."

Thinking was fine. And after Alexa really was asleep, maybe a *bit* more than thinking would be forgivable. Sterling busied himself getting his bedroom ready for her, changing out the sheets and clearing off the random debris that kept settling on the bedside table despite his best efforts to keep it clear. By the time Alexa came downstairs and had negotiated a mutually tolerable show with Jericho, Sterling had his teeth brushed and pajama pants on and a spare blanket and pillow put aside for use on the sofa. He walked back out of his room to find Jericho and Alexa squished together on the sofa, the blanket over their laps, and both giggling.

"We took your blanket," Alexa teased, and started laughing again. "Now when you sleep here tonight, the couch will be warm *from our butts!*"

Jericho rolled his eyes, clearly for Sterling's benefit, but he was chuckling too. "Come on over," he suggested, lifting one corner of the blanket. "We'll all get your bed warm while we watch *Phineas and Ferb*."

"Or *Mako Mermaids*," Alexa added. "If you vote for mermaids, it will be two against one and Mr. J will have to watch it with us."

"Maybe another time." Sterling eyed them both, then snatched up the blanket and wedged himself in between them. "There—now we all can share the blanket, but *I'll* be the warmest."

He and Alexa play-fought while Jericho got the cartoon on. It was a kids' show, but *Phineas and Ferb* was a lot more watchable than most of what else was out there. By the time the episode was done, Alexa was slumped against his right shoulder and Jericho was a comforting presence at his left. Sometime during the dramatics Jericho's hand had ended up on Sterling's knee underneath the blanket and vice versa. They sat there for a few minutes with the TV menu on mute, nobody wanting to move.

Eventually they had to, of course. Sterling carried Alexa into his bedroom and got her tucked in under the covers, where she essentially rolled over and went straight to sleep. Jericho was lying flat on the sofa, on top of the blanket, when he came back out.

"Keeping it warm for you," Jericho said with a sinful smile. One which tempted Sterling to say *the hell with it* and drag him into another room to see how soundproof the walls really were. Jericho sat and stretched, though, then lazily rolled himself up to a standing position. "I don't know about you," he murmured, "but I'm going to go enjoy my nice big bed and my lockable door. Have a good night!"

"Has anyone ever told you you're a total bastard?"

Jericho grinned. “Not when they’re sizing me up like you are.” He ran his palm over his chest, down his lean stomach, and casually caressed the visible bulge in his jeans. Sterling could have sworn there was an extra sway in Jericho’s hips as he and his deliciously round ass walked away.

It took a long, long time to get to sleep.

Chapter 12

Tante Brielle called Jericho three days later with an offer: Would he and his new friends like to come to Camp Ladybug for the bonfire on family weekend? Specifically, would Alexa like to come visit overnight?

"She'll stay in their guest room," Jericho assured Sterling when he first brought up the idea. "Same one I did whenever we were between sessions and I wasn't assigned a camper. I prodded a bit, and it sounds like she actually would be a help. One of the families there this weekend has three kids—twin boys and a ten-year-old daughter. I had one of the boys his first year at camp. They're good people and Kiana, the daughter, is really sweet. She's also neurotypical and her brothers both do best with a lot of one-on-one supervision. Two teenage boys, two parents, and one ten-year-old who's going to feel left out even if she has her own counselor 'buddy' for the weekend...and we'd get a night to ourselves." He winked suggestively, and had to stifle a laugh at Sterling's startled look. Three days into this, whatever it was, and Sterling still rarely flirted back. He always looked so surprised and pleased when Jericho turned on the charm, though, that Jericho started making a point of hitting on him as often as he could without Alexa noticing.

"So they want Alexa to...what? Babysit?" Sterling's forehead crinkled adorably. "She's not really old enough for that..."

"Oh, God no." Alexa was a wonderfully thoughtful and kind girl once you got past her abrupt and sometimes disorienting monologues, but actual child-minding was going to be a few years off yet. If that. "Tante Brielle proposed that she and Alexa and Kiana be a trio for the weekend instead of the one-on-one with campers like they usually do. I know it's a big step to take, especially since you've only met my aunt and uncle the one time, but Alexa would have a blast. Uncle René and Tante Brielle are amazing people. They loved her, and they'll accept her as she is without blinking an eye." He punctuated his argument by giving Sterling a blatant up-and-down ogle. It wasn't entirely feigned—Sterling in a button-down shirt and dress pants was worth mentally undressing any day. Sterling didn't look as surprised the second time around. "Totally incidentally," Jericho added, "us having a day and a half to ourselves would give us time for a few of the things I'd *love* to introduce you to."

Sterling pretended—badly—that he didn't notice the hint. "Things, like..."

"Like however you want it to mean." *Like we both want a repeat and you know it.* He waggled an eyebrow suggestively, and Sterling blushed right on cue.

Sterling later insisted he said yes for Alexa's sake, but they both knew better. Alexa needed no convincing—she was practically ready to jump in the car the moment Sterling and Jericho asked if she wanted to go. Jericho set her up for a phone conversation with Tante Brielle instead.

"They're gonna have a nature scavenger hunt in the morning," Alexa told them both over dinner that night. "Mr. René and Miss Brielle are really nice, and they're letting me stay in their guest room instead of one of the cabins, and we met them before when we picked up Mr. J so I already know what they look like. On Friday we'll get to make our own candles in whatever colors we want, and ride horses, and then after dinner there's a talent show where Mr. J says the counselors all do silly things, and Miss Brielle said there's a girl named Kiana who's ten years old like me, and she thinks we'd get along really well."

Sterling leaned over and ruffled her short hair. "You've always been good at making new friends, Pup," he declared.

She beamed. Then, a few minutes later, piped back up with a more serious observation: "I think Kiana is going to be the first kid I've met who will only know me as Alexa."

"You met those girls at the beach on my birthday," Sterling pointed out.

"Yeah, but we never really told each other our names."

Sterling looked like he didn't quite know what to say, so Jericho put down his fork and gave Alexa his full attention. "How do you feel about that?" he asked. "Excited? Scared? There's no right answer; I'm just curious."

She poked at her mashed potatoes instead of meeting his gaze. "Maybe," she answered slowly. "Happy, but a little scared because I don't want her to find out. And what if she doesn't like me?"

Jericho's memories of Kiana were a bit hazy—she'd been six when their family was at Camp Ladybug to drop her brothers off, way back when—but the reason he remembered her at all was because she'd been so impressively well-behaved. Please, thank you, excuse me, and she'd waited patiently for him to finish talking with her mother before presenting her mom with a bouquet of dandelions she picked from the lawn outside the main cabin. Camp was always a zoo on pick-up day, but she'd whispered to Jericho that he must be very nice because he made her brother so happy. That's not the kind of thing anyone would forget.

"She'll like you," Jericho assured Alexa. "I promise."

So here they were, barely past nine o'clock in the morning, and Jericho's ears were already ringing from Alexa's nonstop nervous chatter during the drive. Sterling had left for work that morning with a kiss on her forehead and a promise to see her at the bonfire. He pointedly did not look at Jericho. Which was probably for the best, because there was a good chance Jericho couldn't have kept his pornographic train of thought from showing on his face. If Sterling finished on time and got home by five thirty, they'd have a whole twenty-four hours together to fill with whatever activities they liked. Preferably sex. Jericho fervently hoped Sterling had been compiling a list so they could compare notes and plan a tongue-in-cheek schedule of mutual orgasm techniques. His own list was *way* too long to finish in one night.

Alexa was halfway out of the car and running for Uncle René and Tante Brielle's house before Jericho even had a chance to pop the trunk. Not that she needed all that much luggage for such a short stay, but she and Sterling had put together a full duffel anyway.

"Alexa!" Tante Brielle called from the doorway. "Thank you so much for helping us this weekend, *mô shè*! I've got the guest room all made up for you, and there are brownies in the oven. Have you ever ridden on a horse before?"

Jericho followed more slowly with the bag. By the time he dumped it on the guest bed and made it back to the kitchen, Alexa was already in deep conversation a mile a minute with Tante Brielle. Uncle René caught Jericho's eye and jerked his head toward the front porch.

They settled into the two rocking chairs, and Uncle René lit his cigarette. Tante Brielle had long ago banned him from smoking in the house, so he'd claimed the porch as his territory. The breeze felt heavenly at the moment, blowing away some of the mugginess in the air.

"She seems like a good kid," Uncle René said. "Brielle's excited to have a houseguest again, even just overnight. How's the babysitting going?"

"We're having fun." It really was true. Alexa *reveled* in the one-on-one attention from Jericho—and from Sterling, whenever he could—and as a result was more cheerful than Sterling said he'd seen her in months.

"I know you said I didn't have to stay, but if y'all need Sterling and me tomorrow afternoon for extra hands to prep the bonfire..."

"Weekends are your time off, right?" Uncle René closed his eyes and exhaled smoke upward, where it immediately disappeared with the evening breeze. "We're not going to ask you to come up early for a silly little thing like this. And you know we'll call if anything goes wrong." He huffed. "It won't, though. Ten is old enough to do a night away from home, and Brielle has plans to feed her up with all sorts of sugary homemade treats while she's here."

Thank God. "If you're sure." He'd made the offer out of habit rather than enthusiasm. No specific commitment meant he and Sterling could head down whenever they were ready, instead of at a set time.

Uncle René fixed Jericho with a *don't be stupid* look. It was one Jericho recognized well. "In a related question," Uncle René said casually, "that father of hers is good looking and single, isn't he? You'd notice more than me."

Jericho couldn't help his reactive huff of laughter. "Are you matchmaking? For all intents and purposes, Sterling is my boss." There was absolutely no way Uncle René could have known what Jericho had in mind for his "weekend off"—or about the time he and Sterling played porn connoisseurs and ended up jerking off together—but the comment hit uncomfortably close to home. "It would make things awkward if I hit on him."

"Might be, but I bet he'd be worth it." Uncle René winked. "I'm just saying, you should make the most of your time off. Drop a hint tonight and see what he says. He seemed like a man with a good head on his shoulders when the two of them came to pick you up before. You never know—even though you're not a woman, you've got a few qualities to recommend you. If he's not too picky." He grinned around his cigarette. "It's been a while since you had someone special, hasn't it?"

Lord, this was *not* a conversation Jericho wanted to have right now. Uncle René was probably hinting about the more innocent aspects of "going steady" rather than suggesting he and Sterling have filthy, wild sex, but still. "I can't think of any non-profane responses to that," he admitted. "Have you been talking to my mom?"

In hindsight, it had probably been a mistake to tell her his real reason for not re-upping with TeachUniversal. He'd been feeling exhausted and lonely at the time, two months left of his third year, and he'd scored a rare half hour alone with the one landline in the school's office. There had been another news account of an accused gay couple being beaten by complete strangers for kissing in public the previous day. One more assault among many. Jericho's closet was getting claustrophobic. Confessing his frustrations was cathartic, but he should have known his mother would blab to Tante Brielle.

"I really and truly came back to the States because I wanted to actually teach," he added. "Not aiming to meet a nice American boy and settle down quite yet."

"Yes, I know." Uncle René regarded him steadily for a minute. "It was good that you went," he proclaimed. "You've matured a lot since then. A little less idealistic, a little more rational. And a lot more confidence. Still a smart-ass—"

"Hey!"

"—but you're an adult now. Not a green twenty-two-year-old, even if you do still happen to be the best dang counselor Camp Ladybug ever had. Two minutes with that girl in there, and I can tell she already thinks you hung the moon." He grinned and stubbed out his cigarette on the well-worn arm of his rocking chair. "Now go enjoy your free evening off-duty, and I'll see you two tomorrow sometime after six. Brielle and I are looking forward to getting to know this angelic child who obviously adores you."

Oh, of course they were. Jericho's mother probably called Tante Brielle immediately every time he got off his regular phone call home, gossiping about this or that activity Jericho told her he and Alexa were doing. Probably with a lot more commentary than he'd provided. Uncle René and Tante Brielle had never had children of their own, so they'd more or less mothered him every summer while he was working at the camp. This felt like that but a little more distant.

Jericho stood and leaned down to hug Uncle René, then headed inside to say goodbye to Alexa and Tante Brielle. A whole twenty-four hours with Sterling? Yes, they could definitely come up with some ideas to fill the time.

It's possible he whistled the whole drive back. *Two hours, two hours, two hours...*

* * * *

Sterling was thoroughly exhausted by the time he managed to make it home, nearly an hour later than he'd hoped and a full forty-five minutes later than he'd told Jericho. He'd been a walking mess of excitement and restlessness all day, waffling back and forth between "wow, this is actually going to happen" and "what the hell am I doing?" Maintaining a professional facade was harder than it had ever been before. Sterling tried to ignore the emotions and focus on dentistry instead, but daydreams about Jericho, beds, privacy, and the intriguing ways those things could intersect kept popping up at the most inconvenient of times. As in, the whole damned day.

Late afternoon brought a walk-in, a fourteen-year-old with severe tooth pain accompanied by her anxious mother. Irene took one look at the girl and squeezed her into the schedule. By the time Sterling saw the extra chart pop up in the stack, Dr. McClellan was already packing up to leave early. Sterling graciously volunteered to take a look, if only to spare the girl having to go to urgent care for what was probably garden-variety irritation concurrent with a slightly premature eruption of her wisdom teeth.

The "irritation" turned out to be acute pericoronitis, including a *lovely* infected pericoronal abscess, which meant Sterling ended up doing an unscheduled wisdom tooth extraction after-hours when everyone else except Ellen had already left. Lord bless her and her surgical expertise making everything easy. She stepped up like a champ and finished both the prep and the clean-up in half the time it would have taken Sterling to do it himself—a reminder of how she'd been working in this dental office since before he was born. They saw the girl and her much-relieved mother off, Sterling locked up the building behind himself, got in his car…and every erotic, non-professional thought he'd been having all day rushed back into his brain at once.

On my way home, he texted to Jericho. *Want me to pick up something for dinner?*

Jericho's return text pinged a moment later. *I've got it covered—hope you're hungry! ;)*

Hungry, eager, a bit nervous, and more than a bit self-conscious. Sterling poked at his hair in the rearview mirror, but there wasn't much he could do to fix the way a few bits stuck out at odd angles above his ears where they got caught the wrong way by the oversized temples of his protective surgical glasses. The nice red line across his forehead from his headlamp was a sexy touch too. Jericho had obviously seen him look worse, but it still would have been nice to have an hour or two to shower and then try on eighteen different outfits before settling on the one he was leaning toward wearing in the first place. Sterling suspected his teenage self would have absolutely done that, if he'd had eighteen outfits to choose from. And a date to impress.

Why did this feel so much like a first date?

Jericho took one look at him when he got home and silently handed him a plate of fettuccini alfredo. The smell made Sterling's mouth water. "I felt like cooking, and you love it when I make alfredo sauce with twice the parmesan cheese any normal recipe would call for," he declared, "so let's skip the part where you feel guilty for having a job that keeps you late, and I'll skip the part where I reassure you it's fine. I'm guessing you're going to want to stick with water instead of wine tonight?"

"Probably best, if you don't want me falling asleep on you." Sterling sank into his chair and gave a silent thanks for Jericho being so perceptive. "I half expected, with Alexa gone, that you might have taken the night off."

Jericho paused for a moment, then smoothly continued filling their glasses from the ice dispenser on the refrigerator door. "Would you prefer me to?" he asked. His voice was steady, but he kept his back to Sterling longer than was strictly necessary before bringing the water back to the table. "I've been looking forward to being able to take my time with you tonight, but if you'd rather read a book and knock off early, that's okay too. Or if you want me to take my dinner to eat back in my room so you've got your space—"

Crap. The last thing Sterling intended to do was to make Jericho think he wasn't wanted. "Food will help," he blurted out. "I just… My last patient was a work-in who took longer than I expected and I'm moving slower than usual at the moment. I'm not kicking you out—don't confuse me being tired with me not wanting this."

"What do you envision by 'this,' exactly? And that's an honest question, not a demand." Jericho slipped into the seat opposite and passed Sterling his glass. There was already a serving bowl of salad between them and some sliced garlic bread—clearly he'd put some thought into making dinner nice. *Romantic.* The only thing missing from the setting was a candle.

The lack was easily fixed. Sterling held up a finger in a "wait" gesture, then dug in the "formal stuff" cupboard (as Alexa put it) until he found a decent-smelling jar candle and a box of matches. Jericho watched with a bemused look as Sterling turned off all the lights except the one over the stove, lit the candle, and set it triumphantly back in the middle of the table. Dinner by candlelight may have been a horrible cliché, but the room immediately felt more intimate.

Jericho hummed thoughtfully, his gaze never leaving Sterling's face. "Whatever you're thinking," he murmured, "I'm game. Especially if it involves the kind of things people tend to do together when turning the lights down low."

"Changing the bulb?"

"Oh, I was thinking something more intimate. Something like…" Jericho paused, then shook his head. "Sorry, I got nothing. I was going to say something else funny, but the only thing I can think of that requires dimming the lights besides sex is when there's a bug flying around the room and you don't want it to come near you. Not exactly what I was going for. That sex thing, though—that's fun too."

God, he looked handsome like that, the golden tones in his skin brought out by the candlelight and the white of his smile even more stark by contrast. Sterling gathered up a forkful of fettuccini and twirled it around a few more times than it strictly required. "Jericho Johnston," he said with an attempt at a straight face which absolutely was not working, "are you trying to seduce me?"

"You said it yourself earlier," Jericho pointed out. "I've got the night off and so do you. Which means until tomorrow at six, at least, you're not 'Sterling Harper the dentist' or 'Sterling Harper the father' or 'Sterling Harper my sort-of boss.' You can't blame me if I'm hoping to see 'Sterling Harper the damn sexy lay' again."

"Good." *Damn well fantastic, really.* Although… "You got that I don't have a lot of experience with this, right?" They hadn't laid out their total sexual histories beyond that one surreal night, but surely Jericho was able to conclude that "there was one guy in my DiffEQ class" meant "I had a crush on him and we made out a few times but nothing involving other bodily fluids." Theoretical knowledge might not be an adequate substitute for the real thing. *Crap.* What if they finally got down to it and he turned out to be the worst partner Jericho had ever had? What if Jericho got sick of "going slow" and decided he wasn't worth the effort? What if—

"I did work out the implications, yes," Jericho drawled lazily. He didn't look put off in the least. "It's fine if you're too tired to do more than go to sleep early tonight, but I'd like to say—for the record—I'd be more than happy to get us both in bed and stay that way for the next twenty-four hours. Preferably the *same* bed, but…"

Yes. What he said. "For that," Sterling declared, "I'll stay awake all night."

Chapter 13

It was a relief to see that Sterling did not, in fact, fall asleep in his pasta. They chatted about the same inconsequential "how was your day" topics they usually did over meals when Alexa was present, but there was a new tone to the conversation even though the content stayed entirely PG. He seemed to perk up once he got some food in him too. Butter, cheese, chicken, cream, and pasta—fettuccini alfredo was one of those "can't get it wrong" dishes, but Jericho had spent most of the drive back to Willow Heights making a mental list of what they had in the fridge, what he could substitute out if he had to, and what noises Sterling might make when he was really enjoying his food and how close they'd correlate to other sounds which might follow later in the evening. Somehow his brain kept getting stuck on that last one.

Sterling insisted on helping load the dishwasher afterward, so they ended up awkwardly dancing around each other in the kitchen. The sooner they got things sorted up to Sterling's standard of cleanliness, the sooner they could do...something. Jericho hadn't been lying—if Sterling wanted to curl up next to each other on the sofa and read for the next three hours, it would still be a good evening. Not *as* good as what he'd been daydreaming about, of course, but nice anyway.

A pale pair of arms winding around Jericho's waist pulled him out of his thoughts. Their height difference meant Sterling's forehead pressed against the nape of Jericho's neck. Sterling slid one palm under the hem of Jericho's t-shirt, then allowed Jericho to spin around in the loose circle of his embrace.

God, the look in Sterling's eyes... Jericho allowed himself to be drawn into a thorough, not-at-all-drowsy kiss. Sterling taking the lead was new, but damned if Jericho was going to complain. It felt like Sterling was trying to make up for whatever enthusiasm he may have been lacking when he walked through the door. The kiss started hungry and slowly softened, until it was less a single kiss and more a series of nuzzles against each other's mouths. Jericho finally broke it off and pressed his forehead to Sterling's. "I take it that's a vote in favor of this, then? You're not too tired?"

Sterling slid a hand back under Jericho's shirt and ran his fingertips along Jericho's spine. "I'm still exhausted," he admitted, "but that kiss may have helped me get a second wind."

As it damn well should have. "Would a massage help you feel better?" Jericho offered. Sterling's gentle up-and-down touch was already having an effect on Jericho's circulatory system—with luck, a massage meant he could return the favor. "I may be a bit rusty," he admitted, "but I'm told I'm decent at it. And I suspect you'll feel better once you're not carrying all that stress around in your shoulders."

"That sounds heavenly, but I may fall asleep on you if you try."

Jericho pressed quick reciprocal kiss onto Sterling's lips. "If it gets you to take your shirt off and lets me put my hands on you, it'll be worth it."

Sterling grinned and pulled away. "Don't say I didn't warn you..."

Jericho blew out the candle and they retreated to Sterling's bedroom. Sterling turned on his bedside lamp and something subtle in the master bathroom, continuing the dim-lights-are-romantic thing they had going. He paused then, looking lost, so Jericho toed off his shoes and motioned for Sterling to join him on the mattress. "Strip down to your boxers and lie facedown, if you're comfortable with that?"

The words seemed to snap him out of whatever state he was in. "It'd make certain other things difficult if I weren't," he countered, even as he unbuttoned his cuffs and started on the front of his shirt. "And how do you know I don't usually wear briefs? I don't think I was in boxers the last time you saw me. When—you know."

Oh, that one was easy. "You're slow to get your laundry out of the dryer," Jericho teased. "You've got one pair of tighty-whities, one that's a brighter red than literally anything else you own, and everything else is boxers or boxer-briefs. And okay, maybe I've been primed to notice, but in my defense it's hard not to. I've spent all summer trying not to ogle too obviously whenever you go up the stairs ahead of me."

Sterling laughed and stripped off the rest of his clothes. He was indeed wearing boxers, pale green ones, that pulled temptingly taut over his ass as he crawled onto the bed and lay on his stomach in the middle. "Ogle away," Sterling said, pillowing his head on his hands and turning his face to one side so he could still talk.

"I intend to." Humor was good. Humor meant Sterling was enjoying himself, which was a rather important goal for the evening. Jericho swung a leg over Sterling's body and settled on his heels straddling him, kneeling on either side of the small of his back. "Tell me if any of this hurts."

He started with a lighter pressure until Sterling relaxed underneath him, then went to a firmer touch up and down Sterling's spine until Sterling was sinking helplessly into the mattress and making pornographic sounds of enjoyment.

"Good so far?"

Sterling straightened his head out so Jericho could work at the muscles in his neck. The position smushed his face into the bed, so presumably he'd worked out some way to lie on his hands so he could still breathe. "Feels amazing," he mumbled. "God, you're going to have to teach me how to do that."

"If you want someone to practice on, I'm not gonna argue." Jericho switched to a kneading motion, covering the small of Sterling's back. It let him shuffle backward and finally get in the good, long lecherous ogle that Sterling's ass deserved. One that he'd been wanting to indulge himself with ever since he first met the man at that tiny coffee shop. Sterling didn't have quite the same build as he himself did, was a little squarer and a little sturdier in his shoulders and hips, but the curve where his lower back became his ass was worth all the attention Jericho was able to lavish on it. Everything below the dip of Sterling's hips was still hidden under light green cotton, the fabric shifting minutely as Sterling breathed and whenever Jericho's thumbs happened to brush the hem.

"I spent all day fantasizing about how much I wanted to be touching you," Jericho admitted. "With anybody else I'd be focused on how fast we can get off, but I would honestly be content to run my hands over you like this all night." He traced the waistband of Sterling's boxers with one fingertip, then slid downward to kneel between his feet and relocated his attentions to Sterling's calves. Without any prompting, Sterling shifted his legs farther apart. The new position offered a teasing glimpse of skin underneath the soft cotton. Not even enough for Jericho to say for sure he saw anything, but the shadows between Sterling's thighs suggested the curve of his balls and the line where his thigh met his ass and Jericho's mouth literally started watering. *Damn, the things that body is made for.* To hell with slow and steady, despite what he'd told Sterling ten seconds earlier. Jericho sped through rubbing the tension out of Sterling's lower legs, ankles, and the soles of his feet. Sterling being a novice to actual, real-life dude-on-dude sex meant he'd probably be weirded out if Jericho were to peel those boxers off him and continue the massage on his virgin hole. Didn't mean it wasn't tempting, though. He hadn't covered Sterling's *whole* body under the pretense of helping him relax, yet, but maybe some parts could take higher priority than others.

Yeah, to hell with it. Patience could be a virtue later. Jericho slid back up Sterling's body, laying himself out flat like a blanket along Sterling's spine, and lipped gently at his earlobe.

"You still awake?" he asked softly.

Sterling hummed something affirmative.

"Actually awake?"

"No thanks to your magic fingers." Sterling drew in a giant breath—which created a slightly disorienting sensation as his ribcage expanded with Jericho's torso still on top of it—and turned his head to the side again. "Turns out I can't just drift off with a gorgeous man like you in my bed, I guess. I keep having these really hot daydreams."

"Oh?" Jericho rolled off so Sterling could turn over onto his side.

Sterling immediately twisted around and gave him an obvious once-over. "Yeah," he said. "But in these daydreams, the hot guy pinning me to the bed was naked."

Jericho nodded solemnly, then immediately peeled off his t-shirt. "That makes sense." He rose to kneeling to unbutton his jeans. There was no missing how intently Sterling was watching him, so Jericho unzipped as slowly as he could with a raging hard-on making things difficult. *Strip all the way, or make him wait?* Sterling seemed to be happy in only his boxers, so Jericho left his own on too. "Anything particular this hot guy was doing?"

Some guidance would have been nice, but instead Sterling buried his face back in the bed and made a sound like he was choking on his own tongue. Too embarrassed to ask for what he wanted? Or lost his nerve? "Sorry," he said, his voice muffled by the blanket. "I'm a failure at dirty talk. I don't know what I should—I mean, you know what you like better than I do."

He wasn't saying no. That was good. Jericho sat back a bit and eyed Sterling up and down. Even with his body halfway curled up, the shape of his hard-on outlined in loose green cotton was pretty damn clear. Still, just in case... "Want to stop?"

Sterling shook his head no.

Good. "Trust me?"

A nod yes.

"Lie back and let me do all the work this round then, okay? I want to make you come like this, while you're all sleepy and relaxed."

Sterling stretched and rolled over onto his back with no particular attempt at modesty, and Jericho found himself practically salivating. *Hell yes.* Sterling's slow blinks and contented expression spoke to an awe-inspiring amount of trust. Jericho sat there with what was probably an idiotic expression on his face until Sterling reached out and brushed a hand against his knee. "Less sleepy the longer you're looking at me like that," he teased. "Feels like you're expecting I'll disappear."

Not entirely what he was thinking, but disturbingly close. "I don't usually get to see you with your walls down," Jericho admitted. "You sneak away after dinner to hide in here whenever you're all peopled out. And on the nights we are in the same room together without Alexa, we're usually either reading or silently watching TV. I was admiring."

Sterling shook his head. "I'm not hiding—I'm trying to give you your space."

It suddenly became imperative that Jericho touch this gorgeous man, preferably enough to make him re-think his assumption. He leaned down to nuzzle a cloud of warm breath against Sterling's abs. "I'll show you the amount of space I need," he murmured, and kissed Sterling's navel. "I can give you a hint, though—it's nowhere near as much as you seem to believe."

Sterling let out a strangled laugh, one which in other circumstances Jericho might have termed a nervous giggle. "Go ahead then," he said, and relaxed back into the mattress. "Feel free to demonstrate."

"Mmmm." Jericho smeared his cheek along Sterling's stomach, kissing whatever bits of skin were in reach. The man had the perfect ratio of angles to softness. No intimidating six-pack abs, no fancy manscaping. Just smooth, slightly spicy skin with a darkening triangle where the smattering of light fuzz over his sternum condensed into a happy trail that Jericho was *more* than happy to follow. He nosed along the hem of Sterling's boxers—which made Sterling's dick twitch and literally bop him in the chin.

"Oh God." Sterling threw his hands up over his face. "Sorry, sorry."

"Stop apologizing." Jericho turned his head without changing his angle and captured the tip of Sterling's cock between his lips. The pale green fabric already had a darker spot on it, evidence Sterling enjoyed being teased as much as Jericho enjoyed doing the teasing, and Jericho worked his tongue over it until all the flavor of precome was gone. When he came up for air, Sterling had his eyes squeezed tightly shut and was gripping the blanket at his sides with both hands. Jericho gave him two more teasing kisses through his boxers, making Sterling arch his hips slightly and clench his fists. *Christ, so gorgeous.*

Tugging the hem of the boxers down felt uncannily like unwrapping a long-awaited Christmas present. The slow reveal uncovered an inch of pale hip at a time, until Jericho finally took pity and freed Sterling's cock the rest of the way. Flushed, hard, the well-mouthed head already damp from Jericho's saliva and Sterling's precome even through the cotton. Before Sterling could work up too much anxiety over finally being completely naked, Jericho leaned back down and licked the shaft from base to tip.

Sterling's breath punched out in an audible pant.

Jericho groped for one of those fists without looking up. He steadied the base of Sterling's cock with one hand, holding it still so he could keep his touches light, and slipped the other into Sterling's clenched grip. Sterling squeezed Jericho's fingers and relaxed somewhat, which was excellent. Blowjobs were—Jericho knew well from experience—a hell of a lot better when both parties were into it and not worried about stupid self-conscious insecurities. Sterling wasn't necessarily freaking out about anything specific, but the way his muscles started to relax had to be a good sign. They stayed there, innocently holding hands while Jericho nuzzled Sterling's cock, until Sterling's breathing returned to normal and he was no longer arched off the mattress with tension.

Even though Jericho had mostly just been teasing at what was on offer, licking and kissing and only lightly squeezing Sterling's shaft, it wasn't hard to tell Sterling would go off in about ten seconds if he tried anything complicated. Instead, Jericho shifted so they could make eye contact and slowly sucked him down to about halfway.

Holy hell, I've missed this so much. More than he'd realized. Sterling's cock was warm and fit perfectly in the cradle of Jericho's tongue, and Jericho couldn't resist the urge to let himself go and enjoy the sensation for a bit. Up above him Sterling was gasping and mumbling half-intelligible words of encouragement, which only made Jericho's own dick harder. Which he couldn't do anything about, because Sterling was holding his one hand and Sterling's balls were cradled nicely in the other and trying to rub off on the blanket while delivering a blowjob was probably a recipe for embarrassment and/or disaster.

Sterling's grip tightened around Jericho's hand, which made Jericho abruptly realize that the filthy stream of monologue falling from Sterling's lips had coalesced into actual words.

"—gonna come, *Christ*, Jericho, I can't even—*oooh*, that's it, there, that feels *amazing*, I'm, oh God—"

Jericho had sucked enough dicks to recognize the signs even without the warning, but it was nice of Sterling to have said something anyway. He pulled off and exchanged his mouth for his palm right as Sterling arched his back and cried out. *Still* no free hand to pump his own cock, damn it, but the feeling of Sterling's dick pulsing against his fingers as it emptied his sac was almost as good. Almost.

"Oh my God," Sterling said aloud, once he started breathing again. "That was…" He trailed off into another moan. "Give a minute to regrow my bones and I'll try my best to follow that performance. *Hell.*"

"You don't have to," Jericho assured him. He let his nonsticky hand drift up and down Sterling's arm. "This round isn't about reciprocation, it's about you needing some sleep before we do anything else. And I like blowing you—"

"Wait, you do? Really?" Sterling propped himself up on an elbow and stared at him with wonder on his face until the doubt clouds rolled in. "It can't be the same, though. Sorry, I haven't reciprocated at *all* tonight…"

"What's really getting me off," Jericho continued, talking right over Sterling's budding apology, "is you letting me. Encouraging everything I'm asking you for. God, you don't even know. Seeing you sprawled out under me, totally trusting, it's…*fuck*. Look what you do to me." He took their joined hands and pressed them against his painfully hard cock. The thing was tenting the front of his boxers something ridiculous, not subtle in the least, but Sterling sucked in a sharp breath when the back of his hand made contact with the fabric. *Fuck*. "That's all you," Jericho growled, "with absolutely no effort on your part. I haven't touched myself at *all* and I'm ready to pound nails after getting to taste—"

Sterling batted Jericho's hand away and slid his own through the slit in Jericho's boxers. He didn't even have a proper grip before Jericho was already past the point of no return. Sterling pumped a few times and then stayed perfectly still, holding him loosely, while Jericho felt his whole brain leak out his dick. All he could do afterward was to flop down on the bed next to Sterling and groan. As soon as he could stand without toppling over, though, he got back up and went to find a washcloth in the en suite bathroom. Sterling watched him with heavy eyes. Jericho stripped off his now-messy boxers and left them there, then came back and cleaned them both up as best he could. By the time he managed to bully Sterling into lying *in* the bed instead of merely on top of it and got the top sheet and blanket pulled back over them both, Sterling was already half gone.

"I'll be here when you wake up," he said quietly to the back of Sterling's head. "For now, you can sleep."

He claimed his rightful position as the big spoon and drifted off soon after Sterling did.

Chapter 14

They slept for almost two hours. Sterling would have probably stayed passed out for the whole night if Jericho hadn't shifted in his sleep and jammed a knee into his kidney. As it was, Sterling startled awake to discover that it was still dark outside, the lamp and the bathroom light were still on, and a very naked Jericho was snuggled up behind him. He was on the verge of saying *screw it* and dozing back off while the mattress was still warm, but Jericho sat up before he could figure out the logistics.

"Hey," Jericho said, rubbing his eyes like a tired toddler. "Feel better?"

Oh, he did. Much better rested, definitely, but also terribly mortified to have contributed so little to the encounter. The two emotions evened out to somewhere around "sheepish." Sterling nodded anyway. "You were right—you're damn good at giving massages. Didn't mean to pass out on you like that, though. Sorry."

"Don't be. I straight-up said I was happy for you to get some sleep. Trust me, I wasn't expecting wild, kinky sex for twenty-four hours straight."

"Is that something to aspire to?"

Jericho laughed. "Feels like that would be the equivalent of running a marathon without having done more than a 5K before, honestly. For me too. Waking up together is really nice, though."

"Not your usual?" *Crap.* Sterling was immediately kicking himself—that came out sounding a lot judgier than it was supposed to. "I mean," he amended, "not saying I expect you to only have had one-night stands…"

"A mix of those and longer-term partners, but nobody for the last few years." Jericho yawned and stretched, the movement making his pecs shift distractingly across his chest. "I was meaning more that I tend to be the early bird and am out of bed and raiding the pantry before my partner wakes up. You're worth sleeping in for."

God, he was gorgeous when still a bit dozy. Sterling was struck by the sudden mental image of Jericho as a cat, lazing on a windowsill. Long and lean and muscular and content but capable of so much more when he wanted to be… He found his attention involuntarily wandering to Jericho's nipples and the occasional wiry hair dotted over his sternum. Apparently he wasn't very subtle about it, though—by the time he realized and snapped his gaze back up to Jericho's face, Jericho was silently laughing at him.

"I assumed I'd be the one to get caught staring," Jericho explained with a smirk. "Although in my defense…" He paused, then shook his head. "Never mind; I've got no good excuse. I just like staring at your ass."

Ha. "I may have noticed one or two of those sneak peeks," Sterling admitted. "And reciprocated when you weren't likely to catch me at it. I usually felt guilty about it afterward, though."

Jericho raised one incredulous eyebrow. "You must be better at 'subtle' than I am."

"Well, as far as you know…"

"Oh, *God.*" Jericho guffawed and shoved at Sterling's shoulder. "That was terrible. And speaking of terrible lines, what horrid pick-up cliché do I need to use for you to invite me into that thing?" He nodded toward the garden tub between the window and the bathroom door. "Because I've been having dirty thoughts about what we could do in it ever since that night I got my first look inside your bedroom."

Sterling hummed and pretended he was having to consider it.

"You'll be able to ogle me better when you're not lying on your back," Jericho coaxed. "Um, what else… Oh! It would help us wash off the flakes of dried come I didn't manage to get to before. They itch." He rubbed one such bit off his thigh with a fingertip and flicked it over the edge of the bed somewhere. "I think those are all the objective, logical reasons I've got, but there are probably more. If the dirty thoughts thing isn't enough of an incentive."

Logic had very little to do with how much Sterling wanted Jericho to show him round two, and the tub was as good a place as any. He tried to remember the last time he'd used it for something other than Alexa's occasional bath time. Ages, probably. The biweekly cleaning lady kept it shiny white and ready to use, though, and tub sex sounded a lot less awkward than shower sex.

"I suppose…" Sterling tapped his index finger over his lips. "You do make a good case. And I don't think I've ever done much of anything in that tub, actually. Dana used it more than I did. You did say you were interested in helping me create some new 'firsts'…"

Jericho launched himself out of bed, across the room, and into the empty tub before Sterling could even finish his sentence. His long legs worked against him, for once—the tub was deeper than it looked from the bed, which Jericho only discovered when he failed to stick his landing. "Flippity ding dong dammit!"

He looked more frustrated with his failure to be graceful than actually hurt. Another point in favor of the "Jericho is secretly a house cat in disguise" theory. Sterling barely held in a snicker.

"Go ahead and laugh," Jericho said, but he was already shaking his head and smiling. "*Damn it,* that hurt. Your faucet was pointier than I expected."

"I'm not"—Sterling smothered a snort—"I wouldn't laugh at you getting hurt. That would be rude."

Jericho sniffed and tilted his nose in the air. "At least I still have my dignity, then."

"Oh, not a chance. You lost that with the 'ding dong dammit.'" Sterling did laugh aloud at Jericho's struggle to maintain his haughty expression without joining in. A struggle the man was losing the longer Sterling took trying to get himself back together. "Let me guess—you get creative in your exclamations when you work in a school?"

Jericho finally gave in and laughed too. "Kind of lost my filter halfway through, didn't I?"

"A bit, yeah. I promise not to tell." Sterling took pity on him and got off the bed to go turn on the tap. Jericho sat on one of the two half-height benches and massaged his shin while making increasingly ridiculous faces. He was still taller than the designers of the tub had likely intended—his knees would probably stick out of the water even if he had his feet flat against the opposite wall—but Sterling didn't expect they'd do much actual washing. *In fact…* He waved for Jericho to stay in the tub as it filled, then dashed back to his bedside table and dug out his half-empty bottle of lube and the new-still-in-the-plastic-wrap box of condoms. He'd had to stand in line at Publix to buy them over lunch a few days earlier because their self-check machines weren't working. Even as a theoretically full-grown man, Sterling wasn't keen on some teenage cashier commenting on his brand preferences. The kid hadn't actually said anything aloud, but it was still embarrassing.

"Ambitious, are we?" Jericho caught the box and placed it next to the tub, then did the same with the lube. The water was up to his navel, now. "Come on; get in."

Sterling eased himself in and let his body acclimate to the temperature as the tub continued to fill. By the time it was up to mid-chest and Jericho turned it off, the two of them ended up perched on the benches on opposite sides of the tub with their legs creating a lazy tangle in the middle. Sterling leaned his head back against the tile behind him and groaned. "I think this is a sign of me feeling my age. The massage last night nearly put me to sleep, and now soaking here with you in the middle of the night feels almost as good as getting off."

"Oh, yes, you're a whole three years older than I am. You're positively ancient. And if this is better than what we just did, I didn't do a thorough enough job." Jericho hooked his hands behind Sterling's knees and tugged him closer, until Sterling didn't have any option but to slide off his bench.

Jericho immediately pulled him up into his lap. "You can't tell me you didn't mean that as a challenge," he declared, before leaning in and mouthing a hot, wet spot on Sterling's neck. Their relative positions meant Sterling was taller, for once, and Jericho was obviously enjoying the novelty. Sterling steadied himself on Jericho's shoulders and let himself be appreciated. He honestly didn't realize he was twitching his hips until Jericho groaned and yanked Sterling's ass closer. The movement bumped Sterling's cock against his own and pulled a low groan from them both.

The warm water made it hard to tell which part of Sterling's body had just been electrocuted by the contact. Maybe everything. Water was a conductor; maybe that's why his whole body lit up.

"You bought condoms," Jericho said in a low voice. "The twenty-pack may be a *few* more than we need tonight—"

"Oh, you know I didn't—"

"—but I'm very much in favor of helping you break in your new box." He pulled away from kissing Sterling's neck and collarbone long enough to flash him a dangerous smile.

Not a house cat. A mountain lion, maybe. Something soft and silent until it pounced with the exact right maneuver to get what it wanted. And damn if Sterling didn't find that little bit of imagined danger a turn-on. Deliberately, this time, he ground down harder into Jericho's lap.

"Damn." Jericho shifted Sterling an inch or two, and Sterling could feel the hard pressure of Jericho's dick against his own. He dove down to capture Jericho's lips in a kiss, and they stayed like that for what felt like forever. Finally Jericho tore himself away and hauled in a deep breath. "*Christ*," he groaned. "I swear you're going to kill me one of these days. All my blood's gonna be in my cock and there'll be none left for my brain."

That sounded perfectly lovely to Sterling. "Any particular tips on how to accomplish that?"

Jericho half laughed, half groaned. "Greedy, aren't you? The more relevant question would be, top or bottom? I'm up for either, so which one do you fantasize about?" He hitched Sterling higher and gradually let him slide back down, Sterling's cock making contact in a slow line down his abdomen. "I'm at your disposal," he added. "Think of me as your personal, highly qualified tutor in whatever you'd like to learn."

Oh God, that was *such* a long list. "I think…fluid kinematics, maybe? It was the one unit in my thermodynamics class I never quite got the hang of."

"Ha! So for that…" Jericho stopped groping Sterling's ass and pinched his butt cheek instead. Their cocks both got a tease when Sterling jumped. *Another reaction to think about more later.*

"Hell." Sterling tipped his head back and tried to think. "I, um. I've had thoughts about either," he admitted. "But for tonight, I think I want to find out what you'd feel like inside me. I'm guessing my fingers aren't quite the same as the real thing."

Jericho's full-body shiver hit Sterling like an earthquake. "That's… yes." He arched up to steal another quick kiss. "You like fingering yourself open sometimes, yeah?"

Sterling bit his lip and nodded. "Sometimes. When I'm…when I let myself get carried away. And I've got the time to indulge."

"Oh, we've got *all* the time tonight," Jericho breathed. The heated look in his eyes alone would have probably gotten Sterling halfway to hard. "Want me to give you something to jerk off to in the future? Take you nice and slow? I will, if you can trust me to take the lead."

Absolutely and without hesitation, Sterling returned the kiss and the eye-fuck. "I'm all yours."

* * * *

Now, after all the tough talk, Jericho couldn't decide what he wanted to do first. It felt like Sterling had led him to Willy Wonka's candy room and now wanted to watch him gorge himself. The warm water felt wonderful, even though it only reached to halfway up their chests, but for more carnal purposes… Jericho eased Sterling to standing and turned him ninety degrees so he faced back toward the bed. Sterling stayed delightfully pliant, allowing Jericho to nudge and poke him into a wide straddle with his feet braced against the bases of the two shelf seats.

"Lean forward and brace yourself against the edge of the tub."

"Like this?"

Oh, *yes*. The position put Sterling's cock just barely skimming the surface of the water, which was perfect. More importantly, it let Jericho sink back until the water was level with his collarbone and Sterling's ass was at the perfect height. The view was amazing—Sterling held trustingly still with his shoulders down, cock half submerged, head twisted around so he could watch what Jericho was doing…and his hole was in perfect licking distance.

"God, Jericho," Sterling said in a thin voice. "Are you going to—*Jesus Christ!*"

"You can drop down to lean on your elbows if it's more comfortable," Jericho suggested, then settled his palms on the twin curves of Sterling's ass cheeks and nuzzled his hole again. The angle put his chin almost in the water, but it would be worth half drowning himself if it meant Sterling kept making those little shocked, aroused noises as Jericho licked him open. *Another first, and it's all mine.*

It was a stupid, possessive thought, and Jericho knew it, but right now the concept of being Sterling's first everything felt too good to brush aside. Jericho was never going to be the poster boy for abstinence before marriage—by a long shot, thank you LGBT-friendly high school—but the fact that Sterling had been denying himself all this was… Christ, he couldn't even think of the words. No matter where this summer led, Jericho vowed to at least give Sterling the best "firsts" he possibly could. This, rimming Sterling while crouching neck-deep in a bathtub at fuck-o'clock at night, was a first for himself too.

Oh, and it was something worth repeating if they ever got the chance. Licking someone else's ass was always an odd combination of thrilling and taboo, but Sterling's skin was already warm and wet and clean and soft. Jericho slid a hand around to cradle Sterling's now rock-hard cock. The backs of his fingers skimmed the water as he traced it with a feather-light touch.

Sterling moaned loudly and shifted down so he was leaning on his elbows instead of his hands, giving Jericho an even better angle to eat his ass. Which Jericho absolutely took advantage of. "That feels…damn." Sterling groaned again. "God, *so* much better than my fingers. Going to come from that, if you keep it up. Don't wanna."

Jericho pulled back a moment and replaced his mouth with his thumbs, massaging and stretching Sterling's hole. "You want me to stop?" he asked. "Or you don't want to come like this?"

He was 90 percent sure it was the latter, but Sterling's immediate "Don't stop!" was still reassuring.

Good. He'd happily keep going forever, if he could. Although if he did, they'd never get to open that box of condoms.

Fuck. New plan. "You'd look gorgeous with my fingers inside you," Jericho said aloud.

Sterling rolled his head back and forth on his folded arms, which was probably as close as Jericho was going to get to a yes.

"You able to keep your balance like this without me holding your hip steady?"

A clear nod, even though Sterling's face was still buried.

"You focus on not tipping over, then," Jericho ordered. He slid his butt back up to the submerged bench and grabbed the lube. Sterling's entire body shuddered at the click of the cap. *Distraction—distraction is key.* "You said you like fingering yourself sometimes, right?" Jericho asked, purposely keeping his voice light.

"Sometimes," Sterling admitted.

Jericho didn't see any undue tension in his muscles, other than his shoulders, and that was probably from the angle of his arms. Not freaking out—another reassuring sign. "Tell me about it?"

"Mmmm." Sterling rolled his head to one side, so his voice wasn't muffled by his arms. "Sometimes when I can't sleep, and it's late enough I know nobody else will still be awake, I lie there in the dark and try to imagine what it feels like."

"You haven't tried toys?"

Sterling snorted. "Remind me to show you my collection sometime. It can't possibly feel the same, though."

The mental image of Sterling showing off an old pirate-style treasure chest full of butt plugs and dildos flashed through Jericho's mind, and he had to give the base of his own cock a tight squeeze to prevent anything embarrassing from happening at the mere thought. "You have no damn idea how much I'd like to see that," he said. "With your fingers, though—you start with one, like this?" He traced his lube-slick forefinger around Sterling's rim twice, then pressed gently against his hole. Sterling gasped, then promptly *melted.*

"God, yes, like that, but not as—*oooh.*" Sterling groaned loudly. "Damn, your fingers are so much longer than mine. I can never quite reach—*aaah!*"

Found it. Jericho backed off after that single brief touch, focusing on stretching Sterling's rim enough for a second finger and then a third. By the time he had three fingers inside and was rubbing soft circles on Sterling's perineum with his thumb, Sterling was nearly beyond words. Jericho was just as nearly beyond being able to wait any longer.

"Ready for more?" *Please say yes please say yes ple—*

Sterling's moans turned into a waterfall of *need, please, yes, now,* and a handful of other words all mixed together in a jumble. Jericho raced to get the condom opened and onto his cock before they both went over the edge.

Condom, lube, line himself up, hold Sterling's hip for balance… Jericho knew he was in trouble before he even got his tip past that tight ring. He was trying to go slow, dammit, but Sterling shimmied his ass backward and despite his total lack of leverage, he managed to impale himself on the first inch or two of Jericho's cock.

"Ohgod. Ohgod." Sterling groaned, but he didn't stop leaning back into Jericho. "Christ. You feel so…" He thrust his hips back again, taking another half-inch into his body.

"That's a good feeling, right? Or too fast?" Jericho bit the inside of his cheek and tried to run through his usual mental slideshow for boner control, but none of them worked while he had Sterling's tight, virgin hole around him. "There's no rush," he lied. *I may implode right here, but take your time...*

Sterling whipped around to stare at him over his shoulder. "Jericho Johnston," he hissed, "if you don't pound me into next Wednesday this goddamn *minute* I will never forgive you." He resettled his arms into a firmer brace on the lip of the tile. "I've waited twenty-nine years for this, so don't you dare try to go slow."

Well. No ambiguity there. Jericho grabbed Sterling's hips and pulled himself closer as quickly as he dared. Sterling adjusted their angle and ground back against him, until Jericho's balls were pressed against Sterling's ass and Sterling was minimally verbal again. They might have overdone it with the lube, but *fuck it.* Eating Sterling out and then fucking his gorgeous ass in his posh hot tub was possibly the best idea Jericho had ever had.

After all the build-up—the flirting, the first round, the nap, the making out while halfway submerged in hot water, the rimming and fingering—after all that, Jericho felt like his orgasm was on a hair trigger. Luckily, so was Sterling's. Jericho literally saw black spots behind his eyelids when he hit that point of no return and slammed home for the last time in Sterling's hole. He only barely remembered to do a reach-around with his still-lube-slicked hand, and Sterling came a few seconds after he did.

Neither of them were doing a great job at standing afterward, so Jericho flipped the lever for the drain and sat back down. Sterling collapsed gracelessly into his lap, sideways this time and still mostly boneless.

"Oh my God," Sterling mumbled into Jericho's neck. "Oh my *God.* Why didn't you tell me it could be like that?"

It almost never was, as far as Jericho could remember. What they'd just done was so far beyond "good" that "good" wasn't even in the same zip code. Jericho would have been perfectly happy to give in and fall asleep right there in the tub with Sterling flopped on top of him, and usually he wasn't the roll-over-and-start-snoring kind.

Sterling got heavier as the water level lowered. Jericho took care of the condom, tried not to think about how much jizz the two of them had probably deposited in the water still swirling around their shins, and hauled Sterling to his feet.

"Gotta make it back to the bed," he prodded. "I'd carry you but I'm gonna fall over too. *Christ.*"

They tumbled onto the blanket together with matching stupid smiles on their faces, leaving the world's largest wet spot on the covers. Sterling crawled up to where the pillows were and dragged Jericho along to spoon up behind him, then pulled the less-damp-at-that-end blanket over them both and promptly dozed off.

Jericho managed to stay awake a few more minutes, gaze fixed on Sterling and mind racing, before he succumbed.

Chapter 15

Sterling was trying not to worry whether Alexa was enjoying herself at Camp Ladybug, but her giant grin when he and Jericho got out of the car the next evening put any lingering concern to rest. She attack-hugged him and Jericho, then dragged them both by the hand to where a much more reserved girl was waiting at the edge of the parking lot.

"This is Kiana and we're BFFs now," Alexa declared.

The two girls were a similar height, but Kiana had purple glasses and a waist-length waterfall of frizzy hair that looked like it'd be a nightmare to keep brushed. She gave Sterling and Jericho both polite little nods before turning and whispering something in Alexa's ear. Alexa cracked up, then the two of them dashed back up the path to the main cluster of cabins.

"Like I said," Jericho commented as they watched the girls go, "nice kid and really sweet. A bit shy, apparently, but then most kids are at that age. Alexa excepted."

Sterling shook his head, more in resignation than argument. "I'd say I disagree, but you're not wrong. She's been a nonstop extrovert ever since her transition. Before it, too, but recently she's been particularly exuberant about it. Probably something about hanging around with you." He winked, just to make Jericho laugh. "Should we follow them?"

"Not yet." Jericho led him instead in the opposite direction, to a wide field on the other side of the camp. "I promised Uncle René we'd help set up the bonfire even though he assured me we didn't have to," he explained. "You'd be surprised at how many college-aged counselors don't have the first clue how to build a fire safely. I used to have to give a tutorial every year."

"Not sure I could," Sterling admitted. "Not one of any size, anyway. I think the last time I intentionally lit something on fire, it was with a magnifying glass and I was Alexa's age."

"I can see that. Gung-ho for science, were you?"

"That's what I justified it as, yeah."

"Guess that means Alexa comes by it naturally."

They crested what turned out to be the curve of a gentle hill and Sterling saw the well-used fire pit in a little amphitheater toward the middle. There was a chest-high log pile behind the nearest bench, but the fire pit was empty. The center was a good six feet wide, ringed in brick, and had several rows of varnished wooden benches radiating outward from it in a semicircle. The benches varied oddly in length.

"Wheelchair cut-outs," Jericho explained. "Some campers do better on flat surfaces and others need a ramp, so Uncle René made sure to provide twice as much seating as we ever use." He pointed out how one aisle had stairs, another had the ramp, and the outer edges of the arc were carefully graded and had railings set into the concrete all the way down. "The nice thing about a one-to-one camper to staff ratio is there's no need to *make* everyone all sit and behave to keep order," he added. "As long as you keep eyes on your camper buddy for the week, they can climb around in the back or swing—gently—on the railing and they'll either pay attention to the group activity or not."

"No 'sit down and be quiet'?"

"Not here, anyway." Jericho inclined his head back toward the camp. "Come on—I was hoping they'd have something out here already, but the fact that they don't probably means they do need some help. I'm guessing Uncle René forgot to send someone out with the rest of the gear yet." He dug out his phone and sent a long text, then cocked his head in the direction of the paved path. "Walk with me? You don't have to help lay the fire if you don't want, but I'm still volunteering you to help me haul the kindling. It gets too wet if we keep it out here with the rest of the woodpile."

Back at the camp's main building, a dining-room-cum-theater area, they were met by a cheerful staffer juggling several reusable grocery bags brimming with snapped one-by-two board pieces. He set them down to give Jericho a hearty hug and a pat on the back, then fell in alongside them as they shared the load on the trip back across the field.

"Haven't seen you in forever, J-man!" the camp counselor declared. "How you been? You reclaiming your spot?"

"Nah," Jericho answered, a decidedly Southern twang creeping into his voice. It made him sound younger—fitting, since the kid who'd just joined them looked all of about sixteen. And damn, when had that started sounding so far back? "I finished college, spent the last couple of years teaching abroad, and now I'm aiming to find a permanent teaching position somewhere."

"You end up going for the special needs thing?"

"You know it. You?" Jericho waved the kid toward the fire pit, then stopped. "Darn it, I'm being rude. Sterling, this is Chase. Chase, Sterling. Chase and I worked a couple of summers together, which I'm guessing you probably figured out already. He's Tante Brielle's right-hand man now."

Sterling nodded politely and tried to mentally adjust his estimate of Chase's age upward to somewhere in the early twenties. Which flat-out did not compute. Maybe summer camp administration was a recommended career choice for people who would probably be carded at bars until they turned fifty.

"I help out when I can, for what that's worth." Chase offered Sterling a firm handshake. "I graduated on the six-year plan, unlike some overachievers I could mention." He stuck his tongue out at Jericho. "Still no idea what I'm doing come fall. I'm gonna keep spending my summers here as long as I can, though. I love the work and I love the kids."

"Did you get to meet Sterling's daughter, Alexa? She's the spiky-haired one who's been running around with Kiana since yesterday."

"Oh!" Chase beamed at Sterling. "She's a fun one, definitely. Well done on the whole parenting thing. She was our audience volunteer for the talent show last night—you'll have to ask her about her role in the skit. She looked like she was loving it."

"I'll...be sure to do that," Sterling answered. Somehow, without talking to or even really looking at each other, Jericho and Chase already had a respectable stack of logs positioned in the fire pit. The placement of each piece felt like it could have been a complex mathematical arrangement if not for the thinner kindling stuck randomly underneath the larger pieces and totally ruining the design. Chase and Jericho had clearly done this together many times before. "I wouldn't be surprised if Alexa is asking to come here again in another year or two," Sterling added.

Jericho laughed. "She's not going to wait that long."

He was probably right.

Soon after Jericho and Chase got the fire lit and stable, Jericho's Tante Brielle came trotting up the path to them. "Ten-minute warning," she called. "Hope you boys are hungry, because René overstocked on the s'mores supplies by at least half. Everyone's finishing up dinner now, so families will start to wander this way at their own pace, and we can start once the sun's mostly down."

Belatedly, Sterling realized it *was* quite a bit darker than it had been when they first arrived. The fledgling bonfire's glow lit the meeting circle area and not much else—hopefully some of the parents and counselors had flashlights. The woods ringing the field blocked the actual sunset, unfortunately, but the sky was already turning interesting shades around the tops of the trees.

"Hey." Jericho tugged Sterling to one of the front-row benches and sat down. "Might as well enjoy the quiet while we've got it, right?"

Two hours earlier, Sterling would have snuggled up against Jericho without a second thought and enjoyed staring into the fire. There was something magnetic about the man's build—long limbs, narrow shoulders, his easy grace—that made Sterling want to indulge his inner five-year-old and curl up in Jericho's lap while Jericho held him close. It wasn't a particularly sexual fantasy, it was…nice. Sweet and innocent. Two hours earlier they'd been doing something that might sound remarkably similar, although that was because they'd just finished a wonderfully slow front, and full-body snuggling with a limp, sated Jericho was a phenomenal reward. As was the reciprocation soon afterward.

Voices from the first wave of campers carried from over the hill toward the main lodge. Sterling squashed his *cuddling* urge down and slid away, putting more space between them. "Guess it won't be quiet much longer?"

"Probably not," Jericho said after an odd little pause. Sterling struggled to interpret his tone of voice—he didn't sound excited to be swarmed by campers, but he didn't sound wistful over their child-free holiday ending either. "I should probably help get everyone to wherever they want to sit. Keep my spot open for me?"

"Sure." *Business as usual, then.* Any awkwardness was probably limited to Sterling's own mind, anyway. He swung his legs up and sat sideways on the bench, taking up more than half of it. "I'm assuming Alexa and maybe Kiana will want to sit with us too? I'll stay here and try to look fierce enough nobody will try to claim my territory."

It turned out to be a good prediction—Alexa and Kiana were in the second wave of people coming up the path from the lodge. Alexa leapt down the central stairs two at a time and practically landed in Sterling's lap.

"Wanna see my new necklace? Kiana and I made ours be exactly the same so we could always match." She held up the cord so he could examine the multicolored lumps in more detail. "They let us make our own beads and there's a real kiln here so when we finished we had to put them on these little metal sticks and Miss Cricket—she's one of the counselors—she baked them last night so we could string our necklaces this morning. The middle one's a cat, because Kiana likes cats"—she pointed out the larger pendant, which was reasonably identifiable as feline—"and we picked the rainbow colors together. But look, I did *teeth!* Kiana thought my idea was cool, and she says she might want to be a dental zoologist someday too! I don't think anyone else has a dental zoology necklace," she concluded. "I mean, other than Kiana and me."

"That's probably true." Now that she'd told him what they were, the oblong blobs on either side of the cat did have the general shape of canines and incisors and molars. "Did you make them cat teeth specifically, or all different kinds?"

She rolled her eyes at him. "Obligate carnivores' molars are *totally* different, Dad. No, Kiana thought we should do all kinds of different animals' teeth so they're all the different tooth shapes. Since we both like lots of kinds of animals. Oh, wait—I want to show Mr. J." She dashed back across to the other side of the fire pit. Sterling watched as she enthusiastically introduced Jericho and Kiana, even though they'd apparently already met once upon a time, then Kiana dragged Alexa to come talk with a forty-something couple who were sitting beside identical blond boys in electric wheelchairs. Kiana's brothers, presumably.

"You're Dr. Harper—I remember you from before."

Sterling jumped at the sudden hand on his shoulder, but before he could say anything its owner rounded the bench and he recognized Jericho's Tante Brielle.

"Miss Alexa is the sweetest thing," she continued, sitting down next to him on the bench. "A real bundle of energy, that one, isn't she?"

"That's one way to put it." *A bundle of energy approaching supernova, maybe.* "My mother says 'vivacious.'"

She laughed. "However you say it, she and Kiana and I had a wonderful time. I enjoyed hearing so much about how you and my Jericho are the best people on the planet. It sounded to me like you're doing a marvelous job of raising your daughter with the freedom to be herself—that's all too rare these days, unfortunately."

Sterling wasn't sure whether he was supposed to take that as a compliment or as social commentary on Alexa being transgender, so he smiled and shrugged. "She's an amazing kid, and I love her no matter how she wants to express herself. I'm guessing you heard a lot about animal teeth?"

"Oh, yes." She sighed. "I remember when Jericho was around that age—all knees and elbows and charm." She got a faraway look in her eyes. "René and I never had children, and neither did my sister Delphine. Our brother Claude—Jericho's father—carried on the next generation for all three of us. Delphine got to see our nieces and nephews all the time during the years she lived with them, but René and I had already moved out here by then. We saw all the children when we visited them or vice versa, of course, but Jericho was the one who fell in love with Camp Ladybug right from the first. He was always begging to come out here. I'm probably not supposed to play favorites, but"—she leaned in closer and mock-whispered—"*he's my favorite.*"

Sterling could absolutely picture a much younger Jericho tearing around the camp, being enthusiastic about literally everything and zealously making new friends. "Is that why he went into teaching special education?"

"Oh, I can't take credit for that—he's a special young man." She winked at Sterling. "But you've already figured that out, haven't you?"

"I, um. I've noticed." Was she hinting at something? Her sweet Southern smile made it hard to tell whether she was merely bragging on her nephew or whether she was insinuating there was something going on between him and Jericho. Which, *of course*, but not whatever she was suggesting. "Alexa has loved having him around," he said. "As I assume she's been telling you, probably at great length. It's been a fun summer."

"I'm sure. Are you two planning for him to stay with you on past next month? Alexa seemed to think you were, but Jericho's mother originally told me this nanny thing was a temporary job the same way working here would have been. Is the position he was offered in the fall close enough he can commute? It's somewhere up in Georgia, right?"

Crap. Okay, maybe she wasn't pushing, but if Alexa didn't understand Jericho was leaving… "I see I'm going to have to explain things to my daughter," Sterling admitted. That wasn't going to be fun. "No, it's about an hour away. Although I'd love to hire Jericho for breaks or the occasional weekend if it fits in his new schedule. I know Alexa will miss him a lot."

"She implied the two of you had formed more than a business relationship—that 'Mr. J' was becoming a close friend. For you as well as for her." Tante Brielle raised one eyebrow, but didn't elaborate, which was just as well because Sterling was already probably blushing. He was struck by the strong family resemblance—Jericho sometimes had the exact same doubtful expression his aunt currently did.

Alexa was more right than she realized, of course. *A close friend.* Did he even have friends anymore? Sterling tried to think of the last time he'd done something social and drew a complete blank. Outings with Alexa, sure. Occasional get-togethers with Dana's parents, did that count? The last time he had anyone over was...*dang.* Other than his own mother, it was probably before Dana died. Most of their joint friends were really "her" friends, and had been happy enough to leave Sterling alone when he stopped returning calls. He couldn't even say he had strong work friendships, because Dr. McClellan was more paternal than anything. For everyone else, Sterling was "one of the bosses."

"I didn't mean to pry, hon," Tante Brielle said, the words neatly cutting off his depressing train of thought. "Jericho's all grown up now and heaven knows he's capable of handling his own personal life. We were all so worried for him in Haiti, but of course that turned out fine. Three years is a long time, though—seems like the friends he had before are all moving on. It's always hard, coming back home and finding home has changed while you weren't watching."

"Yeah, it's...that's very true." *Sometimes it changes even when you thought you already had an eye on everything.* "I'm sure Jericho's new school will be another adventure for him, though, and I imagine he'll get to know everyone pretty quickly. New beginnings, right? Sounds like he's always been good at finding somewhere to fit in."

Luckily Sterling didn't have to embarrass himself with any further blather because right then Alexa and Kiana came back to join them on the bench. Jericho slid in smoothly on the other side of Alexa. Uncle René strummed his guitar a few times, quieting everyone down before the songs and s'mores started, and Sterling was able to focus on the fire instead.

* * * *

Jericho made a point of not letting on that he'd overheard Sterling's conversation with Tante Brielle, that night or any of the nights that followed. Things were back to the previous normal once Alexa got back home, anyway. He and Sterling took turns cooking, Alexa talked a lot, and Sterling spent his days at work and his evenings in his armchair. Jericho usually took over the other chair to keep him company, reading or watching TV or poking at Alexa's meager collection of videogames. They still sat in silence more often than not. Hard to tell whether the new "normal" felt anywhere near as awkward to Sterling.

Even on the evenings he and Sterling did talk, they didn't touch until well after Alexa's bedtime. Usually that involved either making out on the sofa or still-mostly-clothed handjobs in Sterling's bedroom. Jericho was getting off regularly—by his hand or by Sterling's—and he was still getting paid a stupidly huge salary for what amounted to being Alexa's sidekick and summertime playmate. He was back in the States rent-free for the rest of the summer and had a lead on a nice little upstairs half of a duplex in Brunswick not too far from his new school with the potential lease available to start anytime after August first. So why did everything in his life feel even more confining than Haiti had?

He was still chewing on that thought the morning Sterling called to say a family of four had all cancelled with no notice and could Jericho bring Alexa into the office? She was almost due for a cleaning anyway and getting it out of the way now meant not having to pull her out of school for it later. Alexa took some convincing, but Jericho prevailed. They got to Sterling's clinic right before ten.

"This almost never happens," Sterling said when he came into view and saw Alexa and Jericho there chatting with the receptionist at the front desk. "Come on back. Usually when it's time for Alexa's checkup, she and my mom and I end up coming in after hours and I do everything myself. Seemed like a shame to waste such a huge time slot, though, so thanks for dropping whatever else you were doing. Keeping busy, I assume?"

"Drawing," Alexa told him. "Mr. J was helping me with my shading. We got out Mom's old work lamps—the ones with the bendy part in the middle—and we were investigating how putting them in different places changed how much detail you could see on my coyote skull."

"You have a coyote skull?" asked a voice Jericho didn't recognize. It resolved itself into an older man with a graying fringe of hair and a bit of a gut, who popped out of a room near the opposite end of the hallway from where they were standing. "Dr. Calvin McClellan," he said, offering Jericho a handshake. "Or Cal, to anyone not in my chair, so I don't get called 'doctor' very often. Hard to talk with your mouth open wide." He chuckled at his own joke. "I'm Sterling's partner in crime here. Although not for long, I hope!" He clapped Sterling on the shoulder. "Young pups need space to grow into big dogs in this world. I keep telling Sterling I'm ready to kick back and retire whenever he's ready to take over. Our Sterling's got it in him to be a very big dog indeed."

"Thanks," Sterling said. He didn't smile. "Cal, this is Jericho Johnston, who's been helping me out with Alexa for the summer. And of course you remember Alexa." He deftly shrugged off Dr. McClellan's hand on his shoulder in the process of putting an arm around Alexa and hugging her tightly to his side. "She might look a bit different than when you last saw her. Taller, for one."

First time at the office since her transition, Jericho assumed. It wasn't hard to read between the lines. Dr. McClellan surely must have had time to get used to the idea of his partner's daughter, though, right? Jericho couldn't imagine it being a surprise after this long.

Dr. McClellan turned to Alexa and offered her a grown-up handshake. "Definitely taller," Dr. McClellan agreed. "And I like the new haircut. Very fetching."

Alexa grinned and gave his outstretched hand a half-dozen unusually enthusiastic pumps. "Dad said I have to let it go back to a normal shade when school starts," she said, "but purple is my favorite color."

It did look good on her, Jericho thought, not for the first time. Her natural blondish-brown showed through at the roots, but the tips of each pixie spike were currently a vivid magenta. Product of a long afternoon the previous week, when Alexa declared she wanted to try a "stylist" who catered to women and not just the pediatric barber Sterling had usually taken her to before. Kudos to the lady at the fancy salon Jericho found for not batting an eyelid when he brought Alexa in with the "purple, please!" request. The trim and dye cost three times more than Jericho had ever paid for a cut when he *had* hair, though, so maybe her expertise and professionalism came standard at those prices.

"It looks great." Dr. McClellan nodded. "Have you been enjoying your summer?"

"Oh, yes! Mr. J and I have been doing all sorts of fun things. Like, we went to the beach, and started a window garden, and he showed me how to use a flashlight to make shadow animals with my fingers, even though I'm not very good at it yet—"

"Alexa," Sterling interrupted gently. "Let's have you go with Miss Ellen to get started on your cleaning and an X-ray, okay? She'll let me know when you two need me to come in and look."

Alexa happily followed an older woman—Ellen, presumably—into one of the small side rooms.

"Kid's a lot bigger than when you had him—*her*—here last," Dr. McClellan commented. "They sure do grow up fast, don't they?"

Sterling didn't react to the slip-up, even though he must have heard it. Maybe it was a regular thing. Dr. McClellan was at least making some effort to be kind to Alexa, which sounded like it was more than her maternal grandparents were doing, and he didn't misgender her to her face. Maybe that's all Sterling had thought he could ask for. Disappointing, if true, but Jericho knew well how hard it was to get other adults to come around from "your identity doesn't exist" to "your identity makes me uncomfortable" to "it's none of my business how you identify, just tell me what you want me to call you." He'd dealt with it from a handful of family friends when he came out as gay, and again at Georgia State when he let himself experiment with the whole clubbing culture. Alexa undoubtedly had it a hundred times worse than he ever did for being a cisgender gay man, and she was in for a lifetime more ahead. *Because people suck.*

"She's nervous about going back to school," Sterling said, lowering his voice enough Alexa wouldn't possibly be able to hear. "Which, I mean, I don't blame her. I'm so proud of her for coming out anyway, though, even though she knew it would be hard. Lord knows I never had that kind of self-confidence when I was a kid."

Dr. McClellan snorted jovially. "You still are a kid," he joked. "But—*oh!* Speaking of families… Have Lawrence and Vivian invited you to the church picnic yet? I don't know if you still consider yourself a member or not, but it's on the front lawn on Sunday at one. Your church family misses you, you know."

Anyone who didn't know Sterling as well as Jericho did by now might have been forgiven for not noticing the slight tensing in Sterling's shoulders, but then again Jericho wasn't "anyone" anymore. "They've mentioned it," Sterling said. He gestured toward his phone, which was clipped into a holster on his belt. "Hadn't really thought about it, but…"

"Everyone already knows about Oscar's transition," Dr. McClellan said once it became obvious Sterling wasn't going to finish the sentence. "I know not everyone's thrilled with your choice, but you're still welcome any time. And you too, Mr. Johnston," he added. "It's a potluck, but don't worry about bringing anything—there are always tons of leftovers."

A red light started flashing next to the doorway for one of the exam rooms.

"Excuse me," he said, already sidling past Sterling. "Looks like Miss Mueller's X-rays are ready. I'm serious, though—you should come. Bring your nanny too."

Chapter 16

Jericho didn't say anything while he and Alexa were still at the office, but Sterling could tell he was bothered by something. Probably something they'd need to talk about soon, if they didn't want whatever it was to bleed over into the good thing the two of them had going. At least, Sterling thought it was a good thing. Lord only knew if Jericho would agree. Sterling finished up his last patient at five on the dot, picked up Mexican from the place two doors down that did amazing fish tacos, and headed home. He tried not to notice that Jericho was a little slower to smile during dinner.

"Mr. J, it's Wednesday! Can I watch you play your game tonight?" Alexa asked as they loaded the dishwasher afterward. "I promise I won't use any of the bad words I hear your friends say."

Jericho let out a startled laugh and tousled Alexa's hair. "For a few minutes, I guess, but I'm gonna warn them not to swear while you're in there with me. Most of them are capable of being polite when they have to." He waved away Sterling's instinctive *but-evening-is-your-time-off* objection to Alexa intruding on Jericho's one regular social engagement. "I'm sure the guys would love to meet her," he explained, "even if it's only over voice chat. It's okay."

Alexa hearing Jericho's friends swear wasn't all that high on Sterling's list of things to get worked up about, honestly, so if they both wanted… "Brush teeth and change into PJs first, then. And I don't want to hear any whining when it's lights-out."

Sterling puttered around the kitchen while Jericho got logged on and Alexa was upstairs. There wasn't all that much left to do, but for once he was too restless to settle down in front of the TV. *How the hell am I going to break it to her that this isn't forever?* "Meet my friends" felt an awful lot like "meet my parents" in terms of permanence. And suddenly, Alexa visiting Camp Ladybug acquired a whole new light. She'd probably want to return someday, when she was old enough to do summer camp. Being in a mix of special needs and neurotypical kids didn't faze her. Which made him proud, even though it wasn't really *that* much of a reflection on his parenting. Hopefully when that time came and she was a few years older, she'd be able to look back on the summer Jericho lived with them as a good memory. One in what would probably be a sea of frustrating incidents with people determined to misgender her, tell her she's wrong for transitioning, or flat-out insult her for it. So far she'd been more cheerful and willfully oblivious to the negatives about transitioning than Sterling had expected, but that didn't mean she didn't notice the sometimes-hateful undertones.

Jericho wandered back out of his room and leaned against the counter, watching Sterling dither. "Come hang out in my room tonight after?" he asked. "Further from"—he nodded toward the stairs—"and I don't want to talk in the living room where she might sneak up on us and overhear."

"About what?"

Jericho leveled him a serious look. "If I knew, I wouldn't be asking. It feels like there's something, though, and I don't like the change. Just a quick talk, okay? Communication is supposed to be important in…well, in lots of things."

In a relationship, he was about to say. Sterling heard the words in his head as if they'd been spoken aloud. Why did that feel so ominous? "I'll come back down after I put Alexa to bed, will that work?"

"Yeah, perfect." Jericho's gaze drifted past Sterling toward the stairs, which Alexa was thumping down one step at a time. "Hey, princess! You ready to beat all my friends on the virtual racetrack?"

Alexa stuck her tongue out at him. "I beat you last time! But—oh! Can I wear the headset? So I can talk back?"

"Ha! Not a chance. I'll put them on speaker, though."

Sterling hung back and watched as Jericho got Alexa set up with his controller and reset the sound so it came out of the TV instead of the gaming headphones he usually wore. He still hung the headphones around his neck, since the microphone was connected to the ear piece, but this way Alexa could hear too.

"Hey, everyone," he said, "I've got Alexa here with me. Y'all want to tell her hi?"

There was a chorus of greetings in a variety of male voices.

"She's still got about twenty minutes before her bedtime, so she's going to play as me for the first few rounds. Don't go easy on her, though—she may be little, but she can be vicious!"

Sterling left them to it. He wandered up to the study upstairs and worked on cleaning off his desk for a bit, pointlessly shuffling things around. When everything that could reasonably be sorted was in its place, he went back down to his bedroom and puttered around in there too. Twenty minutes took forever. Alexa did come in and jump on his bed eventually, chattering about almost winning a race before accidentally going backwards on the track and Jericho having to take over, and Sterling ended up going through the motions of ushering Alexa into bed. She was chattery but cooperative. She also had a million questions right when he was about to leave, but for once he didn't particularly feel like making it a teaching moment. Luckily, she was almost asleep on her feet already. Her breathing was slow and even within two minutes of Sterling turning off the light. Sterling waited a few minutes longer, more for his own sake than for Alexa's, then bit the bullet and went down to face the let's-have-a-serious-talk with Jericho.

"Hey." Jericho waved him in and scooted farther back on the bed, leaving the foot of it for Sterling to sit on.

"Not finishing your game night?"

Jericho shrugged. "Not feeling that social, honestly. The guys understood."

"Alexa approved of them, sounds like."

"They thought she sounded nice too. My buddy Brandon and his boyfriend Paul found out they're expecting a baby a few weeks ago, so everyone's been teasing them about being future parents. My friends have all had children on the brain lately, on Brandon and Paul's behalf."

Sterling took a moment to parse that. "One of them is trans and pregnant? Or they're adopting?"

"Good guess, but no. Paul's got a twin sister who volunteered to be the other half of the DNA." Jericho cracked a small smile. "I didn't pry into the logistics, but I gather it took more planning than most small governments do in a year. And now Danielle confirmed that she's pregnant and due in February, and since I'm the only one in our group with much experience around kids, Paul and Brandon keep asking me for my opinion on things."

"You've worked with babies?"

"Not since Malachi was born, if you count that. Which you shouldn't, since I was seven. Doesn't matter, apparently—Brandon's got three older brothers who are all smothering him with enthusiasm and Paul's not close with anyone in his family besides his sister, so I guess I'm the only safe one left." Jericho leaned back against the headboard. "I always figured

I'd end up a dad. Maybe foster or adopt a kid with special needs since I'm better equipped to deal with that than a lot of people are. The whole concept of being mature enough to be *the* responsible adult for an actual baby, though… The idea seems a lot more daunting the further I get from college and the closer I get to it ever being a possibility."

God, you have no idea. "I'd never felt strongly about kids one way or the other," Sterling admitted, "but I wouldn't give up Alexa for the world. Even with Dana gone, it's…well, indescribable. And terrifying. Nobody tells you you're messing up until it's too late, you know? At least before, Dana and I could muddle through it together."

Jericho sucked in a deep breath. "Right. So, on that note… We've been pretty honest with each other, haven't we? I mean, I know I've told you some things I've never told anyone else, and I'm guessing you've done the same for me."

"…Yes?"

"And I know this is none of my business so if you want to tell me to shove off after I've said my thing, that's up to you. Okay, so. What's the deal with your in-laws?" He grimaced. "I thought you weren't on good terms with Dana's parents because of the whole transphobic thing, but you as good as promised your partner we'd come to some church-wide potluck. Which they've also invited us to and, presumably, they'll be at. From what you've told me, they're always conscious of what everyone else thinks of them—so how are they going to react when you bring Alexa along and she's obviously not presenting as a boy anymore?"

Sterling's immediate, instinctive reaction was to wave away any problem because Lawrence and Vivian *hated* public scenes. He'd have been lying to himself, though. Both that there wouldn't be a scene and that Dana's parents would try to avoid it. "It's complicated."

"So try me." Jericho crossed his arms and waited. He didn't look mad, but he also didn't look like he'd be accepting a bullshit answer.

Unfortunately, metaphorical excrement was never in short supply when Dana's family were involved. "They're wrong, obviously, but they're still Dana's parents. Alexa's grandparents. Much as I don't want to leave that door open, they deserve a chance to be in Alexa's life. They're the only family we've got, other than my mother."

"You could say your biological father was 'family' too, by that logic," Jericho pointed out. "And yet I don't see you running out to chase him down."

"It's different."

"Is it?"

"My father was a total bastard, from what my mom has told me. Constantly threatened her, spent most of his time and money getting drunk, and kept trying to control her entire life. Succeeded, mostly, until she got pregnant with me and decided she'd rather be broke and single than broke and married to an abuser. Lawrence and Vivian aren't bad people, no matter what impression I've given you. They're just..."

"Trying to control your entire life," Jericho finished for him.

"Not—well, they try, but I'm doing my best not to let them. Dana and I got married and kept the baby because we wanted to, which was pretty much the exact opposite of what they were pushing her for."

"And totally without their input whatsoever, you decided to move to Willow Heights?"

Christ. The worst part was, Jericho wasn't entirely wrong. "It was Dana's idea," Sterling countered. "Yes, they suggested it and she wanted to be closer to her parents, but it also made sense. Dr. McClellan was looking to pass the mantle, being part of an independent practice gave me more flexibility with my schedule and my income, and Alexa was seven at the time. This is a beautiful town to grow up in and Dana wanted the best for our kid."

"Look." Jericho sat up straighter and crossed his legs so he could lean his elbows on his knees as he spoke. "I'm gonna be blunt, because there's no other way to say this: I like you. A lot. Alexa too. I'd like to continue seeing you after August, even though I'll be more than an hour away. You've got the life I've always hoped I'd find someday—an amazing daughter, a stable job, all of it—and it's killing me to see you *still* bending over backwards because it's what your wife would have wanted. I want to keep this going"—he waggled his finger between his own chest and Sterling's—"and to be honest, I kind of want to go yell at your bigoted in-laws because you won't. Shit." He scrubbed a hand over the stubble on his scalp. "Okay, I didn't mean to come on quite that strong, but screw it."

"You...you're offering to come back and look after Alexa after school starts?" Sterling couldn't quite get his brain wrapped around the idea that being a widower was an enviable life goal, but that part of Jericho's little speech stood out. "I mean, apart from all the rest. Is that what you meant? Because yes, I'd be happy to pay extra for your transportation time to get back down here, even though I know it's a drive. I'm sure she'd love to see more of y—"

He was cut off by a rough sound and an explosion of movement from Jericho. "Babysitter?" Jericho spat out the word as if it were something much more obscene. "You—you're assuming I meant earning a little spending money offering to babysit. *Fuck.*"

"Was that not…" The light bulb finally went off in Sterling's head. "Oh. You meant, 'seeing you' as in *seeing* me like, what? Dating?"

"I thought we kind of were already," Jericho grumbled, "but apparently not. Since you were thinking in terms of *paying me.* Did my whole shtick about 'we should start messing around with each other because I don't see this as an employer-employee relationship' not suggest strongly enough that I don't care about the damned money?"

Dating? "I thought this was a 'take pity on the gay virgin' thing," Sterling admitted. "You've been in a dangerously homophobic country for the last three years. I was stuck in a sexless marriage with a woman I liked very much as a friend but wasn't physically attracted to…"

He trailed off. Total silence while Jericho gaped at him.

"I mean," Sterling added, "not that I haven't enjoyed everything we've done, but…I thought we both knew this had to be temporary. We're convenient for each other right now, but you're about to go start your own career, and I'm buying out my partner soon and staying here. We'll be tied down in different places. Convenient and long distance don't mix."

"Wait." Jericho finally seemed to recover his powers of speech. "Back up. I know this is totally off topic, but I can't help it. You're buying out your partner?"

"Yeah. I think so." Sterling wasn't entirely sure why he'd been dragging his feet for the last few years, but Dr. McClellan's hinting wasn't going to get more subtle. And hell, it was well past time to commit, right? "That was the original offer when we moved here—he's backed off to part-time, but one of these days I'm supposed to buy out his ownership of the practice and I'll have the whole office to myself. The staff are all wonderful, so no need for changes there. I might look at hiring another dentist part-time, maybe. I'm not sure I'd be able to keep up with all six rooms' worth of patients at once, but I could probably do four."

"Okay, so you're 'supposed to.' But do you *want* to?"

"Does it matter?"

"*Yes!* Of course it matters!" Jericho groaned. "Jesus Christ, grow a spine already! Look, I'm not asking you to move up to Brunswick and buy me a house, I'm just asking you to admit that we've got something good here. You. Me. I *like* you, and I thought you liked me."

"I do!"

"As more than an employee."

Hell. "I didn't mean it like that," Sterling said. "And yes, of course I like what we've been doing. Would have thought you might have noticed that—it's not like my hard-ons are all that subtle." He rolled up to his knees and scooted closer to Jericho, so they were actually eye to eye. "This has been the best summer I've had in a long time. You're gorgeous and so good with Alexa and I really do wish you the best, but it's not like we've committed to anything. In the end I'll make my life decisions and you make yours."

Jericho raised his chin. "And your decision is?"

To beg you to stay? To take you to bed and never let you go? To completely change the plans I've had for the last ten years, solely because you're mad I'm not meaner to my in-laws? There wasn't a simple answer. Instinctively, yes—if it was a forced choice, he'd much rather have Jericho be happy than Lawrence and Vivian. Being a grown-up means doing things you don't want to do, though, because they're objectively the right thing.

The other option, caving in to Jericho and burning bridges with the in-laws, was the coward's way out. Right now, Sterling didn't give a damn if he was being a coward. "In the short term," he said, "what I really want to do is get you naked and gag myself on your cock until you can't take it anymore and you come straight down my throat." He let his gaze pointedly drop to Jericho's lap. "That sounds like a better use of our evening than arguing, doesn't it?"

Jericho was in his pajama pants already, the blue ones with the light gray stripes that made his long legs go on forever, and they didn't do a darn thing to hide the fact that his dick was very much in favor of Sterling's plan. However much Jericho might have wanted to keep the awkward conversation going, ignoring everything in favor of sex sounded much better. And apparently Jericho agreed, because after another moment or two of silence he leaned forward to grab Sterling around the waist and then toppled both of them over backwards. Sterling narrowly missed cracking his forehead on the headboard in the process.

"I take it this means you don't want to talk about it," Jericho murmured, and shifted them farther down on the bed. "Alexa might still get back up, you realize?"

He did, but for once Sterling didn't care. Usually they kept things strictly platonic until at least ten or eleven, when they could be sure she was 100 percent asleep—but now that Sterling had the mental image in his head of himself sucking Jericho off, waiting sounded like a terrible idea. "You'll just have to be quiet," he countered. "And I intend to keep all my clothes on." He tugged at the hem of Jericho's t-shirt. "Get rid of this."

Jericho obediently shucked the shirt.

Sterling tossed it off the bed onto the floor, then pushed Jericho back down so he was flat on his back. "So glad you agree to my compromise," he whispered into Jericho's ear.

Jericho snorted. "Wouldn't call it a compromise, but when you say you want my dick in your mouth I'll probably agree to anything."

"Good." Sterling tapped his hip and slid his fingertips under the waistband of his pajama pants and boxer-briefs. "Lift."

Jericho did, and Sterling tossed the whole balled-up wad in the direction of the t-shirt. He did get up to lock the door—horny as he was, Alexa walking in on them would *really* be a turn-off—and to kick off his shoes. Nothing else, though. There was something incredibly hot about still being in his work clothes, looking respectable, while Jericho was lying there totally naked.

"I'd rather not have to think about you leaving," he admitted. And climbed onto the bed so he could kneel between Jericho's legs. "So I'm going to try to swallow as much of your cock as I can, and I want you to lie there and try not to make any sounds. No bucking your hips—I'm steering, tonight. Got it?"

Jericho propped himself up on his elbows and nodded.

Excellent. Despite all their experimentation, Sterling had never particularly tried to run the show before. The moment he got a good suck in on the head of Jericho's cock and Jericho's hum of appreciation rumbled through both their bodies, he decided he wanted as much practice as possible. Jericho watched for a little while, mouth open and eyes half-closed, but eventually he gave up and lay flat on his back and let Sterling go at it.

And really, Sterling discovered there was something incredibly satisfying about seeing how much he could take without gagging. Sterling ended up planting his elbows on Jericho's thighs and holding his hips down that way, because Jericho was totally unable to keep from twitching whenever he did something particularly electric. Jericho moaned at Sterling literally pinning him down. Sterling pulled off and teased him with tiny little kitten licks for a while just because of that.

He was stalling, though. Actually giving a blowjob still felt like an impossible, theoretical thing. One he loved in porn and when Jericho volunteered, but which looked a lot more daunting first-hand. Jericho's cock was *there*, warm and hard and absolutely gorgeous, and also too huge to fit in a human mouth. Almost certainly. Years of professional experience meant Sterling felt pretty confident he knew more about the capacity of people's mouths than most, but screw logic. He let all those objections fly out the window and gave it a go. The appeal of having Jericho's erection in his mouth was mostly wrapped up in the fact that it was attached to Jericho, but the actual physical sensation was a big plus.

"Christ," Jericho panted from somewhere far above Sterling's field of view. "You keep that up and I'm not gonna last long."

Sterling pulled off long enough to glare at him. "Hush. Busy down here." And he dove back in.

Jericho's strangled laugh mutated into a low moan, and then into a tension that told Sterling he was indeed close. Sterling settled his weight more firmly onto Jericho's thighs and focused on finding the best way to repress his gag reflex. He finally got the right angle and did the impossible. *Holy fuck.* If he exhaled hard and leaned forward the perfect amount he was able to fit the entire cock in his mouth, all the way up to where his lips were almost touching Jericho's balls. That was it, apparently—Jericho let out a long moan and came down Sterling's throat. God, it wasn't even hard to swallow, his cock was that far down. Sterling slid off slowly until the oversensitive head left his mouth with a soft pop.

He sat back and looked up the bed at Jericho's face. God, Jericho looked *ruined.* His arm was flung up over his eyes, so Sterling couldn't study his facial expression as well as he'd liked, but there was no missing the shiny red ring of a bite mark on Jericho's knuckles. The realization—he'd literally been biting his own fist to keep quiet—made Sterling's own neglected hard-on feel that much more urgent.

"Damn," Jericho breathed. "Give me a sec and—"

And what? Hell. "It's okay," Sterling assured him. Any minute now, Jericho would shake off the post-orgasm lethargy and want to reciprocate. Which would lead to them both lying on Jericho's bed, thoroughly wrung out and feeling sappy and in a prime position to start their aborted conversation back up again. Even the promise of an orgasm wasn't enough to make Sterling want to do revisit the elephant in the room. "I actually think I'm going to go take a shower, finish up in there, and go to bed early tonight."

Jericho's eyebrows climbed up toward his hairline, or what his hairline would have been if he had any hair. "You sure? I'm offering anything you want, after that. *Christ.* I still can't feel my toes."

I'm sure. Sterling retrieved Jericho's clothes from the floor for him, tossed them onto the bed, and escaped to the safety of his own bedroom and his own right hand.

Maybe-sort-of-dating was delicious, but messy. And *complicated.*

Chapter 17

The sun was as hot as ever on Sunday afternoon, the day of the potluck, but Jericho was pleasantly surprised to discover that the church's lawn got a nice breeze. It also had a stunning view—the church stood on a bit of a hill overlooking some subdivisions and a chunk of Willow Heights's world-famous golf course. He felt an odd urge to learn how to golf, solely so he could go see all that manicured greenery up close.

"Haven't actually been here in a while," Sterling admitted as they pulled into the parking lot. "Everyone was wonderful right after Dana died—casseroles for months, lots of offers to help with everything, I'm sure you know what it's like. Church never felt the same without Dana, though, so I stopped dragging Alexa here on Sundays." He sighed. "Not sure whether I miss it or not, to tell you the truth."

"It's okay," Alexa chimed in from the back seat. "I didn't like going anyway. Walker and Sam are nice, but none of the other kids my age are very friendly." She paused, then made a thoughtful noise. "They haven't met me as Alexa, though," she added. "Maybe the girls will be nicer now..."

Jericho wouldn't usually put "church" high on the list of places to find trans acceptance, but maybe from the other kids? *God, I can only hope.*

Despite Dr. McClellan having said they didn't need to bring anything to contribute to the potluck, Sterling had picked up a store-bought crumb cake for the dessert table. They had folding chairs and a brand-new picnic blanket in the back of the SUV—Sterling said he didn't want to bring his regular bed-sized blanket to sit on again like they had at the beach—but it looked like the church had seating covered already. The lawn was studded with little groupings of folding chairs all arranged together like mushroom circles. Jericho opened the trunk and pretended to survey the contents anyway, which brought Sterling to his side.

"This is Alexa's first time seeing her grandparents since before I came, right?" he asked Sterling quietly.

Sterling nodded.

"Did you sit her down and talk her through what to do?"

He earned an odd look for that. "They're Dana's parents," Sterling said. "Alexa has known them her whole life. She can handle herself."

"Wait, seriously?" The upcoming fake smiles and awkward conversation were pretty much guaranteed to be painful and awkward even in the best case scenario. Why the heck wouldn't Sterling prep his daughter for what was to come? *Jesus Christ.* "She's *ten*, Sterling," Jericho pointed out. "I doubt there are even all that many adults who'd be confident in the face of what we both know is coming."

"You're getting all upset over nothing," Sterling countered. "It'll be fine; Alexa's heard it all before so it's not going to be a surprise if they're awful. And they probably won't be—not in public, anyway." He nudged Jericho out of the way and shut the trunk, leaving the unneeded picnic supplies inside. "Right. Everyone ready to eat?"

Alexa lifted her chin and straightened her spine, looking for all the world like a miniature general marching into battle. "I'm ready."

Jericho wished he had half her confidence. Meeting a large group of new people was one thing, but meeting them when they all believe they knew you as a different gender and a different name and they probably all have opinions on your transition was something else entirely. It took... well, not balls, but *something.* Guts. Chutzpah. Alexa may have been brave, but she understandably stuck a little closer than usual to Sterling's side.

Dr. McClellan met them halfway across the lawn. He was accompanied by a tall, thin woman in an unflatteringly tailored dress.

"So glad you were able to make it!" he said as they approached. "Seriously, I am. And glad the rain has held off so far. Oh, can I get that for you?" He took the boxed cake from Sterling. "I know you and Wanda have met before, but it's probably been a while. And not since before Oscar changed his name to Alexa, I'm sure. With them they've brought...is it Joshua? Starts with a J? Sorry, I'm terrible with names. At least at the office I can cheat and read the patient chart first!"

The woman offered Jericho and Alexa both a nod. Sterling immediately jumped in to finish the introductions. Alexa stood at Sterling's elbow and smiled uncertainly back.

It soon became apparent that even though Sterling and Alexa weren't regular churchgoing members anymore, everyone knew who they were. Jericho had a sneaking suspicion the familiarity was based more on gossip than on remembering them from when they were more regular attendees. The next fifteen minutes were a parade of polite handshakes, painful fumbling around Alexa's name and pronouns, and a truly fascinating range of responses to Jericho being hired as the summer nanny. Sterling didn't call it that, merely introduced him as Jericho and mentioned he was helping watch Alexa for the summer, but everyone seemed to have drawn their own conclusion about what that meant. Probably didn't help—Jericho took a surreptitious look around as they approached the food tent—that he was the only dark-skinned person there. Certainly not the first time in his life he'd been the odd one out, but it did feel strange after so long in Haiti where dark skin was actually in the majority for once.

"They're not sure what to make of you," Sterling commented, quiet enough not to be overheard. "You don't mind that I'm telling people why you're staying with us for the summer, do you? I'm afraid if I introduce you as a 'friend' everyone will start to get the wrong impression."

Wrong, or perfectly accurate? Jericho forced himself to shrug and mumble back a noncommittal answer. "Fuckbuddy" wasn't exactly something you busted out in church, but it hurt. Sterling didn't consider him a friend, even? Technically "employee" was still accurate, even though he'd stopped feeling that way weeks ago. Or had, until recently…

"Oh, goodness! You came!"

Sterling didn't see his in-laws approach from behind him and visibly jumped when his mother-in-law spoke. She offered an awkward hug to him and then, oddly enough, to Jericho. Alexa strategically hung back behind one of the folding chairs so her grandparents couldn't smother her with affection. Or eat her—it was hard to tell which she thought was more likely, judging from her expression. Jericho managed a "nice to meet you" and a polite nod.

"Calvin—Dr. McClellan—mentioned you might come," Vivian Butler declared brightly. "And of course you never replied to my text, Sterling, so I didn't know, but I'm *so* glad you could make it. We've missed you on Sunday mornings. Oh, and you must be Jericho." She smiled at him, all teeth and no heart. Lawrence Butler merely nodded. "We were disappointed we didn't get to see much of Oscar this summer, of course, but I'm happy the two of you are having fun. Sterling has been giving us updates on your adventures."

"Oh?" Presumably not *all* their adventures. At least, not the nocturnal ones. Or—right, she probably meant his adventures with Alexa. Sterling flushed and looked away, which probably meant his mind went in the exact same direction.

Vivian didn't seem to notice his reaction. "Of course!" she declared. "Dana was our only child, I'm sure Sterling's told you. Having her gone feels like missing a limb sometimes. The way she could light up a room by walking into it… You never quite get over the death of your child, you know. Lawrence and I haven't been the same."

Lawrence Butler nodded again and mumbled something that probably translated to "yes, dear."

"Of course, it's nice having Sterling and Oscar in town too," Vivian continued, "even though Dana's gone. We don't see these two anywhere near often enough." She crouched down slightly, the way adults do when trying to interact with a very small child, and held out her arms to Alexa. "A hug for your grandmother?"

Alexa moved forward stiffly and allowed herself to be encircled by Vivian's arms.

"You've gotten taller," Vivian teased. Totally ignoring Alexa's body language, which even an idiot could tell read *back off.* "I like the spiky hair. More androgynous, if that's the compromise you were going for. Don't you think he looks better with the shorter hair, Sterling?"

Sterling still didn't correct her. Alexa looked embarrassed and tense, Sterling was too afraid to call his mother-in-law out on her continual misgendering of his daughter, and Jericho had suddenly had *enough* of their bullshit. *Fuck. This.*

"*She*," he interjected pointedly. "Your *granddaughter's* hair looks great. A pixie cut is in no way masculine, even though her hair is short. And *she* would like you to remember her name, please. Right, Alexa?"

It may have been Jericho's imagination, but Alexa seemed to stand slightly taller. "It's Alexa Jean Harper now, Grandma," she said in a slightly shaky voice. "I don't want anyone to call me Oscar anymore because that's a boy's name, so I picked out my own new one."

Jericho pulled her into a side-hug and pointedly left his arm draped around her thin shoulders. "I know it's hard to remember since you've known her presenting as masculine for most of her life," he told Sterling's in-laws, "but you need to understand that Alexa herself hasn't changed. Only her name. She's the same girl now she was before, only now she's letting everyone know it."

Vivian's lips puckered like she got a taste of something sour. "I understand Oscar is going through a phase," she said slowly, "but calling him a girl's name won't make him a girl." She turned to Sterling. "You've let your nanny encourage him about this all summer?"

Come on, Sterling. Speak up speak up speak up speak—

"I want my child to be happy," he said with a weak shrug. "They've gotten along great. And Jericho isn't exactly Alexa's nanny—at least, not a regular one. It's kind of complicated."

Vivian's eyes narrowed as she glared at Jericho. "You're...oh God. You're gay, aren't you? I didn't pick up on it at first, but..." She looked from Sterling to Jericho and back again, then scrubbed her hand over her face. "Sterling," she asked more quietly, "have you gone over to men now that Dana is gone? You hired a homosexual man to *live* with you and Oscar? Are you crazy?"

Oh, that was damn well *it.* Sterling was still standing there, looking uncomfortable, but he wasn't telling her to fuck off like she deserved. Useless. His father-in-law stood back a little way from the conversation, frowning and nodding at various places, but wasn't stepping in either. Best Jericho could tell, it looked like he agreed with his wife through most of her outburst. The only other one in the conversation was Alexa, and of course she shouldn't be expected to speak up and tell off an adult. That left Jericho. To ream out someone else's mother-in-law. *Fuck. It. All.*

"I am gay, not that it matters," he declared flatly. She'd have to be deaf not to hear the come-at-me-and-you'll-regret-it in his voice. "So yes, I'm queer and I'm Black and I'm not stupid-ass rich like you, and yet it seems like I'm the one who actually gives a shit about Alexa in all this." He squeezed Alexa's shoulder, and she leaned more heavily into him. It was hard to tell whether the movement was in shock or in thanks, but Jericho chose to believe Alexa appreciated *someone* standing up for her. "Pardon the language—but I guess that's another mark against me, right? That I speak my mind when you get me mad enough? I've never lost my filter in front of a child before, but Alexa damn well deserves *someone* in her corner. Since it seems awfully fucking empty at the moment."

Vivian glared, not at Jericho, but at her son-in-law. Jericho, she ignored entirely. "You wanted us to trust you!" she whined. "Sterling, why are you doing this? You want to pamper Oscar through his I'm-a-girl phase, fine. Stupid, but fine. But then instead of letting us help him get over it, you hire a total stranger to spend the summer with him. Alone and *unsupervised.* A gay stranger, even—I know you're insistent on letting Oscar call himself a girl's name, but he's still got a little boy's body under that haircut and that ridiculous dress. Did it not occur to you what danger you're putting our grandson in? You don't know what they get up to while you're at work!"

Sterling was, if anything, shrinking away instead of yelling back at her like she deserved. A quick look around proved that even though nobody was intruding on their argument, a dozen people were all openly staring at them and eavesdropping. If they all didn't like cussing at their church picnic, too damn bad.

"If you're going to accuse me of being a pedophile," Jericho said in a dangerously polite tone, "at least be brave enough to use the word. 'Pedophile' and 'gay' aren't synonyms. Excuse me."

As much as he wanted to take Alexa and get the hell out of Dodge—preferably somewhere Sterling would have to thoroughly grovel to his daughter before Jericho had to see the man's face again—kidnapping probably wasn't a good idea. Jericho gave Alexa one last reassuring squeeze and then turned, nodded to Sterling, and walked back toward the car. Thank God Sterling had been thorough enough at the beginning of the summer to give him a copy of the keys for "in case of emergency." This counted.

As he started backing out, though, Alexa came running and waved for him to stop. "I'm coming home too," she declared, yanking open the door and sliding into her usual seat. "You left and Dad started dragging Grandma and Grandpa away from the tent so they could yell at each other in private and I decided I don't want to be at this picnic anymore."

Pretty damn understandable. God, every curse felt like getting a punch in at Sterling's in-laws, and Jericho resolved not to worry about a filter until later because he was *fucking angry* on Alexa's behalf. "I probably shouldn't take you since I'm not actually family," he said, "but to hell with that. Yes, let's go home."

He left the radio off. They were both silent for the entire drive, which was probably just as well for Alexa's ten-year-old ears. By the time Jericho pulled into the garage, he'd run through all the mental yelling he could think of and it really did help. The righteous fury inferno had burned itself down to hot coals—still dangerous, but controllable. *And deserved.*

Alexa surprised him when they got back inside with a long, tight hug. Her nose fit comfortably under his sternum. The raw edge to her demeanor echoed perfectly with his own and Jericho couldn't help but hug her back. Despite Vivian's allegations, he and Alexa had probably touched more in the last day than they had the whole rest of the summer.. He also couldn't bring himself to feel bad about it—Alexa seemed to need the quiet contact as much as he did.

"It'll be okay," he murmured, rubbing gentle circles on her back. "Your dad loves you, and I expect he'll be home soon. Someone will give him a ride, I'm sure."

"He says he loves me no matter what," Alexa whispered, the words muffled into the buttons of Jericho's nicest shirt. "And I know he doesn't *really* wish I were a boy. But sometimes… I think sometimes Dad wishes I weren't trans. That I could go back to being called Oscar and wearing boy colors and he'd call me 'Pup' again without it feeling like the nickname was supposed to be for someone else. He's had such a hard time since Mom died…but I've made everything harder, haven't I?"

"No! No, no, no." Jericho stepped back out of the hug, then dropped to kneel on the floor so they were eye to eye. "No matter what happens, you're *you* and you should never, ever be embarrassed about that. Wear the colors you want, cut your hair however you like it, tell everyone your name and your pronouns. And if anyone gives you grief, tell them I said they can go to hell."

Her laugh came out more like a sob. "Thanks, Mr. J," she said quietly, and sagged back against the wall behind her. "Are you…are you going to stay? I want you to, but Grandma made it sound like you being here was a bad thing."

"Yes, she certainly made it clear she thinks I'm bad for you." Part of him, a large part, wanted to entrench himself and play Papa Bear for Alexa since Sterling apparently wasn't doing it. The rest of him simply wanted out, though. And if Sterling, her biological and legal father, was letting himself be swayed by his mother-in-law… "It's time for me to move on anyway, though, don't you think? You've only got a week of summer break left anyway."

"A week and a half."

"Right." Jericho attempted to summon up a cheerful expression. "I have a bit longer than that, but it's going to take me time to move to my new house and get unpacked before I start my first day at school. I know your dad didn't want you home alone all summer…maybe the two of you can figure out a compromise for the rest of break? You'll want to do your back-to-school shopping for all your supplies, I'm guessing, and you can psych yourself up to go back to fifth grade with a shiny new name and killer fashion sense. Miss Regina said you look gorgeous and fierce, and she should know."

Alexa smiled weakly at that. "She was nice."

"Yeah, she is. And she said the same of you." Had mentioned Alexa in several texts since their shopping date, actually, mostly prodding Jericho for updates on how she was doing and if the new clothes worked. If Alexa ever wanted a Mama Bear for backup support when her own father wimped out on her, Regina would probably jump at the chance.

"The end of last year was horrible," Alexa admitted. She slid down the wall so they were sitting side by side on the hallway carpet. "I didn't want Dad to know, but even thinking about the first day of school feels scary. What if everyone is mean to me and they keep calling me Oscar? The kids I can ignore, but I don't know what to do if my teacher does it."

That, at least, I can help with. Jericho got up and went to dig out the pencil and notepad Sterling kept by the phone, then wrote down his email and his cell. "Just because I can't be here," he promised, "that doesn't mean I'm not happy to talk or give you advice if you need it. Any time, okay?" God, the idea of Alexa becoming a mere former "student" felt painfully final. It had to happen eventually, of course, but he'd hoped it would be more of a long-distance hiatus while still seeing Sterling. Not a pivotal life event.

Alexa nodded and took the paper. "Should I—what do I say to Dad?"

"The truth." Sterling deserved at *least* that. "And I promise you, none of this mess is your fault. Truly. For the moment, I'm going back to Camp Ladybug to see whether Uncle René and Tante Brielle need help with anything." Thank God for habitually packing light—he'd probably be able to get away the moment Sterling walked in the door, if he hurried.

She smiled weakly. "I can do that. Will you... Are you leaving right now?"

"Once I get my stuff together, yeah. I'll wait with you until your dad gets home and then—like I said—I'm only an email away. I'm not sure how I'm going to get the car back, but could you please let your dad know I'll sort it out as I get something else arranged?"

"I can do that." She sucked in a deep breath and squared her shoulders. Once again the tiny general marching bravely into battle. "So...what can I do to help?"

* * * *

By the time Sterling gave up on making his in-laws see reason and had called a cab for the ride home, he was thoroughly exhausted. Lawrence and Vivian were draining even on good days; actually having it out with them after keeping his mouth shut for so long left him wishing he could curl up in bed and sleep for a week. He didn't realize his brain had added "...with Jericho" to the wish until the taxi was almost back to the house. Because yes, sleep sounded good, but even better would be to have Jericho spooned up behind him, their fingers laced together like a keyboard of alternating dark and light skin against the sheets. They'd never actually had a chance to *sleep* together, other than the one night Alexa was at camp, but more often than not they both felt lazy and sated after sex so they snuggled a while. Sterling never thought he'd be a snuggler—Dana definitely hadn't been, on the odd occasions they shared a platonic bed—but then Jericho was causing Sterling to learn lots of new things about himself. If only they'd met during freshman year…

Jericho and Alexa were sitting on the front porch swing when the taxi pulled up in front of the house. Sterling waved, then had to fumble in his wallet for the appropriate cash. When he stepped out of the cab and looked up a moment later, Alexa was alone and Jericho's car was pulling out of the driveway. Sterling looked from her to Jericho's car and back again.

"Where's he going?"

Alexa flashed him a dark look. "Away," she answered in a monotone. "He said he's sorry and he'll get the car back to Willow Heights as soon as he can. I wanted him to stay but he left."

Fuck. Sterling sank down onto the bench beside his daughter and gathered her up into his lap. Even at ten, she was still small enough to curl up against his chest and cover her face. She stayed silent, but her shoulders hitched in a jagged rhythm which didn't hide anything at all. They stayed there for some unknown number of minutes, Alexa crying and Sterling desperately trying not to.

He made them both sandwiches afterward, since neither of them had actually gotten to eat anything at the picnic. Alexa took hers up to her room and locked herself in. When Sterling came up and knocked on her door several minutes later, though, it was already open a crack.

"Pup?"

Alexa looked up at him from the pile of blankets she'd made on the bed, the cordless phone to her ear. The protective hamster nest was something she'd done ever since she was little on occasions when she was feeling too overwhelmed, but this time she managed to look both tiny and defeated. Her cheeks were wet. "It's Nana," she whispered, and put the phone on speaker. "Dad just got home, so can you tell him what you told me?"

"Hey, Little Buddy," Sterling's mother said.

"Hi, Mom. Nice weather we're having?"

Her laugh was brittle, the noise distorted through her iffy cell reception. "Alexa was filling me in on why you need me to come up there for the next two weeks," she said softly, "and the answer is, of course I'll come."

Sterling glanced over at his daughter, but she was tracing where the stripe of wallpaper border encircling her room met cream paint on top and lavender paint below. Jericho had painted the top part on that wall, Sterling had done the bottom, and they both worked together on the border. *Will everything keep making me think of him?* "We're always happy to have you up here," he said in the general direction of the phone, loud enough he didn't have to pick it up, "but you really don't have to if you already have other obligations."

"You and my granddaughter will always be my first and most important obligation. Helen only had me scheduled for two mornings this week anyway, and I'm sure the new girl will be happy for the extra hours. Have I told you about the new girl? Kimberly something. Temporary, only hired for the summer, but sweet and a good worker. She's headed off to college at the end of August, and I get the impression she's saving up all the money she can before she leaves. Anyway, I'm going to let you go so I can pack up—you two hang tight and I'll see you in the morning."

"Mom, it's a ten-hour drive!" Longstanding experience proved she was, and had always been, a morning person. Driving the entire length of Florida, probably through the night, was a recipe for disaster.

His mother snorted, though, unfazed. "You forget I used to do that trip all the time when you were in college. I'll be fine—plenty of motels along the interstate. I'll stop when I need to, but even if I take a full eight-hour snooze, I'll get to Willow Heights early in the morning. Sterling, what time do you leave for work?"

"I can stay home alone for one morning, Nana," Alexa declared. "Or Dad can take me along to work or something." She finally quit fidgeting and met Sterling's gaze full-on. "I'm going to give the phone to Dad, though, because he needs to tell you the real reason he's sad. He didn't want Mr. J to leave either." She handed the cordless to Sterling and made a shooing motion toward the door. "Go on," she told him, and rearranged one of the blankets in her nest. "I need time to draw right now, I think, but tell Nana more about you and Mr. J."

Sterling took the phone off speaker and obediently backed out of Alexa's room. She actually got up off her bed and locked it in his face. *Ten going on sixteen, indeed.*

"So start from the beginning," his mother prodded as he headed back downstairs. "Alexa said you and Jericho had gotten close. She also said he's the first real friend you've had since Dana passed."

That was probably true, if Facebook friends didn't count. "Most of our old group were Dana's friends more than mine, and I'm terrible at keeping in touch."

"And maybe...were you and Jericho more than friends?" Her voice was gentle, encouraging. "I know you and Dana loved each other, in a way, but I've always been sad you never got to experience the big giddy rush of emotion you get from starting in a new relationship, when everything you find out about each other seems amazing and perfect. From what Alexa's told me over the last few months, it sounded like 'Mr. J' was becoming a real part of the family. So what happened?"

Her question was innocent, but Lord knew she could always get him to talk if she wanted to. Especially if she was making the drive to come grill him in person. No point trying to make excuses. It hadn't worked when he was five years old and Sterling expected she'd still be able to guilt him into confessing things to her when she was a hundred.

Sterling abruptly realized where he was standing. Entirely without thought, his feet had carried him to the spare bedroom. Guest bedroom. *Jericho's room.* It was achingly, painfully empty. "Lawrence and Vivian happened," he admitted aloud. "They were horrible and he left."

"Ah." She made a thoughtful noise. "I'll refrain from adding commentary on Dana's parents—if you can't say something nice, etcetera, etcetera. Was this about them calling Alexa by her old name? Are they still stuck on that?"

"Old name, old pronouns, everything. Vivian thinks it's a 'phase,' apparently." God, he was torn between wanting to cry and wanting to give his mother-in-law the punch in the nose she deserved. "That was only part of it, though. We went to the church picnic and she as good as accused Jericho of being a pedophile. Since he's gay and Alexa has a penis and apparently all gay men are rapists. I'm sure him being African-American didn't help either."

"Oh, *Sterling.*" If she could have hugged him through the phone line, she probably would have. "They know about you, though, right? That you're gay too?"

"I thought they did. Or at least, I assumed Dana might have mentioned something to her parents in the last, oh, *decade.* Maybe she did hint to them, I don't know, but apparently today was the day Vivian and Lawrence got their confirmation. I was...less than polite in my response to Vivian's accusations. Jericho went to leave right before things got really ugly and Alexa ran off to go with him. I didn't give a crap anymore, so I told Vivian exactly what I thought of her homophobic, transphobic attitude. Lawrence, too, although he's quieter about it. And she... They..."

"Mmm?"

"They're petitioning for custody of Alexa." Sterling flopped heavily onto the bed. The mattress, really, because Jericho had stripped off the sheets and blanket and left them neatly folded on top of the dresser. "Apparently they'd been planning this behind my back for a few months—ever since Alexa transitioned. I'm an unfit father, I'm endangering her, and she'd be better off with 'a family who can raise him right.' Direct quote."

"Like hell she would! They're not ones to talk—Dana was real-world challenged for a long time, if I remember correctly."

Sterling had never thought of their early years together in that light, but he had to admit it was accurate.

"Yeah, well," he sighed. "Did you know that 'allowing' your child to be trans can be used as evidence of mental child abuse?" Sterling had already researched it a bit, because he'd looked up every terrifying eventuality he could when Alexa first started talking about transitioning to live as a girl, but at the time it had seemed like a far-off, unlikely worry. "It can, if you have the right judge. Oh, and if your in-laws are wealthy and well-connected and you live in a generally rich and conservative town. Vivian said they've got the paperwork all filled out and ready to file, all sitting there at their lawyer's office. I'm not surprised that today was enough to make them want to actively follow up."

His mother was silent for a long moment, the only noise the sound of the wind blowing past her phone. Standing out in the driveway, then. "You and I both know that's not going to happen," she finally declared. "Because if they try that bullshit, I swear I will kidnap Alexa myself if I have to. In the meantime, though, I'm coming up to stay with you until this is resolved, and I don't want to hear any self-sacrificing nonsense about how you should have to do this alone. You've put up with that crap for two years already." Her tone softened. "You know Dana wouldn't have wanted you to entomb yourself in Willow Heights, Sterling. You need to move on, make your own life. You're not broke and pregnant and running from an abusive boyfriend like I was—you have *choices*. Make them."

"I'm trying." *So, so hard.* "I can't up and disappear in the middle of the night, though, especially since Lawrence and Vivian have apparently started the custody appeal in motion already. My only chance to keep my daughter is to keep my head down, say all the right things, and show everyone I'm the upright, respectable father I ought to be."

"Are you going to force Alexa to go by Oscar again?"

"No. Never." He might end up celibate and lonely forever, but damned if Alexa would have to go back to the way things were before. "If a judge thinks I'm 'abusing' her by letting her use the feminine name she herself picked out, I'd never win in that courtroom anyway. I haven't seen the actual papers yet—Vivian said she's formally having me served at the office sometime this week, so hooray for that—but I absolutely believe that they'd try to take Alexa away from me and force her through some gender repair clinic malarkey. They've got the money and know all the right people, and they have no interest in trying to understand what Alexa really needs."

"They won't win," his mother declared. "Because I believe in you, and I believe in Alexa being able to speak her mind, and any judge worth his salt will see that she's happier now. You *are* a good father, Sterling. You just have to start believing it too."

Chapter 18

"Mr. J? It's me."

Jericho switched the phone to his other hand so he could talk and finish putting groceries away at the same time. "I'd know you by your voice even if I didn't still have your dad's number in my contacts list, Alexa," he answered. "How are you?"

Alexa didn't answer. Then… "It was the first day of school today."

Oh, right. The Willow Heights schools started their year a bit earlier than Jericho's new district did. He'd had a whopping two days of orientation and back-to-school training so far, but there was still another week and a half before he got to meet his students. "How was it?" he prompted. "You don't sound like your usual vivacious self. Was it not what you hoped for? Some of your classmates being mean?"

"Not only classmates." There was a thump, which sounded very much like her flopping on her back onto her bed. "Dad talked to my teacher ahead of time—I got Miss Hooper this year—so she was pretty nice about it. A bunch of the other grown-ups weren't, though. My two best friends from last year both said they're not going to be my friends anymore if I'm a girl now."

It was no more and no less than what he'd expected, but Jericho's heart broke for her anyway. Lord, he couldn't even imagine what it must be like to walk back into school with a whole new identity. Especially something as personal as gender presentation. "Maybe you'll make new friends," he offered. Not much of a consolation, but Alexa wasn't exactly shy. Rebuilding her social circle was probably a matter of time. "Girls and boys tend to relate to each other differently at your age—boys bully each other with shoves and fart jokes and picking on anyone physically smaller and weaker than they are, but girls usually use more social manipulation. It's all about who's popular and who's not, and it's *ridiculously* complicated to figure out just what makes someone 'in' and someone else 'out.' I wrote a paper on it once."

"In teaching school?"

"Yep."

He got the last of the groceries in from the car—new car, at least new-to-him—and slammed the trunk, then went to go find places in the kitchen to put them. He had gotten the place he liked from earlier in the summer, the upper half of a historic house which had been renovated into a duplex. It had "antique charm" and the price was right, plus his landlord was fine with him sticking to a month-to-month contract in case his long-term sub position suddenly got retracted, but the downside was the weird layout. Namely the way he had to carry everything through the living room, the laundry-room-slash-hallway, and past his bedroom to get to the kitchen. Where the walk-through pantry doubled as the bedroom closet.

"My point is," he said as he set the bags on the tiny kitchen counter, "your clothes and your name aren't the only thing your classmates have to re-learn. People got used to thinking of you as a boy, and even friends who like you a lot are probably going to mess up sometimes. It's going to take time for everyone at school to adjust."

"I wasn't surprised when everyone laughed at me at the end of last year," she said quietly. "I thought a whole summer would be long enough for them to understand, though."

Oh, Alexa. "For some people, it will have been. For others it might take a while. Years, even. You're lucky you have a wonderful father who loves you very much and supports you being yourself, whoever you turn out to be."

"Yeah, I guess. And Nana is here, which is good. Dad's been really sad since you left."

Jericho had to close his eyes against a wave of guilt at that. "I'm sorry I had to leave early," he admitted. "I wish I could have stayed until you started school again, but I… Well, I couldn't. I know that's hard to understand."

"No, I get it," Alexa said. "It really was because of what Grandma Butler said, right? That you're gay? Dad said people sometimes don't like gay people."

Oh, lordy. Jericho had promised Sterling back in May that Alexa could ask him questions about LGBT matters in general and transitioning in particular, but this was the first time she'd ever broached the topic of his sexuality. *Where to begin?* "You know what that means, right?" he hedged.

She gave an affirmative little hum. "It means you want to marry another boy instead of marrying a girl."

"Yes, exactly. Some people think men who choose to spend a lot of time around children are weird or creepy. A lot of those people also think being gay—or bisexual, which is when you're flexible and you can fall in love with someone no matter what their gender is—they think it makes men like me want to hurt kids. And *you* know that's not true, and *I* know it's not true, and your dad knows it's not true. If I stayed, though, those people would think your dad wasn't taking very good care of you. That I'm dangerous and he shouldn't have let me near you in the first place."

"That's stupid, and it didn't help," Alexa said in a flat voice. "I heard Dad and Nana talking about it last night. Grandma and Grandpa Butler want to make me come live with them. They said Dad and I have to go to see a judge and they'd come too and the judge would decide who I should live with. I…I don't know if the judge will even ask me which one I wanted more."

"Oh, for…" Jericho held the phone away from his body so he could swear with the appropriate vigor. Judging from how Alexa was giggling when he put it back to his ear—a slightly panicked laugh, but giggling nonetheless—he must not have held it far enough away. And seriously, screw it—filters were for when you weren't so angry you were literally seeing red.

"You swear like Dad does," Alexa teased. "He never used to, when Mom was still alive, but ever since you left and Nana got here, he's been swearing a lot whenever he thinks I can't hear. I didn't think he knew all those bad words."

"Most adults do, but it's not polite to actually *say* them. So let's pretend I muted the phone before I blurted all that out, okay?"

"Okay." She was smiling; Jericho could hear it in her voice even through her entirely reasonable fear of her life being torn apart. "I won't tell."

"Good. So. I don't get to tell you what to do anymore, now that I live so far away, but I'm going to tell you anyway: let your dad worry about your grandparents. You're perfect just as you are and I'm sure the judge will see how happy you and your dad are as a team."

"Yeah, I guess."

"Maybe a *bit* more enthusiasm than that?"

She snorted. "You know what I mean." A long pause. "I miss you, though," she added quietly. "Dad does too, even though he's trying to pretend he doesn't care. I can tell."

I miss you both. So, so much. The last he'd heard from Sterling directly was the church picnic. The day after Jericho showed back up on Uncle

René and Tante Brielle's doorstep, his bank texted to notify him about an unusually large deposit—Sterling had been incredibly generous with the final paycheck. Jericho took the money, returned the silver Mazda 3 to the dealership listed on the paperwork in the glove box, and went to browse the other cars in their lot. Between his bonus from Sterling and what he had in savings, he ended up being able to turn around and buy a used Nissan free and clear. Nowhere near as decked-out as the Mazda had been, and his new car had quite a few miles on it, but for the first time in his life he actually owned his own transportation. *Adulting: achievement unlocked.*

"I'm glad your nana is there," he told Alexa after what was probably a too-long awkward silence. "We knew I was only going to be hanging out with you for the one summer, though, so I would have had to leave eventually. Change is hard on everyone."

"Can I call you again? If—if Grandma and Grandpa Butler really are… are…" Her question dissolved into a dispirited mumble. There was no positive ending to that question.

"Of course," Jericho said with more cheerfulness than he felt. "You know we're all proud of you, right? Your dad and your nana and everyone. You're very brave, and even though this is going to be hard, I know you'll come through okay."

Alexa took a deep breath and let it *whoosh* out again over the speaker of the phone. "Thanks, Mr. J. Maybe if the judge asks me where I want to live, I can tell him to ask you how nice my dad is. A lot nicer than Grandma and Grandpa."

Jericho would have used a stronger word than "nice." Then again, he would have done a lot of things if Sterling had only asked. "I'd be honored," he said.

Chapter 19

Alexa met with her court-appointed "guardian ad litem" for the first time on a breezy October morning, and it was perhaps the first non-terrible thing to happen to Sterling in the two months since Lawrence and Vivian filed their custody dispute. His mother had stayed with them for almost three full weeks, but there were some things a tight hug and Mom's comfort food couldn't fix. Like the frustrating bureaucracy of the Willow Heights courthouse, for one example. The behavior of the rest of the town, for another.

You'd think there'd never been another trans person in north Florida, judging by the way acquaintances and strangers alike were gossiping behind his and Alexa's backs. It felt like their family was the news story of the year. Sterling didn't get it so bad—his patients spent most of their time sedated or with a mouth full of tools—but Alexa was struggling. A lot. She broke down once, a few days into the school year, and Sterling's mother had been an absolute godsend in how she talked Alexa back down off the ledge while she let Alexa cry on her shoulder.

Sterling and Alexa met the law guardian at the public library downtown, where Sterling could stay in line of sight of the small room where his daughter and her advocate were meeting but wouldn't be able to listen in or interfere. Alexa tugged on his hand and smiled up at him as they rode the elevator to the second floor, which made Sterling realize he was drumming his fingers on his leg like a hyperactive middle-schooler.

"It will be okay, Dad," she assured him. "Nana showed me a website that explained this, and she told me all about what's supposed to happen next. The lawyer lady is supposed to listen to what I want and tell it to the judge, and I'm going to tell her I want to stay with you."

Sterling's stomach stayed in knots anyway, all the way through the reference department and to the little collection of meeting rooms at the end. There, they were greeted by a forty-something Hispanic woman with short wavy hair, bright purple glasses, and a genuine smile. "Alexa and Sterling Harper?" she asked, offering Alexa and then Sterling a handshake. "I'm Gabriela. It's nice to meet you."

She called her "Alexa," not "Oscar." Without needing correction. Without sputtering about Alexa's legal name and the gender on her birth certificate. Even though almost all the legal paperwork said Oscar because Vivian was a stubborn, vindictive shrew. Sterling felt himself relax a tiny bit for the first time in ages.

After a brief introduction and an explanation of what would happen next, Gabriela politely but firmly showed Sterling from the room and pointed him toward the tables in the middle of the reference section. She went back in, shut the door, and she and Alexa proceeded to stay in there for the next forty-five minutes. Sterling tried to distract himself on his phone, but he didn't even have the brainpower for stupid easy games.

So much of this custody battle would rely on factors outside what any father could control. It was maddening. The good news, according to the lawyer Sterling found as soon as he possibly could, was that Florida's laws on grandparents' rights changed in 2015 and were now stacked strongly in favor of the parent. The bad news was, his in-laws' easiest route to getting temporary or permanent custody was to prove him unfit—which was the tack they had been taking from the beginning. It all came down to whether the judge agreed that "allowing" Alexa to be a girl was abuse or not, and whether that was enough to warrant her getting taken away.

"Dad?" Alexa was waving to him from the doorway of the meeting room. Sterling practically sprinted to rejoin her.

"Dr. Harper." Gabriela gestured for him to take a seat across from her at the table. "First off, did you prep your daughter in any way, or coerce her responses? Not accusing you," she added immediately, "but it's something I'm required to ask since you're the custodial entity for the duration of the challenge."

"No, I…" He looked up at Alexa, whose eyes were wide. "If I did, it certainly wasn't intentional."

"Okay, that's a no. Good." Gabriela quickly scribbled something on her note paper. "That's what Alexa said too, lest you think she told me otherwise. Well, then." She flipped the notepad closed and flashed him a smile. "I appreciate you making the time to bring Alexa here to talk with me today; she had a lot to say and it was extremely helpful. I'll have my notes back to the court and to your legal counsel within the next two weeks—my recommendations are confidential from both parties, Dr. Harper, but your lawyer will be able to read through them and can give you a summary of the parts that don't impinge on your daughter's right to privacy. If you and your late wife's parents aren't able to come to a settlement following that, you'll be assigned a date for a first appearance in front of the judge, and you or your legal representation will be able to have a mediated discussion with each other to determine what's in Alexa's best interests." She paused and adjusted her glasses. "I will note, however, that only a small percentage of custody challenges in your situation go that far. Generally speaking, a protracted debate is rarely what's best for the child. If it should come to that, I will be meeting with Alexa again in a few months. Alexa, you've got my card?"

Alexa jammed her hand into her pocket and nodded.

"Excellent." She offered handshakes to Sterling and Alexa again. "I sincerely hope I don't ever see you again, Dr. Harper, and I mean that in the best possible way."

* * * *

Jericho cursed the traffic, the Georgia road construction, and the myriad list of other factors slowing down his progress on I-95. What should have been just over an hour, from Brunswick to Willow Heights, became closer to ninety minutes. Which, if he got to the courthouse too late, might mean he drove all this way for nothing.

He found the courthouse, found parking, and got through the metal detector at the entrance at right around eight thirty. Alexa's email had said their official appear-before-a-judge time was first thing in the morning, which the Willow Heights municipal website said was eight o'clock sharp. *Please still be there please still be there please—*

Alexa spotted him before he saw her. His frantic flipping through his phone trying to find the judge's name and thus the room number was interrupted by a yell from two stories up. "Up here!"

Jericho, and everyone else in the lobby surrounding the central staircase, looked up. Alexa was leaning over a balcony from the third floor, waving furiously. She didn't seem to be in *actual* danger of falling over and cracking her head open on the tile floor, but there may still have been a little extra speed in Jericho's steps as he took the two flights up at a run.

"You came!" Alexa cried, and met him at the top of the stairs with a bear hug. "I'm supposed to stay in the cafeteria down there"—she indicated toward an open doorway—"but I was really, really, really hoping you'd be here. And you *came.*"

There were tears pricking at the corners of Jericho's eyes, but he focused on the feeling of Alexa's arms squeezing around his waist instead. "Of course I came. With a request like what you sent me, how could I refuse?"

She huffed into his pinstripe dress shirt. That and a dark gray pair of trousers were the nicest outfit he owned, both relatively new purchases and which he absolutely did *not* dither over for forty-five minutes the night before. Getting it right was important, though, since it was for Sterling and Alexa and at court. "I thought maybe you'd have to be teaching," she mumbled. "Dad let me skip school this morning for this."

"Even we substitute teachers get substitutes sometimes." Jericho eased her stranglehold from his waist and made a motion ushering her toward what was presumably the door to the cafeteria. "Let's go back to where you're supposed to be waiting," he suggested, "and we can have second breakfast. We'll pretend we're hobbits."

Jericho's only prior courthouse experience was a failure-to-yield citation his junior year of high school, which merely meant he had to show up and pay a fine. Willow Heights's courthouse was a *lot* nicer than the one back home. The cafeteria turned out to be small but brightly lit. It was decently stocked with a variety of snack foods, and there was a woman behind a counter assembling made-to-order sandwiches. Jericho bought himself and Alexa each a muffin and a bottle of juice, then they snagged one of the handful of booths.

"So first question—where's your dad?"

Alexa made a face. "He and our *lawyer*, Mr. Rowe, are talking with Grandma and Grandpa Butler before we all go see the judge. Mr. Rowe is old and he passes gas a lot, but Dad said he's a good lawyer and it's important to have a lawyer when you go to see a judge the same way it's good to have a hygienist when you go to see the dentist. Except each person's lawyer argues with the other one, I think. The judge isn't here yet so I didn't get to look in the courtroom."

Jericho decided to let the flatulence comment pass without correction—Lord knew Alexa would probably still be speaking her mind when she was Mr. Rowe's age. Hard to tell whether Sterling and his in-laws "talking" was a good sign or not, but at least it meant Jericho wasn't too late. "I take it they're not letting you listen to them argue?"

She shook her head. "Dad was really mad about something, but he said not to worry and that he'd be back in a little bit. Oh—he let me play with his phone, though!" Alexa dug a familiar cell phone out of her pocket and put it on the table between them. "He doesn't have very good games on it," she added with a sigh.

"Not sure if I have any better, but we can look." Jericho pulled out his own cell, which was at least a generation older than Sterling's, and let Alexa have a look at his games folder. She then proceeded to spend the next twenty minutes thoroughly whooping him at Disney trivia. They were only interrupted when someone came into the cafeteria, got halfway toward their table, and stopped dead.

"Hi, Dad!" Alexa chirped. "Mr. J has better apps on his phone than you do."

Sterling kept staring like he thought Jericho was a ghost.

"Dad?" Alexa clambered out of her seat and pressed his phone into his unresisting hand. "Do we have to go to see the judge now?"

"Oh." Sterling shook his head and refocused on his daughter. "No, Pup, we don't. That's why I had to go for a bit—Mr. Rowe and I were talking to your grandparents and their lawyer, and"—he let out a breath which started as a sigh and ended as a laugh—"and their lawyer told them they don't have a case. We're done. You don't even have to ever see them again if you don't want to. If they want to *earn* a chance to visit, they'll have to apologize to both of us *and* prove that they won't treat you like you're a boy."

"Wow," Jericho murmured. From what Alexa had told him in her semi-regular emails, her grandparents were dead-set on convincing the court and their social group at large that Sterling was a dangerous degenerate who wasn't safe to be around his own daughter. "Sterling, that's… I'm so happy for you both. Truly."

Sterling snapped his gaze back up to Jericho's face, and Jericho felt it like a physical jolt. Not of pain, but of electricity. Sterling dropped a hand on Alexa's shoulder as he moved past her, slowly but smoothly, and came to a stop with his body mere inches away from Jericho's. "I'm happy too," he said, so quietly it was almost a whisper. "And I owe you the biggest apology in the world, for letting you go. Or pushing you away. I know you've moved on and are putting down new roots, but can we… Would you…"

Alexa was hovering behind her father with a humongous grin on her face. As much as Jericho wanted to yank Sterling in for a loud, messy make-out session while they apologized to each other sans words, they did have a ten-year-old to think about. "I heard you have a vacancy," he said with his best attempt at a straight face. "Nanny was a seasonal job, I know, but…are you still in the market for a significant other?"

Sterling's worried expression cracked into one of giddy relief. "Oh my God," he breathed, chuckling. "Yes! Yes, of course. I thought I had someone lined up for the position, but then I was a complete idiot and drove him away. You remind me of him, a bit. I think… Would you care to accompany me and my daughter to the park next door? She's already missed an hour or so of school, and I think finally having her immediate future settled is a good enough reason to play hooky a little longer."

The three of them practically floated downstairs and out to the municipal park in the square in front of the courthouse. Several permanent sculpture installations doubled as "touchable art" and—for a few—abstract jungle gyms. Alexa was clearly more aware of the undercurrents between her dad and Jericho than she let on, because the moment they got to the main grassy area she took off for an interesting-looking sculpture with lots of bars to climb around on. Jericho and Sterling found a park bench on the opposite side of the lawn and sat. Jericho didn't mind at all when Sterling slid in close enough for their thighs to touch.

"So," Sterling said.

"So?"

"So that thing you said at the church picnic, the day you left. About me not speaking up. I didn't get a chance to tell you, but I did know you were right. About all of it." He shifted and slumped some of his weight against Jericho's side. Putting an arm around him and pulling him in closer felt like the most natural thing in the world.

"I should have at least waited until you got home before I disappeared," Jericho conceded. "That wasn't fair of me to leave you with a week and a half left before school started."

"No, I mean…" Sterling relaxed further into Jericho's embrace. "They *were* being awful to Alexa, and I did know it. Wasn't surprised, even—they were the same with Dana, a lot of the time. Vivian speaks her mind no matter how wrong she is or how much she's hurting anyone else, and…" He sighed. "Well, let's say that I've had ten years' experience in not saying anything. Or me wanting to confront them and then Dana convincing me I shouldn't look to start trouble. But then when Vivian started in on you, I couldn't let it go any more."

"Like the thing about the frog in a pot of boiling water? Supposedly it won't jump out if the water starts out cold and gets heated up?"

Sterling nodded against Jericho's shoulder. "Up until this summer they'd still been rude and needy, but it was easier to smile and nod and then do what Dana and I wanted to do anyway. Then when Dana died, I wasn't up to making any decisions at all for a while. Didn't have the emotional energy. I guess I got in the habit of not wanting to make everything a big fight."

The sad thing was, Jericho knew exactly how that nonconfrontational dynamic could play out. His sister Naomi was like that with her own in-laws, although theirs was more of a cold war than an open battle, and there were no children in the mix. "I'm glad you finally did," he confessed. "Some things are worth fighting for."

"I'm glad too." Sterling gave a little hum of contentment. "This whole custody challenge broadsided me, to be honest, but it made me realize some things. About myself, mostly. I'm good at trying to make other people happy, but I need to work more on making sure I'm happy too. Dana and I were married for nine years because she desperately wanted to be a mother and an underpaid artist, and I wanted my best friend to get the life she'd always dreamed about. I don't regret going to dental school, but that dream wasn't mine. I don't know exactly what my dream was, at eighteen, but I know what I want now. And it's not in that big house all by myself."

Jericho's heart literally skipped a beat. "Are you asking me to move in with you? Because I'll warn you I'd probably say yes just so I could hang out more with your charming daughter."

Sterling laughed. "As long as that's not the only reason."

"No, it's not. It's really, really not." Jericho did some quick mental math. "I'm in Brunswick until Christmas break, at the earliest, but I don't *have* to look for another contract there after the teacher I'm covering for gets back. Do you think the schools in Willow Heights would accept a substitute with a Georgia teaching license?"

"I was actually thinking something else altogether," Sterling said quietly. "Alexa is miserable in school this year, for exactly the reasons I was afraid of."

"Transphobic teachers, cruel peers? Yes, she's told me some about it. I wasn't sure if you knew she emails me sometimes or not, but I think she mostly needs an occasional shoulder to cry on without putting more of a burden on you."

"Damn it." Sterling shook his head. "I did know, and you're exactly right. It's not *all* her teachers and her peers, but it's more than I expected. She's being brave, so amazingly brave, but I can't see her hurting anymore." He shifted so his forehead was cradled between Jericho's neck and breastbone. "Sorry, I'm extra clingy right now. Feels like I need to make up for lost time."

Jericho felt the same way, so he responded by turning and planting a kiss in Sterling's hair.

Alexa managed an impressive flip off another one of the jungle gym sculptures, one with a monkey-bars-like section across the middle. She bounced up, looked over to where Sterling and Jericho were sitting to see if they'd been watching, and promptly turned her back to go try again. *Kid knows what's up.* Jericho couldn't see her expression from all the way across the square, but he'd have bet anything she was grinning like crazy.

"I'm thinking," Sterling continued, "that maybe we'd all be happier if we made a fresh start. Alexa in a new school with new friends, me at a new practice, both of us somewhere a lot farther away from Dana's parents. And—I know it's ridiculous to ask this soon, considering you only applied for the position of 'significant other' less than half an hour ago—"

"Yes." Jericho didn't even need to let him finish the sentence. "I'd be happy to move in with you as soon as we're both able to uproot. Although… How would that work for you? Do you still have to take over your practice after your partner retires?"

"I have to give him an answer. I don't have to buy in the rest of the way." Sterling shrugged, as much as he was able while slumped into Jericho. "It's—I've got money invested in some office improvements already, and it would mean walking away from that, but I'd rather let Dr. McClellan have my money and find a new partner to buy him out than go through with it and be stuck in Willow Heights. Vivian and Lawrence weren't happy at *all* when their lawyer told them they don't have a case, and I don't expect they'd be particularly gracious about it if we stayed."

Jericho had been meaning to ask about that. "Was this whole custody suit a bluff, or…?"

"Unfortunately, no. A long shot, but if they'd been able to convince the judge that I'm an unfit father, they could have won guardianship. We got very, very lucky that the neutral third party assigned to Alexa turned out to be a woman with a family friend who transitioned late in life. Alexa told me afterward. The advocate interviewed Alexa, concluded she's a well-adjusted girl whose only 'fault' is that she's transgender, and apparently wrote a scathing report saying that Vivian and Lawrence's lawyer was unethical to take on this case and it never should have been filed at all. And it turned out their lawyer, being the most expensive man money can buy in this town, hadn't personally read the report until today. I guess because his time is too valuable for little things like that."

"Damn."

"Pretty much. I went in ready to yell at them this morning, but their lawyer was already apologizing for having wasted our time. And that was that. I'm out court costs, lawyer's fees, and two months of sleep, but the upshot is now Vivian and Lawrence would have to provide positive proof of abuse before anybody will listen to them complain about me and Alexa again. For all intents and purposes, they're out of our lives for good."

"And how do you feel about that?"

A long silence. "I don't know," Sterling finally admitted. "Dana loved them despite their faults, and I cared about Dana a lot. But I can't be sad that her parents aren't going to be around to poison Alexa's life. Maybe they can apologize someday, but honestly I doubt they will." He stretched and stood, then offered Jericho a hand up. "I don't know about you," he added, "but I made sure I had the whole day off. And social issues or not, we should technically get Alexa back to school. That leaves you, me, an empty house, and several hours to kill." His vague smile acquired a world of promise. "I feel like I might need to go back to bed this afternoon. You?"

Epilogue

"What's this?" Sterling hefted the gift bag higher, gauging the weight, but Alexa took it from him before he could venture a guess about the contents. Jericho rounded the corner from the kitchen, laughed, then bounded out to the front porch to envelop his much shorter friend in a hug.

"Lito, this is Sterling," Jericho declared. "Sterling, my friend Lito. I'm assuming you brought—yep, here he is. Dave, nice to see you again, dude." A man nearly Jericho's height but with a much broader build sauntered up the walkway to Jericho and Sterling's new house and greeted Jericho with a clap on the shoulder.

"It's a movie!" Alexa squealed. She'd taken the tissue paper out of the bag and was peeking at the housewarming present.

Lito grinned. "My Little Pony, complete first season. Don't laugh—I was dubious at first too, but Dave's little brother is a total brony and he got us both hooked. And since you two actually *have* a girl as your excuse for watching cartoons…"

"I'll give it a shot," Jericho vowed. "Come on in! Paul and Brandon are in the living room, although you may have to stand in line to meet Emily. Apparently she smiled for real for the first time on Sunday, and now she can't stop showing off her new trick. Adam and Chris got here right before you did. Ian said he's going to be late, but he promised he'd come. Not sure if he's bringing his flavor of the month or not."

"Zack?"

"That sounds right. Something that started with a Z, anyway." Jericho sidled over next to Sterling and casually draped an arm over his shoulder. "I'd make more fun of Ian for never settling down," he said, "but I'm not really one to talk. I didn't until suddenly I did. Turns out I just had to find the right man to settle with."

"Instant family," Dave agreed. "Speaking of which—young lady, you must be Alexa. Nice to meet you face to face, after hearing your voice on game nights for so long!"

Alexa very properly jumped to her feet, abandoning the new DVD set, and accepted Dave's handshake. "Mr. J says I can play with y'all again sometime soon," she declared. "He and I have a chart of all our games and write down who wins. So far his side has more checkmarks than mine, but I can usually beat him at the racing ones. He's a better driver in real life."

"Oh, so you're good at gaming, hmmm?" Dave raised an eyebrow. "You're on, young lady."

"So…dentist?" Lito asked, dragging Sterling's attention back to the other conversation going on in front of him. "Which of you got the new job first?"

"He did," Sterling admitted. "It's a lot harder to find teaching positions specifically for special needs kids than it is finding a spot at a dental practice, and there was the whole issue of transferring his teaching license to a new state. Jericho ended up with a few offers, actually, but we both liked Fort Myers and we're within an afternoon's drive of my mom down in the Keys. I mean, it'd be a *long* afternoon, but still."

"I'm from Miami—believe me, I've done both ends of that drive many times over." Lito laughed quietly. "I was actually living there again for about six months early last year, but I finally got the chance to move back to Alabama to be with Dave. Long distance sucks."

"Tell me about it." Sterling and Jericho had been making the hour-long commute back and forth from Willow Heights to Brunswick for months too. Occasionally at first, and then a lot more frequently once the teacher Jericho was subbing for came back from maternity leave and he was jobless for a bit. "He and I both have sworn never to do that again—*way* too much time spent in transit."

"Worth it to see him though, right?"

Sterling couldn't help but smile. "Yeah. Always."

It had been helpful that Jericho's Georgia teaching gig had come with an end date already in sight. By the time they got to Christmas they'd still only known each other for seven months, but living together for the first two of those made it a lot easier to commit to the living together part. Picking *where* was harder. Alexa was the been the real impetus for the *when*, though—even after a full semester living out as a girl, less than half the adults at her school were making an effort to accept her new name and new presentation. Several more had inconsistent success, and a few flat-out refused to change unless she had whatever they considered good enough proof she really meant it. She was making new friends among the other girls, slowly, but the majority of her classmates had been having a tough time making the mental switch as well.

Lito clapped Sterling on the back. "I'm excited for you, dude. The whole time I was in Miami, I couldn't wait to get back to Black Lake. Dave's got these two ridiculous dogs, huge but sweet as pie, and my own pup didn't understand why she didn't get to see her best friends anymore. I've got a cousin in town I got to see every so often, but it's not the same as having roots, you know?"

Sterling knew. It had been scary as hell to break the news to Dr. McClellan and to then put the house up for sale—Dana's dream house, the one they'd committed to together—all to uproot and move to a totally new city, but so far the move was worth it. Alexa was happy as a clam at her new school, where nobody remembered her from before her transition. Jericho took her in every morning because the elementary school she attended and the middle school he taught at were right across the street from each other. Sterling was settling in at his new office, a six-dentist practice where they rotated who was "on call." One curtailed weekend every month and a half wasn't bad. Three of his partners also had kids, so they even had something to talk about besides teeth. He never mentioned Alexa was trans and darn well didn't need to. It was none of their business.

"Earth to Sterling!" Jericho pulled him in for a quick kiss, then turned him around and propelled him down the hallway to the kitchen. "Let's let Lito and Dave pay court to the new baby princess, and we can get the grill fired up. Do we still need to chop anything, or are the shish kebabs all in the fridge and ready to go?"

Sterling stopped and pulled his partner in for a longer, much more thorough kiss. Alexa made gagging noises behind him, but tough cookies. Part of having your dads stupidly, ridiculously in love with each other was having to put up with occasional smooches. Jericho broke away eventually, though, and wrestled Alexa into a mock noogie. "Don't you distract him, missy—I happen to like your dad quite a lot. You'll understand someday."

She squirmed away and rolled her eyes. "I *know*," she groaned. "You don't have to keep telling me."

"Yeah, well." Sterling pulled her in between himself and Jericho and squashed them all into one big hug. "I think we might have to let him stick around. Lord knows I won't be able to keep you out of trouble all by myself."

"It's a tough job," Jericho said with a straight face. "Luckily, I know the right family to handle it."

If you enjoyed *Worth Fighting For*, don't miss any of the books in Wendy Qualls' Heart of the South series, including

Most gay men wouldn't expect to see their dreams come true in a small town in the Deep South. But the road to true love can lead to the unlikeliest places . . .

Disowned by his conservative Peruvian parents, Lito Apaza headed for gay-friendly Atlanta. Resilient, charismatic, and successful, he's built a life on his terms—with a new family of friends and the unconditional love of his dog, Spot. Then his job forces him to relocate to tiny Black Lake, Alabama. Here, being fabulous isn't exactly the town motto. However, Lito can't help who he is any more than he can curb his feelings for a certain sexy ex-soldier.

A former dog handler in Afghanistan, Dave Schmidt now runs a volunteer K9 search-and-rescue team. Until he met Lito, his nights were free. As their hook-ups grow hotter, Dave and Lito have to admit this could be something nearer to romance. It's not what Lito expected. And Dave isn't used to the scrutiny of being visibly gay. Yet everything they've been secretly searching for could be right here in Black Lake. If Dave and Lito want a future together, one of them will have to make the first move . . .

Keep reading for a special look!

Chapter 1

The local pet store was painted an eye-searing yellow, the "Pawse Awhile" logo a vivid orange above it. It was tucked away on a side street behind the Publix and *completely* not what Lito expected, which was why it had taken him forty-five minutes to find. One of the frustrating things about moving to a small town (considered "almost a city" if you asked the other residents, who clearly had never seen a real city to compare it to) was having to find replacements for all the chain stores that seemingly didn't exist outside Atlanta. PetSmart included. Lito's old neighborhood had been quirky, more "poor hipster" than urban chic, but he'd relied on corporate mega-marts more than he'd realized.

Case in point: Black Lake had exactly one Starbucks. It also had a farmers' market, a six-screen movie theater, approximately eight thousand different flavors of Baptist church, and no nightclubs for at least an hour in any direction. Spot had finished the last of her hard-to-find brand of kibble, though, so "Pawse Awhile" it was. Lito clipped her on her leash and headed inside.

The painfully bright color scheme extended to the interior as well. The building was bigger than it looked from the front—not quite on a PetSmart scale, but still promising. It was busy, too. A surprising number of people wandered the aisles with various-sized dogs, although nobody looked like they were actually shopping for anything. Spot whined and sniffed the air but stayed at Lito's side. He gave her a proud scratch behind the ears for being on good behavior.

"Take another minute and then bring them back in," a perky blonde in a Pawse Awhile polo shirt called out from a little partitioned-off area in the middle of the store. "Remember your 'heel' command if your pup starts pulling—they need to know you're there on the other end of the leash and you're paying attention. Use your clicker when they look at you."

Obedience class. That explained how busy the store was. Lito skirted around a woman with two toy poodles and an older man with a wrinkly bulldog puppy and headed for where the dog food section seemed likely to be. Spot kept craning her neck up at him, tail wagging at half-mast, but she trotted alongside like she was trying to show those upstart mutts how it was done. She probably was, honestly—Lito had never done the formal obedience training thing with her, but even when he first took her in, Spot had been determined to prove she was better-behaved than all those other, more *boring* dogs out there. Maybe he spoiled her a bit, but it was nice to not be making this move to a new place all by himself. Even if the only "person" he knew here outside of work wasn't actually a person at all.

"Heel! No—*heel*, Sherman!"

Lito didn't have any more warning than that before some sort of hound mix was suddenly right behind him, nipping at Spot's hip. Spot whirled with a growl, warning the dog to back off, but Sherman merely growled back. Within seconds the two dogs were clinched together on their hind legs, mouthing and gnawing and generally making aggressive noises at each other. The hound's owner, a tiny brunette with giant earrings and way too much makeup, stood frozen in place. Which was completely useless, damn it. She didn't look like she'd be able to overpower her dog anyway, meaning Lito was going to have to break up the fight. All hundred and thirty pounds of him. *Yay.* Because wading into a literal dogfight was exactly what he'd wanted to do today.

On the bright side, neither Spot nor Sherman looked like they were trying to cause any real damage. Spot was annoyed, definitely, but the growling and batting at each other's necks didn't have any malice to it. Lito grumbled right back at them and lunged for Sherman's trailing leash.

"Hold up," a male voice interjected. "Lumpy, Woozy, *down.*" A sturdy shoulder brushed past Lito's, then Lito found himself at eye level with the man's collarbone as the guy deftly inserted himself into the fight.

And *damn.* There were probably better times to notice some seriously impressive biceps, but since the dude was a good head taller than Lito was and the biceps in question were right there for the ogling, Lito couldn't help but ogle. He smelled nice, too, from the quick impression Lito got when his nose was near the guy's shirt. More importantly, though, the dude seemed to know what he was doing around dogs. His two huge Rottweilers (he named his dogs Lumpy and Woozy? Really?) were now lying across the entrance to the aisle, panting happily. Neither looked like they were planning to move anytime soon.

Lito sidestepped as best he could within the confines of the shelves and tried to find a way to be useful. Seriously Built Dude had Spot's collar in one hand and the hound's in the other and was hoisting them both back and up, onto their hind legs. It couldn't have been easy—Spot was seventy pounds on a good day and the hound was a bit shorter but much fatter. Lito ended up having to twist under the man's arm to reach Spot and get a hand on her collar. Seriously Built Dude let go and focused on the poorly-trained hound, keeping it off balance but without choking it. When he turned the dog so his body was between it and Spot, Lito did the same. Spot settled immediately.

"Easy, Sherman," the man crooned. "There you go. Down—good boy. You can come get him, ma'am. He knows he wasn't supposed to do that—see how he won't make eye contact and keeps looking at your feet? Just be firm with him and keep him at heel while you walk him back to class and he'll get the idea." The guy surrendered the dog's leash to the apologetic woman, then turned his attention to Lito and Spot. "Yours okay?" he asked.

"Fine, I think." Lito ran a hand over Spot's shoulder and hip where the other dog had been mouthing her. Her tan fur was dark with dog drool, but she seemed both uninjured and unbothered. Now that the fun had ended, she was much more interested in the new guy's own dogs, who were still lying flat on the floor like they'd been glued there. Lito cleared his throat. "Yours are really well-trained," he ventured. "Spot doesn't usually have an issue with other animals, but that doesn't mean she's happy about being jumped from behind."

The guy laughed. A nice, full laugh, his whole frame relaxed now that the woman had reclaimed her dog and was a safe distance away. "I wouldn't be too keen on it either," he said, and extended his hand. "I'm assuming we haven't met before—I'm Dave Schmidt. You're welcome to let your pup introduce herself to my two, if you want. They both love attention and they're not picky about who it's from."

Dave didn't seem to be in any particular hurry to go, so he probably wasn't involved with the puppy class. Scratch that—the two Rottweilers blocking the end of the aisle were *still* lying quietly on their stomachs, panting happily. No way they needed obedience classes. Lito let Spot have a bit more slack in the leash and took a few steps toward the dogs. Spot looked up hopefully, her brown eyes searching for permission.

"Good girls," Dave said in a clear command voice. "Up. Go on; greet."

Both dogs heaved to their feet. Within seconds, they and Spot were circling and sniffing each other in little huffs. The Rottweilers met with Spot's approval, clearly, because she was back to her normal, friendly self almost immediately. It was a bit awkward to stand there next to a total stranger while their dogs made instant friends, but Dave was watching them with a faint smile on his face that totally had Lito scrambling for something to say that wouldn't make him sound like an idiot. "How old are they?" he finally asked.

That faint smile turned on him. "Got 'em as puppies, almost eleven years ago. Time flies. Yours?"

"Around two, as far as I know. Friend of a friend found her last year."

"Ah."

Damn it. Really not going so great with the "don't make yourself sound like an idiot" thing. "It's a bit of a long story," Lito explained, "but the short version is that she was wandering around downtown Atlanta by herself. My friend's ex passed her on his way to work for three days in a row and finally decided screw it, might as well see if she's friendly. She was, obviously. The vet said she'd be fine once she had her shots and a few good meals. The ex couldn't keep her, so he asked my friend, who brought her to me."

"She's lucky to have landed with you, then," Dave said. "Were you looking for a dog at the time?"

"Vaguely." Telling Ian *yes* had been a totally impulsive thing, but Lito would have been lying if he'd said he hadn't already been considering getting a pet. Plus Spot had good timing. Lito had earned a promotion—with the accompanying raise—the month before, and as of three days earlier he was suddenly down two apartment-mates. Todd and Trixie had been shit apartment-mates, but without them his crappy little two-bedroom was already feeling empty. "I think it's more that he knew I couldn't say no," Lito added. "She was all ribs and wagging tail back then."

That faint smile morphed into a grin. "I've been there a few times. Obviously you're taking good care of her." Dave folded his arms and shifted his weight to his rear foot, all but leaning back against the shelf. He looked totally up for a nice long chat with a complete stranger in the middle of a pet store.

Lito didn't mind the chat either, truth be told. Two weeks in Alabama and this was the first semi-decent conversation he'd had with anyone outside work. If the guy was packing some serious eye candy under that t-shirt, all the better. His posture and the tone of his voice suggested he might have been flirting a bit, even. Maybe. It was hard to tell whether that was observation or wishful thinking. Dave didn't *sound* gay, at least not the way guys back home tended to talk when they were plugged into the whole Big Gay Scene thing, but there was a reason Atlanta barely counted as "the South." That smile, though, and the approving eye-check when he looked Lito up and down right before they shook hands . . .

"You said Atlanta." Dave was nominally watching the dogs, now snuffling at each other and waggling their entire butts with excitement, but his body stayed angled toward Lito. "Are you in Black Lake for a visit, or . . ."

"Been in town a few weeks," Lito admitted. "The company owners wanted me on a project here instead of back in Atlanta and the chance was too good to refuse. It's been an adjustment." *Bit of an understatement.* "I assumed you could tell I was new because I was the one person in town you didn't already recognize—isn't that how it's supposed to work in places like this?" He realized how much the question made him sound like an asshole a moment too late, but it really had been bouncing around in his head for the past two weeks. Backpedaling would have made it even worse, though. Christ, everyone in earshot was going to think he was some douchebag city boy.

"Black Lake isn't *that* small," Dave said. He snorted. "I'm sure there's five or six people I haven't met yet, at *least*. Maybe even as many as a dozen." His eyes sparkled and he shot Lito another tiny smile. "I'm pretty sure I know all the dogs, though. The big ones, anyway. I tend to keep an eye out."

"Oh?"

"You ever heard of K-9 search and rescue?"

"Like the guys who go through the wreckage after a hurricane and try to find survivors? I've seen it on the news, I guess."

"Not as much for hurricanes around here, this far from the coast. We mostly get lost hikers and kids who wander away from home." Dave jerked his thumb toward his dogs. "These two have been doing it with me since they were pups. My buddy Rick and I started a team—hell, guess it's been ten years ago now. North Alabama Search and Rescue, or NALSAR for short. We respond to call-outs all over Alabama, plus a few up in eastern Tennessee and some parts of north Georgia." He cocked his head slightly to one side. "Don't suppose Spot likes running around outdoors and getting lots of exercise, does she? Two's a good age to start, and she's the right size for it."

The question felt a bit out of the blue, but it was nice to *finally* get a social invitation after being cooped up in the new rental house for so long. Well, a semi-social invitation. And from someone who hadn't side-eyed

Lito's hot pink shirt or his earring like he was going to spread gay cooties. "She never got to run as much as she wanted to in Atlanta," Lito answered, "but I can't imagine she'd object. She usually gets along well with new people and with other dogs. Has so far, at least."

"How about you?"

"Get along with other dogs?"

Dave huffed. "You know what I meant." He fished in his jeans pocket and procured a slightly worn business card. "If you're new in town, it might be fun to come out to a practice or two and see how you like it. The team are all friendly and it's good exercise. Plus, you know—it's great volunteer work. Make a difference and all that. Anyway, Spot seems to have made new best friends with Lumpy and Woozy, which is a good sign. We're always on the lookout for new recruits."

"Which of us is the recruit?"

Dave grinned. "The pair of you, if I have anything to say about it. There's no pressure if you try a few times and don't like it, obviously, but I promise it really is fun. For you and your dog both. We practice twice a week up on the mountain at the state park, weather permitting. The website with directions and all the details is on the card." He pressed it into Lito's hand. "I'd love to see you there on Tuesday, if you can make it."

"I . . . yeah, I think I'd like to." Lito's palm tingled where Dave's fingertips had brushed against it. "I've never been an outdoorsy type, but it sounds interesting."

"Oh, it is." Dave snapped his fingers twice, and both his dogs jumped to attention. "I've got to get going, but when you come on Tuesday you can tell me all about why you named a solid-yellow dog 'Spot.'"

"It's not nearly as interesting a story as you're probably imagining."

"I look forward to hearing it anyway." Dave patted his thigh, which brought his dogs over to sit on either side of his legs with an almost military precision. He didn't even need to bend down to pick up their leashes—they each leaned in so he could dispense a good ear-scratch before tracing the leash back from where it clipped onto their collars. Spot whined and looked up at Lito's face, clearly disappointed that playtime was done, but she let her new friends go without any further protest.

Lito got in one last gawk as the man walked away. He looked just as good from the back as he did from the front.

Damn.

Meet the Author

Wendy Qualls was a small town librarian until she finished reading everything her library had to offer. At that point she put her expensive and totally unrelated college degree to use by writing smutty romance novels and wasting time on the internet. She lives in Northern Alabama with her husband, two daughters, two dogs, and a seasonally fluctuating swarm of unwanted ladybugs. She's a member of both the Romance Writers of America and way too many online writers' forums. Wendy can be found at www.wendyqualls.com and on Twitter as @wendyqualls.

Worth Waiting For

A small town in the Deep South isn't where most gay men would choose to go looking for love. But open hearts will find a way . . .

Growing up in the Bible Belt, Paul Dunham learned from a young age to hide his sexuality. Now he's teaching psychology at a conservative college in Georgia—and still hiding who he really is. If Paul hopes to get tenure, he needs to keep his desires on the down-low. But when an old college crush shows up on campus—looking more gorgeous than ever—Paul's long-suppressed urges are just too big for one little closet to hold . . .

Brandon Mercer has come a long way since his freshman year fumblings with Paul. Now he's confident, accomplished, proudly out—and the sexiest IT consultant Paul's ever seen. When Brandon asks Paul to grab some coffee and catch up, it leads to a steamy reunion that puts their first night of passion to shame. But when Paul's longtime crush turns into a full-time romance, he receives an anonymous email threatening to expose their secret to the world. If Paul stays with Brandon, his teaching career is over. Yet if he caves under pressure, he risks losing the one true love he's been waiting for . . .

Praise for Wendy Qualls

"Qualls provides a sweet romance with some spice while tackling issues such as coming out as an adult, family relationships, and religious acceptance or denial of LGBTQ lifestyles."
—*Library Journal*

"Sexy, fun and well written, Wendy Qualls' new novel, *Worth Waiting For*, is the perfect book for a cozy night at home reading. I can't wait to see what Ms. Qualls has in store for us next."
—J.L. Langley, bestselling author of *The Tin Star*

"A charming, sexy, and beautifully crafted tale that tugs at the heartstrings. Can't wait to read more from this talented author!"
—Sara Brookes, award-winning author

Printed in the United States
by Baker & Taylor Publisher Services